I0762078

LEFT

TO

FEAR

(An Adele Sharp Mystery—Book Ten)

BLAKE PIERCE

Blake Pierce

Blake Pierce is the USA Today bestselling author of the RILEY PAGE mystery series, which includes seventeen books. Blake Pierce is also the author of the MACKENZIE WHITE mystery series, comprising fourteen books; of the AVERY BLACK mystery series, comprising six books; of the KERI LOCKE mystery series, comprising five books; of the MAKING OF RILEY PAIGE mystery series, comprising six books; of the KATE WISE mystery series, comprising seven books; of the CHLOE FINE psychological suspense mystery, comprising six books; of the JESSE HUNT psychological suspense thriller series, comprising nineteen books; of the AU PAIR psychological suspense thriller series, comprising three books; of the ZOE PRIME mystery series, comprising six books; of the ADELE SHARP mystery series, comprising thirteen books; of the EUROPEAN VOYAGE cozy mystery series, comprising six books (and counting); of the new LAURA FROST FBI suspense thriller, comprising four books (and counting); of the new ELLA DARK FBI suspense thriller, comprising six books (and counting); of the A YEAR IN EUROPE cozy mystery series, comprising nine books; of the AVA GOLD mystery series, comprising three books (and counting); and of the RACHEL GIFT mystery series, comprising three books (and counting).

An avid reader and lifelong fan of the mystery and thriller genres, Blake loves to hear from you, so please feel free to visit www.blakepierceauthor.com to learn more and stay in touch.

ISBN: 978-1-0943-9231-8

BOOKS BY BLAKE PIERCE

RACHEL GIFT MYSTERY SERIES
HER LAST WISH (Book #1)
HER LAST CHANCE (Book #2)
HER LAST HOPE (Book #3)

AVA GOLD MYSTERY SERIES
CITY OF PREY (Book #1)
CITY OF FEAR (Book #2)
CITY OF BONES (Book #3)

A YEAR IN EUROPE
A MURDER IN PARIS (Book #1)
DEATH IN FLORENCE (Book #2)
VENGEANCE IN VIENNA (Book #3)
A FATALITY IN SPAIN (Book #4)
SCANDAL IN LONDON (Book #5)
AN IMPOSTOR IN DUBLIN (Book #6)
SEDUCTION IN BORDEAUX (Book #7)
JEALOUSY IN SWITZERLAND (Book #8)
A DEBACLE IN PRAGUE (Book #9)

ELLA DARK FBI SUSPENSE THRILLER
GIRL, ALONE (Book #1)
GIRL, TAKEN (Book #2)
GIRL, HUNTED (Book #3)
GIRL, SILENCED (Book #4)
GIRL, VANISHED (Book 5)
GIRL ERASED (Book #6)

LAURA FROST FBI SUSPENSE THRILLER
ALREADY GONE (Book #1)
ALREADY SEEN (Book #2)
ALREADY TRAPPED (Book #3)
ALREADY MISSING (Book #4)

EUROPEAN VOYAGE COZY MYSTERY SERIES

MURDER (AND BAKLAVA) (Book #1)
DEATH (AND APPLE STRUDEL) (Book #2)
CRIME (AND LAGER) (Book #3)
MISFORTUNE (AND GOUDA) (Book #4)
CALAMITY (AND A DANISH) (Book #5)
MAYHEM (AND HERRING) (Book #6)

ADELE SHARP MYSTERY SERIES
LEFT TO DIE (Book #1)
LEFT TO RUN (Book #2)
LEFT TO HIDE (Book #3)
LEFT TO KILL (Book #4)
LEFT TO MURDER (Book #5)
LEFT TO ENVY (Book #6)
LEFT TO LAPSE (Book #7)
LEFT TO VANISH (Book #8)
LEFT TO HUNT (Book #9)
LEFT TO FEAR (Book #10)
LEFT TO PREY (Book #11)
LEFT TO LURE (Book #12)
LEFT TO CRAVE (Book #13)

THE AU PAIR SERIES
ALMOST GONE (Book#1)
ALMOST LOST (Book #2)
ALMOST DEAD (Book #3)

ZOE PRIME MYSTERY SERIES
FACE OF DEATH (Book#1)
FACE OF MURDER (Book #2)
FACE OF FEAR (Book #3)
FACE OF MADNESS (Book #4)
FACE OF FURY (Book #5)
FACE OF DARKNESS (Book #6)

A JESSIE HUNT PSYCHOLOGICAL SUSPENSE SERIES
THE PERFECT WIFE (Book #1)
THE PERFECT BLOCK (Book #2)
THE PERFECT HOUSE (Book #3)
THE PERFECT SMILE (Book #4)
THE PERFECT LIE (Book #5)

THE PERFECT LOOK (Book #6)
THE PERFECT AFFAIR (Book #7)
THE PERFECT ALIBI (Book #8)
THE PERFECT NEIGHBOR (Book #9)
THE PERFECT DISGUISE (Book #10)
THE PERFECT SECRET (Book #11)
THE PERFECT FAÇADE (Book #12)
THE PERFECT IMPRESSION (Book #13)
THE PERFECT DECEIT (Book #14)
THE PERFECT MISTRESS (Book #15)
THE PERFECT IMAGE (Book #16)
THE PERFECT VEIL (Book #17)
THE PERFECT INDISCRETION (Book #18)
THE PERFECT RUMOR (Book #19)

CHLOE FINE PSYCHOLOGICAL SUSPENSE SERIES
NEXT DOOR (Book #1)
A NEIGHBOR'S LIE (Book #2)
CUL DE SAC (Book #3)
SILENT NEIGHBOR (Book #4)
HOMECOMING (Book #5)
TINTED WINDOWS (Book #6)

KATE WISE MYSTERY SERIES
IF SHE KNEW (Book #1)
IF SHE SAW (Book #2)
IF SHE RAN (Book #3)
IF SHE HID (Book #4)
IF SHE FLED (Book #5)
IF SHE FEARED (Book #6)
IF SHE HEARD (Book #7)

THE MAKING OF RILEY PAIGE SERIES
WATCHING (Book #1)
WAITING (Book #2)
LURING (Book #3)
TAKING (Book #4)
STALKING (Book #5)
KILLING (Book #6)

RILEY PAIGE MYSTERY SERIES

ONCE GONE (Book #1)
ONCE TAKEN (Book #2)
ONCE CRAVED (Book #3)
ONCE LURED (Book #4)
ONCE HUNTED (Book #5)
ONCE PINED (Book #6)
ONCE FORSAKEN (Book #7)
ONCE COLD (Book #8)
ONCE STALKED (Book #9)
ONCE LOST (Book #10)
ONCE BURIED (Book #11)
ONCE BOUND (Book #12)
ONCE TRAPPED (Book #13)
ONCE DORMANT (Book #14)
ONCE SHUNNED (Book #15)
ONCE MISSED (Book #16)
ONCE CHOSEN (Book #17)

MACKENZIE WHITE MYSTERY SERIES
BEFORE HE KILLS (Book #1)
BEFORE HE SEES (Book #2)
BEFORE HE COVETS (Book #3)
BEFORE HE TAKES (Book #4)
BEFORE HE NEEDS (Book #5)
BEFORE HE FEELS (Book #6)
BEFORE HE SINS (Book #7)
BEFORE HE HUNTS (Book #8)
BEFORE HE PREYS (Book #9)
BEFORE HE LONGS (Book #10)
BEFORE HE LAPSES (Book #11)
BEFORE HE ENVIES (Book #12)
BEFORE HE STALKS (Book #13)
BEFORE HE HARMS (Book #14)

AVERY BLACK MYSTERY SERIES
CAUSE TO KILL (Book #1)
CAUSE TO RUN (Book #2)
CAUSE TO HIDE (Book #3)
CAUSE TO FEAR (Book #4)
CAUSE TO SAVE (Book #5)
CAUSE TO DREAD (Book #6)

KERI LOCKE MYSTERY SERIES

A TRACE OF DEATH (Book #1)
A TRACE OF MURDER (Book #2)
A TRACE OF VICE (Book #3)
A TRACE OF CRIME (Book #4)
A TRACE OF HOPE (Book #5)

CHAPTER ONE

The heiress to the Akbulut fortune stared across the Danube River, watching the wavering streaks of moonlight reflect off the surface. Zeynep Akbulut hailed from Germany by way of Turkish immigrants. The headscarf she wore, though, was a fashion statement more than a cultural one. The two nose jobs and cheek lifts were neither cultural nor fashionable, but had intended to be so when first administered.

Now, Zeynep's plastic features were arranged in a scowl as she stared across the beautiful water, one white-gloved hand extended over the metal railing, though not quite making contact. Who knew what sort of germs from the general public found their way onto such things?

"Ms. Akbulut," one of the riverboat attendees was saying over her shoulder, "please, I am happy to carry your bags for you."

The riverboat swayed and shifted gently with the flow of the water. Couldn't they make these things still? It would give her a stomachache before the night was out. And that horrible, horrible smell? What was that...? Disgusting.

Zeynep turned, lowering her hand from where it had never touched the railing to begin with and fixated a wary eye on the riverboat's attendee.

"Are we still in Austria?" she said, her tone clipped.

The attendee was a young man in a black, silk suit. He winced at her expression, both his hands dangling at his side where he clutched her two suitcases. The small carry-on cage with the fluffy pink warmth sheath sat at his feet where her cat, Kaya, was mewling in the dark.

"No, Ms. Akbulut," the man replied, quickly. "We're heading towards Regensburg now."

"What is that?"

He blinked. "Umm, Germany, ma'am. It's near your home town."

Zeynep was no longer listening though. She wasn't a geography expert—geography was for chauffeurs and poor people. "Well," she said, "I want to go back. Turn this ship around."

The attendee blinked, and swallowed, doing his best, it seemed, to keep his tone even. "I... I don't know what to tell you, Ms. Akbulut. We can't turn around. The other passengers—"

"Ugh!" she groaned, rolling her eyes at the thought of *others* hampering her wishes. "I'll pay you!" she said. "How much do you want? Five hundred. Five thousand? I don't care. Just turn this thing around."

The attendee winced, shaking his head. "It isn't possible. Please, if you would just let me, I can show you to your room. It's one of the best we have. People rave about the view."

Zeynep was already shaking her head, though, not that she was listening too closely to begin with. "My rooms are *horrible,"* she declared. "Absolutely terrible. And they smell funny."

"They... they smell?" The attendee paused. "How so?"

"They smell like the rest of this little ship."

"The riverboat, ma'am? Do you mean the water? You don't," he coughed delicately, "find the scent of the river somewhat pleasant? We could shut your windows for you, if you like."

Zeynep sniffed. "They're *not* my windows. Because it isn't my room." She crossed her arms. "You're the ones who begged me to be on this ship."

"I'm afraid I don't understand."

She threw her hands back in frustration, but her knuckles grazed the railing and she yelped, withdrawing her hand and rubbing it in frustration. "I'd like to speak with your manager."

The man hefted the two suitcases. "I am the manager. That young woman you yelled at earlier, she said you weren't satisfied with your rooms. I could move you to a lower deck, if you'd like."

"No!" Zeynep said, horrified. "No. That lady, what was her name—Tiffy?"

"Bernice," the man replied, unblinking.

"Right. Bernie. Well, she said there was a *larger* room. Above mine. A better room. I want that one. Yes. I want it."

"I—I'm afraid someone is already staying there. But we do have nice rooms on the same level as yours. Perhaps we could—"

"No! I want the larger one. *Now!*"

By now, the manager was breathing through his nose, in and out as if counting the number of seconds between inhalations. His lips had tightened somewhat, and his cheeks seemed tinged with red, even in the night beneath the moon. The riverboat continued to churn up the Danube River—this second longest river in Europe moved from Austria into Germany, past the countryside, and the occasional town lining the waterway. Smaller watercraft could occasionally be glimpsed tied to docks or lining the wharf. A couple of boats were being loaded onto the back of a trailer at a dry dock as they passed.

Zeynep didn't much notice any of this. She could feel her temper rising. How *dare* this little boat man tell her she couldn't have the room! She was an Akbulut! The disrespect alone... If her father was here...

She gritted her teeth, shaking her head and wagging a finger. She was so angry that she couldn't even find the words. "No," she said, simply. "No!" she said, even louder, yelling in the manager's face. "I want that room! Or I want you to turn this boat around."

The attendee's posture had changed a bit now. He'd lowered her bags to the deck again, on either side of the little pink cage. His eyes were hooded, his lips tight as he said, softly, "This is not possible, I'm afraid. And no, I cannot take your money, Ms. Akbulut."

"I want to speak to the captain."

"This—that isn't how the riverboats work..." he trailed off, though, rubbing his jaw and glancing to the side. A couple of lights were on down the side of the boat, but most of the passengers were either sleeping, or in their rooms, or still lingering in the dining hall. After a moment of consideration, the manager seemed to reach a decision. He nodded slowly as if suddenly realizing something and his brow furrowed in consideration. "You know," he said, snapping his fingers against his silk pants. "Actually, that's a good idea. I'll speak to the, er, *captain*. You wait here, okay?"

"I don't want to wait! I want that room."

"Yes... Yes, I understand. I'll be right back. Just hang tight. I'll see what I can do about that room."

Zeynep smiled now as the manager began to march away, leaving her bags on the deck, next to the railing. She knew she'd get her way eventually. The Akbuluts always did. Her family hadn't built a fashion empire by taking no for an answer. It was the way things had to be.

She watched as the bellhop... busboy? What had he said he was? She snorted. Not that it mattered. As long as she got that room. She didn't like having to wait, standing out in the open, but she supposed it would have to do for now. Of course, she'd lodge a complaint. Maybe try to speak to one of the owners and get the little bellhop fired.

For now, though, she turned, looking over the railing again and frowning at the river. So much water... It was all just *too* wet. She never should have accepted the invitation for the riverboat. They had wanted her here for the sheer clout of her last name, no doubt. It's how things often went. But this time, they hadn't even comped her with the best room.

She heard the footsteps of the busboy against the metal stairs at the far end of the deck. She watched as he circled, his hand trailing against the metal railing as he moved up a level. As he left, she thought she heard him mutter something beneath his breath before spitting over the railing.

She frowned at this. Now she *definitely* would speak to the owners about the rude man's job.

She waited... And waited... Nearly five whole minutes passed. Her temper was beginning to wear thin. Five entire minutes. Who did they think she was?

"Hello?" she called up, towards the front of the boat. Above her, from the dining level, she could hear the sounds of footsteps, of passengers moving about.

Then, suddenly, from behind her, she heard the noise of quickly approaching feet.

She turned, looking past her luggage and frowning as a shadowy form neared. "There you are," she began. "I've been waiting for hours. Well? When can I move into my new roo—"

She trailed off. It wasn't the bellhop.

The approaching figure only picked up pace though, running now. She took a hesitant step back, frowning. "Stop!" she said, suddenly, her voice rising. "Hey—you. Stop!"

But the form kept coming, fast. An arm shot out, grabbing her neck. A voice whispered in her ear, "You look so lovely tonight." And then the fingers around her throat began to squeeze.

She yelped, struggling, gasping, trying to strike with her hands. Her fingers flashed forward, and one of her pasted-on nails broke off. The man had her throat tight. Another hand reached towards her neck, though, grabbing the strand of pearls around her throat. There were diamonds inlaid in the pearls.

"Thief!" she tried to choke out. But the words were muted. She could still hear, muffled and faint, the sound of passengers above. But no one seemed to hear her. No one else was around.

The shadowed form above her ripped the necklace from her throat.

"Thief," she groaned again. "Stop! Stop it!"

But he didn't take the pearls and run. Instead, still holding her neck, his other hand descended, clutching the pearls between thick fingers. He jammed the strand of pearls and diamonds against her lips.

"I'll tell daddy you miss him," the man whispered in her ear.

She gagged now, choking. What was he doing? What was—

The pearls jammed past her lips, into her mouth. The fingers followed and she tried to bite, but now his hand around her throat squeezed at her cheeks, holding her jaw open. He shoved the necklace into her mouth and kept pushing, hard, shoving the invaluable piece of jewelry further back until it tickled her throat.

She started gagging, retching, trying to bend over. But the thick hands kept her upright, gasping, unable to breath, unable to scream.

"I'll tell him," the man was whispering. "I'll tell your family. I'll tell them you miss them."

And then, choking on her own necklace, darkness descended.

CHAPTER TWO

"This is your idea of a date?" Adele said, trying to hide her smirk.

John paused, one hand extended, holding a pair of orange earmuffs. He was wearing a second set askew, his left ear protruding past the padding so he could still hear her.

"You don't?" he said, hesitantly.

The sound of loud *bangs* retorted through the underground shooting range. Two men, on the far side of the room, facing down twin ranges, peppered cardboard cutouts with lead. The veneer of barely concealed excitement across John's features diminished somewhat at Adele's words.

She rolled her eyes, allowing the grin to show now, so John would know she was kidding. She snagged the second set of earmuffs from him, then turned to face the range, brushing her blonde hair out of her eyes, and pulling her full frame upright. She was a few inches taller than most women, but Agent Renee was taller still, dwarfing her with his six-foot-five frame. The tall, muscular Frenchman faced the range next to her. One hand rested on his holster, but out of the corner of his eye he was watching her.

"How about a little wager?" Adele said, her hand on her own firearm.

John's eyebrows went up; the burn scar under his chin was pale beneath the glow of unnatural lights in the underground bunker. The place, apparently, was operated by one of Agent Renee's old military buddies. Shooting ranges weren't commonplace in France, but for law enforcement and active military, sometimes special licenses were issued. Not that anyone had checked to see if John or Adele qualified for the range. They hadn't even had to show ID when John had walked into the place. A couple of grunts had served as greeting, and John had provided his own ammunition.

"Your friend didn't seem too concerned about letting us back here," Adele said.

"That's the wager?"

"No, I was just observing."

John shrugged one massive shoulder. "Jacques owes me. I get in free, plus anyone I bring with."

"I spotted him wiggle his eyebrows as I passed."

John snorted. "Jacques has a nervous twitch."

"Mhmm, likely."

The tall man grinned but returned his attention to the range. "So, what's the wager?"

"Most shots in the bullseye," Adele said. "Loser buys lunch."

John nodded as if in gratitude. "Thanks."

"For what?"

"For lunch."

He drew his weapon, aimed, sighting and firing all in one smooth motion. He emptied the clip in a matter of seconds and, by the end, the two other shooters were both looking over. They frowned at first, but when John hit the red button next to his lane, and the target whirred on the track, drawing nearer, both other shooters' frowns turned into looks of mild admiration. They hid the expressions quick enough.

John's finger tapped the bullseye on the yellow and black target. "Looks like a full dozen, hmm?" he said, smirking. "How do you feel about pizza?"

"Hang on," Adele retorted. "I haven't gone yet." She shifted uncomfortably, squaring her shoulders, one hand still resting on her firearm. For a moment, she was grateful for the ability to focus on something else for the moment.

Not that she didn't like looking at John.

But things between them... had never been normal. Certainly not average. For one, who took a girl to a legally questionable shooting range on a first date?

But then again, that's what she'd signed up for, and she'd made her peace with it. She liked John, and she was relatively confident the feelings were mutual. Besides, dating Agent Renee came with perks. Adele knew she was often too hard on herself, and also too hard on others.

For a moment, firearm rising in her grip, aiming down the range, she exhaled slowly, closing her eyes for a second if only to force herself to concentrate. Not on the target, not even on the weapon. But to focus on allowing herself to enjoy the moment.

Enjoyment was all too easy to lose amidst distraction. She was standing next to a handsome man who was interested in her. Her career was going well. Her closure rate on cases for the DGSI and Interpol was at an all-time high.

She smiled, nodding to herself.

And then she unloaded. The first two shots winged the target. The next missed entirely. Bullet four hit the outer circle. By the time she'd finished, though, two of the shots had struck center eye. Most found the target's outer rings. Solidly average—that's what she'd been told about her shooting during field training, and things clearly hadn't improved.

"One," John said before the target had even reached them.

This time, Adele didn't have to feign her offense. "One? That's two!" She said, adamantly, jabbing a finger towards the swishing target moving towards them on the track. The two other shooters were no longer looking over. One of them seemed to be trying to hide a snicker.

Adele's mood only darkened further, and she lowered her earmuffs and pointed angrily towards the center mark. "See. Two."

"That second one barely hit."

"It's two," she insisted.

John snorted but then swallowed as if trying to hide the sound. He nodded delicately, and said, "Alright, two..."

For someone like John, this was nearly the same as an apology. He really was trying to make it work. He'd even picked her up outside her place in a regular sedan for once, instead of one of the sports cars he used government money to lease. He'd also brought her flowers.

Well, really, one of them had been a flower. The others were technically weeds but John clearly hadn't known. The Frenchman got credit for trying in Adele's book.

She looked up at him, smiling now, and shaking her head. "Maybe one and a half."

He chuckled. "We can split lunch."

"Psh. No. Fair and square; a wager is a wager. I'll pay." She reached up, holstering her weapon and patting John affectionately on the cheek. "I might have to take out a loan, though, with the portion sizes you order."

John snorted. "They'd deny the loan. You're a shifty character, Agent Sharp."

For a moment, one hand still grazing John's stubble, the other resting on her holster, Adele met her partner's gaze. His eyes twinkled with mirth and his lips twitched with a smile. More loud retorts echoed from the two lanes further down the track.

A strange place for a first date, but also fitting after a fashion. She supposed violence and flying bullets were only another feature of whatever *this* between them was. Still, standing there, her hand trailing down to rest against John's chest, she found her own smile returning, a soft warmth of contentment in her chest.

Sometimes, she decided, it was nice to simply enjoy life, to enjoy this moment with John, and not concern herself with killers and murderers and victims...

A slow chill crept up her spine at the thought, though, and her fingers left the warmth of John's chest, lowering to her side now. Her other hand still brushed the leather of her holster, her skin touching the cold metal of her weapon.

Not *all* killers could be ignored, though...

Not for Adele. Not until it was all said and done. She'd always known one of them would end up in the other's sights. When the time came, she knew it would all depend on whoever squeezed the trigger first.

Her mother's killer was still out there.

"Best of two?" Adele said, finding her voice a bit more hoarse, her tone grim.

"You sure, Sharp? I don't want to take your money."

"Best of two," she snapped back. She reattached another target, hit the button and listened to the whir as the outline of the bullseye got further and further away, carried off on the spinning metal wheels towards the darker portion of the underground shooting range.

Even at a distance, though, no matter how many shots it took, Adele eventually always found her target.

This would be no exception. She'd check in with Foucault before bed to see if there were any leads on the Spade killer—a nighttime habit she'd started to develop in recent weeks. No hits yet, but maybe, just maybe, tonight would be different.

CHAPTER THREE

Sculptors often used knives, as did some painters. A whittler might do the same, and in the old days, authors, when preparing their pages, would incline to a blade as well.

The painter smiled at his own tool of choice. A fisherman's knife, this time. A special blade for a special target. No masterpiece could be completed without the proper medium.

His car was parked two streets over, a rental, under a false name. He'd walked the rest of the way, limping against his frail leg. He was sweaty and breathing heavily. Sometimes, the drawbacks of his own body would bother him, but tonight wasn't a night for despair. Soon, it would be one of celebration and crowning achievement.

He inhaled the night air, his feet firmly on German soil as he faced the small house, his eyes trailing up the steps to the porch, and the two white painted columns on either side of the rail.

"Hello there," he murmured softly.

A pulsing blue light emanated from the front window through the blinds. Someone watching TV. His favorite friend's father lived alone. The painter had been scouting for the last three days, and he knew well enough how careful he had to be for this particular painting.

He glanced over his shoulder at the other houses along the street. No witnesses. No one watching at all as he waited for night to fall. Sergeant Sharp always woke at exactly seven AM. The man liked to make soup, and he liked to watch TV late into the night.

Not that it mattered. A sleeping target would be easier to subdue. But someone in a stupor in front of a buzzing screen was nearly the same thing anyway.

Besides, he'd already planned his entry point. A window, in the dining room, on the side of the house, always left half ajar.

The painter winced as he stepped onto the curb, adjusting his balance, and putting most of his weight on his good leg. He blinked his good eye, and reached up, adjusting the fake, glass eyeball into a more comfortable position. He pressed the fish knife into his sweater pocket, and then slowly limped up the driveway, onto the grass, around the side of the house.

Part of him wanted to whistle, wanted to listen to music. Oftentimes, he would play one of his favorite symphonies as the prelude to a kill.

But this time, he knew his full attention would be required. Besides, there would be time enough for music, punctuated by the shrill screams of Adele Sharp when she saw the corpse of her daddy.

"I'm coming home, friend," he muttered beneath his breath.

The painter reached the window. And while his bones were weak, and he was small of stature, he was still wiry. He reached up, his fingers pressing on the flecked paint, and the window emitted a soft scraping sound as he shoved it a bit further.

He waited, listening. No alarm, as he'd determined earlier.

Now, though, the silence from the dark house was deafening. The painter pulled his frail form up and then, sliding through the gap in the window—head followed by torso—he rolled into a bit of a somersault as he deposited himself on the carpeted ground in the dining room.

There, head against the wall, body on the floor, he let out a loose little sigh of relief.

Even now, he could feel his fingers twitching, could envision the swirling patterns, the beautiful work of ornamentation he would inflict. He would make it slow. Very, very slow. This time, he was determined to record the process itself. A behind-the-scenes look into a master craftsman and his procedure.

He would send the video to Adele. His dearest friend would appreciate it most of all.

He wondered if she'd cry at the squeals of her father. Or maybe she might get angry. Both thoughts amused him. Slowly he pushed to his feet, one hand pressing into the soft carpet. He could hear the muted sound of the TV from the other room. Could see, through the door frame of the living room, the very top of the TV screen, flickering with colors.

The carpet softened his footsteps as he moved forward, brushing past the doorway, and coming to a halt in the hall. There, sitting in a chair, he spotted a balding head, leaned back—Joseph Sharp. And by the looks of things, he'd fallen asleep.

The painter smirked widely now, his pale skin stretching like taffy. He winced, briefly, though, as his teeth hurt thanks to the ice they had given him on the plane. It would take another week for his mouth to feel the same again, but all the best artists suffered. Van Gogh had cut off his own ear, after all.

The painter frowned. Maybe that's what he'd been missing with his other sacrifices. Maybe that's what he'd failed to realize. His own pain had to be as much a part of the art as the pain of his subject. He thought about it for second, and stood in the doorway, feet on the carpet in the hall, watching the news broadcast over the top of the reclined armchair, and Joseph Sharp's sleeping form.

They were alone in the house. No one else lived here.

His fingers pulled the fish knife from his pocket, and he absentmindedly pressed it against his left hand. He traced his palm, following the lines with the tip of his blade. He frowned for a moment, considering Van Gogh. And then he pressed the blade, hard, into his palm. Blood immediately began to pool, and he kept his hand facing up. No droplets could be spilled. No DNA evidence.

His eyebrows were shaved again, his eyelashes plucked like he always did before a masterpiece. Like he had done with Robert, Adele's old mentor.

How the Frenchman had screamed.

As the pain flushed up his arm, he smiled at the memory; the way Robert's feet had kicked. The way he had grit his teeth, snarling like a pig.

He had cut pieces and patterns for hours.

Could he make Joseph Sharp go even longer? Maybe he ought to restrain the man. Take it even slower. Quality couldn't be rushed.

The painter licked his lips, glancing down the hall, feeling the blood against his palm. He pressed his hand to his shirt, allowing the bleeding to soak into the fabric. No. He wouldn't look for ropes. He was too excited. He'd been anticipating this moment for too long to tarry any longer. For a moment, his eyes skimmed across a couple of pictures on the wall. A woman he recognized, and a smiling child he also knew.

He grinned at the nearest portrait of Adele's family. He'd killed the mother too. One of his earlier works. And now, he would take the second. At the end of it, all three of those smiling faces would be a part of his portfolio. A true artist could only be judged by their body of work, rather than simply a snapshot at a time.

No more time wasting. He'd come here for a reason.

He stepped through the doorway from the hall, approaching the sleeping form of Joseph Sharp.

The floor creaked beneath his foot, and the painter paused.

Sharp continued to slumber. The sound from the TV droned on, drowning out any other noises.

The painter reached the back of the reclined armchair. The fish knife extended in his hand, still slick with the warm blood from his own palm. His fingers trailed against the top of the armchair, feeling the warmth of the fabric, from Joseph Sharp's body heat.

"Sleeping beauty," whispered the painter. "I will turn you into something magnificent."

The knife began to descend, towards Joseph's throat.

And just then, a hand shot up. A thick, muscled forearm went taught. Fingers squeezed around the painter's wrist, and Sergeant Sharp's head spun around, eyes wide. He'd been faking the snoring sound.

"I thought I smelled a rat," the man snarled.

***

The Sergeant had a weapon in his other hand. A silver pistol, which was rising with his arm, twisting towards the painter. The painter, though, wasn't a man given to panic. No time for emotion, only action. With a snarl, the painter lashed out, slamming his other hand into the base of Joseph's neck.

The s Sergeant had been expecting him.

The painter forced his own calm, striking at the Sergeant a second time. Then, he ducked. The gun fired with a loud *bang*. Plaster fell, trickling from a hole in the ceiling. Joseph Sharp sneezed and winced at the blows to his head. He jerked the painter hard, throwing him over the arm of the chair, and trying to rip the knife from his hand.

The gun wavered, and the painter lashed out, surging forward with the same momentum Joseph had used to pull him. Instead of trying to retreat, the painter dove at the gun. Another *bang*. Something hot and sharp across the painter's cheek. He yelled incoherently, grateful he could still speak. The bullet had missed. His fingers scrambled at the gun. The painter's other hand was still in a vice of a grip, his fingers being crushed. His knife nearly dropped, but he held on for dear life.

"Who are you?" the Sergeant snarled.

The painter didn't reply, desperately trying to push the gun down, away. His fingers gripped the muzzle, shoving the weapon off to the side. A fourth gunshot. The painter's ears stung, ringing with a vibration.

Now, laying atop Joseph, who was still reclining in the chair, the two of them struggled. One hand for the knife, the other for the gun.

The Sergeant tried to push out of his seat, but the painter's body, across the larger man's torso held him back.

The Sergeant yelled, and jolted sideways, and the chair toppled. Another *bang*. This time from the furniture striking the floor. Joseph howled like a wounded grizzly bear. He released the grip on the painter's knife, going for the gun completely now.

The painter felt large fingers prying his own from the muzzle. He couldn't let the Sergeant aim. If he did, the masterpiece would be ruined.

And so he lashed out, stabbing down and hitting the closest target. The Sergeant's arm.

Joseph howled, struggling where he lay, propped against the toppled chair, the painter draped over him, both trying to scramble for their weapons.

The painter managed to extricate the gun, stabbing again at Joseph's arm. The Sergeant twisted his grip, no longer trying to aim, but rather doing his best to recover his firearm.

The painter's fingers bent, and he snarled—he didn't have a grip on the trigger, no time to orient—and tossed the weapon away, out of the Sergeant's reach. It clattered against a radiator, then struck the floor, motionless.

Another slash at the Sergeant's arm. But this time, thanks to his discarded weapon freeing up a hand, the Sergeant caught the painter's wrist. He rolled out of the chair, onto the ground, and began to rise to his feet. The painter was already standing now, quicker to his feet.

"Stinky little rat," Joseph growled. The bear of a man tried to crush the painter's arm with sheer willpower.

The masterpiece-maker yelped, dropping the bloodied knife. It tapped to the ground while the painter's blood-smeared palm streaked across Joseph's shirt, the crimson spread staining the plain white T-shirt of the old police officer.

The American kept coming, charging forward, head down like a bull. The Sergeant's thick skull caught the painter's chest, sending him reeling backwards into the hall. The Sergeant followed. The knife was on the ground. The gun discarded behind the radiator.

The painter lashed out, snagging one of the framed photos from the wall. He used it to bludgeon the man. Glass shattered. Another strike, and the photo ripped.

The Sergeant yelled incoherently and flung the painter across the hall, through the door into the living room. The small man toppled over a chair, bringing it and himself crashing to the carpeted floor. A splintering sound, and the chair broke beneath him.

Groaning, and gasping, the painter regained his feet. But the Sergeant was already coming, picking up a second chair and wielding it like a club. He brought it crashing down, and the painter narrowly avoided the attack by clambering underneath the table.

Joseph's fingers groped beneath the table towards the smaller man. The painter yelped. He heard the sounds of voices through the open window, followed by shouting from the street.

Undoubtedly, they'd heard the gunshots. Someone would call the police soon. The painter needed to get out. This masterpiece was a botched job. Even the masters knew when to call it quits.

"Come here little rat," Joseph snarled, scrambling beneath the table after the painter. The smaller man was quick, though. He kicked out, viciously, catching the Sergeant in the chin with his foot.

The larger man spat blood, and the painter scrambled from beneath the table, speckling the carpet with blood of his own. Gasping, clutching his fingers against his chest, he hurried to the open window.

He tried to climb out, but Joseph reached him first. Hands latched onto slim wrists. The painter whirled around, trying to kick again. But Joseph flung him. Hard. Sending him through the glass window. It shattered around the painter, and shards fell with him into the lawn. A hard *thud*. Pain and aches. His eyes flashed with dark spots.

Wheezing, gasping, and groaning, the painter got to his feet, one of his legs unsteady.

Joseph was climbing out the window now too. He brandished one of the shattered legs from a chair like a club. He pointed the club towards the painter, saying something incoherent through bloodied lips. The painter had heard enough. He ducked his head, and hurriedly limped away, rushing as fast as he could. He heard the sound of Joseph's feet thumping into the yard behind him. The painter broke into a sprint, wincing against the agony jolting through his bad leg. He ran, his fingers twisted and bloodied though they were, reaching for the keys in his pocket. He needed to reach his car. He needed to get away.

The sound of the Sergeant's footsteps behind him were slower, now. The larger man clearly wasn't built for movement over the longer haul. In the distance, he could hear a siren wailing. He heard more shouts, voices from one of the houses across the street. He ducked his head, gasping, bleeding, in pain. His face twisted in fury and frustration. So many plans wasted. So much potential ruined.

He continued to gasp and sputter and curse as he stumbled away from the house, racing back up the sidewalk towards where he had parked the rental car. He needed to get out. He needed to get out fast.

CHAPTER FOUR

Anika moved along the edge of the boat, heading towards her room on the second deck, whistling softly. She felt a flicker of worry along her spine as she paused outside her room—she glanced over her shoulder. No one had followed her. Ever since she'd heard about that poor girl murdered on another boat, she'd been jumpy.

Anika paused outside a blue door and slid her key card into the lock. She stepped in, closing the door behind her, feeling the air conditioning against her skin. The window faced the front of the ship, peering out at the passing countryside. In the distance, she spotted a vineyard. She smiled, inhaling the cool and clean air of her cabin and wondered what it would be like to stand amidst the grapes, inhaling the scent of fruit, destined to become wine.

Not all sweet things would turn sour. And not all sour things would be allowed to age and mature properly. But sometimes, something destined for a bottle ended up in a bowl. And sometimes, the rot got to it before anything else could.

Anika liked to hope she'd escaped the rot.

She began to approach her bed, where she'd rested a small copy of the first Harry Potter book which she'd read at least fifteen times. It was one of her favorite series; plus, as far as entertainment went, it came on the cheap. As she sat on the bed, feeling the gust of wind through the cracked window, she heard a quiet tapping sound.

She frowned, hesitantly, and glanced towards the door.

The tapping increased.

The light from the bathroom shone out into the bedroom, an orange glow spreading from the cracked door to her own private shower. A small little fridge sat next to her bed, filled with all manner of bottled drinks. Also paid for. She hadn't touched those, yet.

The tapping sound grew louder.

"Hello?" She called out.

The tapping stopped.

"I'm sorry," she said, "is someone there?"

Silence reigned for a moment. She could hear the whistle of the wind through the window, feel the rustling pages of her book beneath her fingertips. She lowered the book slowly onto the bed. Silence. Then, more tapping.

With a soft sigh of frustration, she got to her feet, smoothing the front of her shirt, and approached the door. She reached out, opening it, half expecting to see one of the porters waiting for her.

But when she opened the door, the deck was empty. She stared at the rail, and then leaned forward, glancing up and down the deck.

No one there. She frowned quizzically and glanced towards the doors on her left and right. Closed. No movement. No indication that anyone had been nearby.

She swallowed. For a moment, it felt like she might have a lump in her throat. She shook her head in frustration, closed the door with a click, and returned to her bed. No sooner had she crossed the gap, though, and felt the breeze against her cheeks again, then there was another louder tapping sound.

She turned around, finding her voice. "Yes?" Still polite, but annoyed.

Again, no response. She approached the door again, and this time flung it open. No one. No sound of hurriedly retreating footsteps. She wondered if maybe some children were playing a joke. But she didn't see or hear anyone. No heads poking around the edge of the boat, looking in her direction. No one was nearby at all.

She waited for a full minute now, wondering if she could catch a glimpse of whoever the nuisance was.

But again, she spotted nothing. She closed the door, locking it this time, and returned to her bed. But now, she'd only crossed halfway, before there was another, louder tapping noise. Now that she stood in the middle of her room, no longer next to the window which had messed with the acoustics, she realized her mistake.

The tapping wasn't coming from the front door.

She turned, slowly, feeling a slow prickle up her spine. Anika stared toward the cracked bathroom door and the strand of orange light spreading into her room.

Her heart leapt into her throat. The tapping sound grew louder. Knuckles against wood. No mistaking it.

Her knees knocked, and she felt like she might collapse; then she turned, with a quiet little yelp, and raced back towards the front door. The bathroom door swung open, and a shadow stretched along with the orange light towards her. Anika's fingers scrambled desperately towards the lock. Why had she locked it? How stupid could she be?

She heard the steady thump of footsteps. She wheeled around, staring as a shadow descended over her.

"Please!" she yelled, "No!"

But the figure was taller than her, stronger. She tried to scream, but a hand clasped over her lips. She felt fingers scrambling towards her. She tried to jerk away, but the fingers were groping at her pants.

Panic flooded her. But the hand only wanted what was in her pocket. It pulled out her wallet, hard. She'd already given away the last of her money.

"Take it," she gasped in a trembling voice. But the fingers locked over her lips preventing further sound. She wasn't a very large woman. Short, small. Still, she tried to push the hand off her. But it was like shoving a brick wall.

The shadowy form was breathing heavily, and the man's features stretched into a scowl.

"I'll tell him you miss him," he whispered. "When they cry, I'll send them flowers."

She shook her head, desperately. "What?" She tried to say, but her voice was still muffled. Panic shot through her, jolting through her body, and causing her hands to tremble horribly. She watched where knuckles clasped against her forearm.

The man had her wallet. Hopefully that's all he wanted. He didn't let her go though. She was lodged against the door, feeling the cold metal against her back. Why had she locked it?

He pressed the wallet against her cheek. The man leaned in, kissing her on the forehead and whispering, "I'll tell them you said goodbye."

She tried to scream now, tried to bite his fingers. But he pressed hard, and then he shoved the wallet into her mouth, jamming it past her lips. The pain was instant, something ripping along her mouth.

She couldn't yell now, her voice muffled. She could barely breathe. He'd jammed the wallet, hard, slamming his palm into her lips. She began to choke, trying to gasp. She couldn't breathe. He continued to slam at the wallet, slammed her face. He said, again, louder, "I'll tell them you miss them!"

She tried to struggle but wasn't able to breathe. Dark spots scattered her vision and she was gagging now, feeling the wallet against her throat. What was he doing?

She was choking, trying to spit it up, desperately, but there was nothing she could do.

The black spots grew wider; her vision fluttered. And then, it all went dark.

CHAPTER FIVE

Adele jolted awake to the sound of a ringing phone chirping in her apartment bedroom. Her eyes snapped open, instinctively, and one of her hands reached out, snagging the device off her nightstand. She glanced at the clock. Nearly midnight.

She groaned, rising into a sitting position, and allowing the phone to ring a second longer as she gathered her wits about her. She left the light off, and, clearing her throat, she answered, "Agent Sharp."

"Sharp?" Came the sound of a familiar voice.

"Executive Foucault?" Adele said, sitting up a little bit straighter, and opening her sleepy eyes even wider.

Heart hammering, for a moment, she wondered if she was in trouble. Briefly, she thought about her trip with John to the firing range. Of course, they hadn't told anyone they'd started dating. The executive had warned them in the past about fraternization between coworkers. They had decided to keep it on the down-low. The shooting range had been an interesting excursion, but the waterfront restaurant they'd gone to afterward had been downright pleasant. John had been on his best behavior, which meant he hadn't made any off-color remarks about the waiters, though he had eaten the lemon garlic salmon he'd ordered with his fingers instead of a fork.

"I've got a case. First thing tomorrow morning, so I need you briefed."

Adele swallowed. "Of course. Need me to come in?"

"No, that's fine agent. Minimal information as it is. Two women have been killed on water boats on the Danube."

"The river?"

"That's the one."

"Heading which direction?"

"Two different boats. Two different victims."

Adele frowned. "Different boats?"

"That's what it looks like, Agent Sharp. Are you awake? Listen, I need you to focus for this one."

"Yes sir. I'm focused. First thing tomorrow morning. Are the boats being held over somewhere?

"The one with the second victim is right now. In Vienna. We're keeping it docked until eight tomorrow. That's when you'll need to get on board."

"Am I going to have a partner for this one, sir?" Adele said it innocently enough, but the executive must've sensed something in her tone. It almost sounded like he growled, and then spoke, a bit more sternly than he might normally have ventured. "Yes, John's going with you. Is that going to be a problem?"

"No, of course not. Thank you. I mean, thank you for the case. Not John. Just, yes. Thank you." Adele resisted the urge to throw her phone across the room. She cringed where she sat, banging her head gently against the wall, and staring wide-eyed at the ceiling, wincing at the executive's response. If he'd noticed anything, he decided not to say it. She heard a soft fluttering little sigh, and then, the executive in his deep voice said, "On that boat by eight AM. We can't hold it a second longer. And Adele, one of those victims was an Akbulut."

Her heart skipped a beat. Adele swallowed. Even for someone who'd spent most of her time in work clothes or running outfits, she'd heard of the fashion empire. "Which one?"

"Eldest daughter."

"And the second victim?"

"We're still looking into her. MO is the same, though. I hope you understand how delicate the situation is. I need a rush on this one. Already I'm getting calls. Last thing we need is for the media to find out before we can notify the parents."

"The Akbuluts don't know yet?"

"We called them back from a business trip yesterday. They're still in transit."

"Shit."

"That's right. Eight AM. That means you'll have to leave Paris bright and early. Think you can do that?"

"Yes sir. Of course."

The executive hung up, and Adele sat there with the phone still pressed to her cheek, feeling the cold metal and glass against her face.

She exhaled softly, her blonde bangs fluttering from the air. Her head rested against the cold concrete of the wall above her headboard, and her back pressed to the wooden barrier. For a moment, in the dark, staring across the small space of her apartment, Adele could feel a flicker of worry. Two bodies, in two days, on two boats. Moving crime scenes were always the worse. But when one threw in the daughter of a billionaire, and her infamously unstable mother, things could get dicey. Adele gritted her teeth, bracing herself for the possibility of interacting with paparazzi on this one. She would just have to warn John beforehand not to throw anyone overboard.

She set her alarm two hours before she'd intended, giving ample time to reach the docked ship in Vienna. Then, Adele lay back down, closing her eyes, and breathing softly, reaching out to place the phone on the nightstand. The moment it made contact with the wooden surface, the phone suddenly began to vibrate.

Adele looked over, frowning. A different number this time. One she didn't recognize. It took her a second to realize the area code was from Germany.

For a moment she considered letting it go to voicemail. She would need to get up early, as refreshed as possible for tomorrow's case. But a small, niggling sensation in her stomach caused a jolt of unease. Swallowing, she lifted the phone, answered it, and put it on speaker, her eyes closed again, resting against the pillow, the phone next to her face.

"Adele Sharp?" said a voice.

Adele's eyes were still closed, and she could feel the sleepiness returning, her mind foggy, drowsy.

"Who is this?" she groaned. Not quite rude but bordering on it.

"I'm sorry for bothering you so late, Adele Sharp. My name is Dr. Mueller."

Adele's eyes snapped open. "Doctor?"

"I'm afraid I have some bad news for you. Your father..."

"What about my father?" she said, fully awake now. Once again, she was sitting upright, the phone was no longer on speaker, but pressed to her cheek.

"He's here. Injured. I'm afraid he was attacked at his house earlier tonight."

Adele's heart leapt into her throat. Her pulse quickened, and for a moment it almost felt like all the blood in her body had frozen solid. She could feel her heart hammering and could even hear her own ragged breaths puffing in her ears. For a moment, it almost felt like her head had been dipped into water, and everything was echoing around her. It took her a second to refocus on the words. "Joseph Sharp? You're sure? Are you talking about Sergeant Joseph Sharp?"

"Yes. I'm sorry Adele, but your father was attacked. He's alrigh, and should make a recovery."

Adele's heart dropped from her chest to her stomach. She tried to latch onto the words towards the second part of the sentence, but found her fingers were trembling so badly she thought she might drop the phone. She was out of her bed before she realized it, stalking towards the door, throwing it open. She was still in her sleeping clothes, but she didn't care; she hastened towards the front door of her apartment, pausing only long enough to grab her wallet, which had her identification. She moved over towards the cupboard next to the fridge, where she kept her passport.

"I'll be there. You said he's going to be fine? What happened? Who attacked him?" She shot off the questions like a military commander barking orders. But she didn't need to. She knew the answer. Who else would attack him? Only one person was out there, hunting everyone Adele loved. It was the same person it had been ten years ago. The same person from a few months ago. The same person it would always be, until one of them caught lead.

"I'm afraid we don't know. A stranger. Your father isn't really speaking with anyone right now. I did have something else to mention, though," the doctor said, hesitantly.

"What?"

"Your father asked me to tell you not to come."

Adele felt a jolt of sheer frustration. *Typical.* "He asked—are you joking? Is he there? Put him on. Is he there?"

The doctor cleared his throat uncomfortably. And then, she heard muffled voices in the background. A second later, the doctor said, "He's going to be fine. Just some superficial wounds on his arm, and some bruises on the back of his head. He'll be fine."

"He's there isn't he? Put him on, dammit. I mean it. Put my father on *now!*"

The full force of Adele's words seemed to weigh and then shift. The doctor gave a stuttered apology, his voice muffled, suggesting the phone had lowered from his cheek. Then, a moment later, she heard the soft clearing of a throat, and then a familiar voice.

"Adele," her father said.

"Dammit, Dad, what happened?"

"I'm fine, Adele. Some little rat skunk got in my house. I gave twice as good as I got."

Adele felt her heart still pounding. She retrieved her passport now. Wallet. Check. Passport. Check. Was she forgetting anything? She needed to get a ticket.

She gritted her teeth, moving back towards her computer. How fast could she get a ticket? Maybe they would just have one available if she rushed to the airport now.

"Are you okay? The doctor said you're gonna be okay. You're okay, aren't you?"

"I'm fine. It's barely a scratch."

"Dad, what did he look like? The guy who did this?"

"Small, runty little fellow. Ugly. Stupid."

Stupid wasn't so much a descriptor of his appearance as her father's mood, but the rest of it was telltale enough. Adele knew she'd been right. The same little runt of a man she'd seen. Who John had seen. Who Robert's private investigator had spotted heading into a police station. The man who'd killed her mother. Who had killed Robert.

"Adele," her father said, "Really, I'm fine. You have work, don't you?"

"I just got a case. But I'm turning it down. Foucault can get someone else."

"Not a chance," her father snapped.

"Christ, Dad, I'm coming."

"Watch your language."

"*Dad.*"

"I don't need you here. I'm fine. Don't you dare leave that case for me. You have a job to do."

Adele let out a strangled little sigh of frustration. She still had her passport and wallet gripped in the same hand, her other palm still pressing her phone to her cheek. She wanted to scream, to lash out. Being the daughter of someone like Joseph Sharp had to be the most frustrating thing in the entire world.

"Like I said, I'm fine. Besides, Adele, I'm a cop."

Those last three words gave her pause. She hesitated, swallowing. She pictured the small station where Joseph Sharp worked out of. She knew how cops got when someone hurt one of their own.

"They're looking for him?"

The Sergeant gave a soft little snort of laughter. It was the most amused she had heard him in a while. "Shut down two airports for me. Three precincts emptied looking for the guy. If he's out there, they'll find him. You're just going to be one other set of boots on the ground. You'll get in the way more than anything. Some of my buddies are keeping a tally at the station. They think they've got something like a hundred guys out there looking for the little rat."

Adele exhaled, slowly, feeling the pressure in her chest released in a steady, shaking breath.

"They're looking for him? Did they find anything?"

"An abandoned car. A rental. Fake ID. That's it, though. They have some of his blood, too. The lab is running tests. DNA."

Adele shivered, leaning back against the counter, placing her hand with the wallet and the passport on the smooth marble to steady herself. She stood in the dark apartment, staring off through the window which faced the city for a moment longer. "Promise me you're okay?"

"Never felt better. I threw him through a window," Joseph said, actually giving a snort of laughter now. He cleared his throat delicately, and chuckled. "You should've seen him, all wide-eyed and scared. It was hilarious." He gave a little laugh, but then started coughing as if in pain.

"Dad," she said, sharply.

"I'm fine. Just swallowed spit. Really, you're overreacting. Look, Adele I'm serious. Do your job. That's what Sharps do. Do your job. If you come here, I'll refuse to see you."

"You're ridiculous."

"Show some respect. I mean it though. I'll refuse you. You better not come. I don't need you here, Adele." Her father spoke firm, harshly as he often had. Then, though, he cleared his throat, and in an attempt at a gentler tone, which barely qualified, he said, “Er, how are you doing by the way?"

In the dark, Adele rolled her eyes. If he was making efforts to try his best and be polite, perhaps it was true he wasn't in such a bad way after all. She could picture a hundred German police officers combing the city, checking passengers and setting up roadblocks. Cops often got that way when one of their own was harmed. She supposed her father was right. It wasn't like she could do much more. If they had blood evidence, then they'd be able to get even more help narrowing down the identity of this guy. There was no guarantee he was in the system, but every little bit helped.

"I'm doing alright, Dad. Look, are you sure I can't do anything?" she said, her voice hoarse.

"I'm fine. Do your job. I'll call you when I can." And then, her father hung up.

Adele sighed, staring at the phone for a moment to make sure she'd been disconnected, and then lowering it, frowning. Fate had never cursed someone so much as the daughter of Joseph Sharp. It was like trying to hug a cactus. But maybe he was right. Maybe she couldn't do anything to help.

Of course, that didn't mean she wouldn't *try*. He might have refused to see her in Germany. But there were still strings she could pull on this side of the continent. She placed her passport back in the cupboard and pocketed her wallet. She stood for a moment in the dark of the apartment, running over her options.

Her mother's killer was still out there, hunting everyone she'd ever loved. He would pay. He had to pay. She needed to stop him, soon. Before it was too late.

She closed her eyes and massaged the bridge of her nose.

It was too late for her to fall asleep again anyway.

Her father in a hospital. Her mother's killer at large. The German police force out in droves, hunting him. Maybe she'd get lucky. Maybe she'd wake up tomorrow to find the news that the small, little bastard had been caught. Or better yet, shot.

She gritted her teeth, a grim resolve falling over her.

Eventually, this would all be over.

A killer at large. Two bodies on boats on the Danube. An heiress to a fashion empire, dead. Another young woman being investigated. And now it was too late to fall asleep again. Best to just get moving.

Never a dull moment. She supposed this was the sort of life she deserved for agreeing to go on a date to a shooting range.

CHAPTER SIX

"You look like death," John muttered as he settled in the seat next to her.

Adele didn't reply, but instead lowered the tray and buckled her seatbelt. She lifted the blind to the window, allowing the sun to shine through and warm her forearms.

She hadn't slept well the previous night. She'd been lucky to get the few hours she had.

All night, she'd been kept up with horrible nightmares of a small-statured man with one dull eye limping towards her father, a knife in hand.

She shivered, shaking her head and forcing herself to focus.

"Everything okay?" John said. He stretched his long legs as far as they would go beneath the seat in front of him. The executive had permitted business class for the short trip. But even the business seats were a tight fit for the tall Frenchman. When Adele didn't reply right away, John lost interest, closing his eyes, and leaning back. For her part, Adele placed her phone on the tray, ignoring the look of the flight attendant who passed by, checking everyone's seats.

"Do you still have the number of Agent Marshall?" Adele said, at last, cycling through her phone a second time.

"Marshall?" John said, feigning ignorance.

"Beatrice Marshall. You hit on her for an entire year. Don't think I did notice. Have her number?"

"Marshall," John murmured, his eyes still closed. "*Marshall...*" and then he snapped his fingers. "Right, right, I think I remember something about her. She worked for BKA?"

Adele wasn't in the mood to call John on his bullshit. "I don't care that you had a crush on another person. I just need her number."

"Why?" John said, opening an eye and glancing at her.

"It's nothing. Look, I just need the number. Do you have it?"

John shifted uncomfortably. His seat leaned back, but his long legs still wedged up against the chair in front of him. "This isn't a test, is it?"

"No, John. It's not a test. I just need her number."

"Pretty sure you have to tell me if this is a relationship test. There's a rule about that."

"I'm serious, John. Do you have her number or not?"

Muttering something about entrapment, John pulled out his phone, slid it over to her, then closed his eyes again, shifting uncomfortably once more.

Adele cycled through John's contacts to “Beatrice Marshall”, and then quickly copied over the number. She waited, tapping her fingers impatiently against the lower tray. One of the flight attendants passed a second time, staring at Adele's fingers. She cleared her throat, and pointedly said, "Please raise the tray until we're in the air.”

Adele complied, gritting her teeth. Her phone continued to ring, and then a voice answered. "Agent Marshall. Who is this?"

"Hello, agent," Adele said, quickly, feeling a flush of relief. Her cheeks prickled as the blood returned, and she glanced out the window, towards the stream of sunlight warming her forearms. "Hey, this is Agent Adele Sharp. Do you remember me?"

"Umm... Adele... Oh! Of course. From the case at those resorts."

Adele hesitated. That hadn't been the only time they'd met, but she decided now wasn't the time to remind the younger woman. She had no doubt that if she'd brought up Agent Renee's name, it would've clicked far faster. "Look, I'm calling for a professional favor."

"How can I help you Agent Sharp?" Came the soft, careful voice of the young woman on the other end.

"You're still with the BKA, yes?"

No answer.

"I'll take that as a yes. Look, my father was attacked in Germany last night."

"Oh no," said Marshall suddenly, her voice losing some of the cautious quality to be replaced by a jolt of horror. Adele felt John shift next to her and could feel him staring at the side of her face.

“Look, I know it's a big ask. I'll owe you one. But please, could you keep an eye on hospitals in the area. It would be a huge help. Anyone who came in with injuries. Especially cuts from glass."

"Glass?"

Adele snorted. "My dad threw his attacker through a window. Could you just have people keep an eye out?"

"I'm sure the police are already doing their best."

"They are. But my hands are tied. I have to work a case of my own. But I feel like I'm doing nothing. This will help."

There was a stretch of silence, and a softly clearing throat. And then

John leaned in past Adele, and said, "Hey Beatrice. It's me." He didn't even give his name.

Marshall gave a sound like a squeal of delight. "John!" she said, cheerful and chipper all of a sudden. "What a pleasure to hear your voice. How are you?"

John cleared his throat delicately. "Doing fine. Partnered with Adele on this case over here. Say, it would be doing both of us a huge favor if you could just look into the hospital thing."

No hesitation, no pause. "Of course. I'm happy to help. How's that new car you were telling me about before? I haven't heard back from you after I sent you that text."

It may have been Adele's imagination, but it looked like John's cheeks suddenly reddened a bit.

"That was a very nice text," he said, in a sort of robotic voice. "A very, very nice text."

Marshall giggled on the other end. Adele found herself scowling.

"I can send you another one if you like," said Marshall. "Or maybe you could send me one; I really liked it when you—"

John coughed, and quickly interrupted. "Maybe now wouldn't be the best time for more texts. Thank you, though. Really. I appreciate the offer."

"Well, if you're sure. I'm looking forward to hearing from you again," said Marshall, quietly. She didn't sound disappointed. If anything, she sounded even more excited.

"I," John coughed, "I'm not sure when that'll happen. Or if ever. Or, well, thank you. Could you just check those hospitals for us?"

"Anything for you, John."

Adele rolled her eyes. And then, she said, "Thanks." And hung up.

Adele looked at John, turning completely to face him. He scratched at the corner of his chin, and glanced off into the aisle, pretending he didn't notice her attention.

"Very, very nice text?" Adele said, innocently.

"She has a way with words," John said, coughing into his hand.

"And with pictures no doubt. You always were one for a visual aid."

"We were *texting*," John coughed again, "before you and I were, well, you know. It was only a brief thing. Nothing at all. She's far too young for me." He added this last part quickly, as if worried he might have offended Adele.

She glared. "Too young for you? Are you saying I'm old?"

"What? No. What?"

Adele crossed her arms, frowning out the window again. She resisted the urge to elbow her partner. Partly, it was in good humor, but most of the humor was drowned by her own worry. Worry for her father. Fear of the unknown. Fear of what awaited in Vienna.

Another case, more dead women—she had to focus. She couldn't let what was happening in Germany distract her. Police were already on it. And Marshall would keep an eye on the hospitals. It wasn't like there was anything else Adele could do. Her father was fine. He had refused to see her. He wanted her to solve this case.

It was all so convincing, and yet Adele felt a jolt of guilt in her stomach. It felt like she should have been on another plane, flying to Germany.

But the choice had been made. Not by her, but for her. There were others out there counting on her doing her best.

Still, the killer was on the prowl. He had murdered her mother. Cut her to pieces. *Bleeding, bleeding, always bleeding*. The warmth of the sun against her arms felt cold all of a sudden. The plane began to move, pulling out from the airport and jockeying onto the runway.

John was leaning back again, eyes closed once more. "You didn't tell me your father was hurt," he mumbled, still reclining.

"He's fine. Barely even scratched."

"Who was it? It was the Spade killer, wasn't it?"

Adele sighed softly. "He's coming after everyone John. Everyone I care about." She looked at her tall partner now, her eyes tracing the scar along the underside of his chin, up to his sharp nose, and to his closed eyes. Would the killer come for John next? Probably not again. Even the Spade killer wasn't stupid enough to tangle with someone like Agent Renee twice.

Who then? Who else might he hunt and try to snatch from Adele?

John frowned slowly, watching her. He shook his head once. "He's already dead," John murmured, his eyes narrowed like a snake's. "He just doesn't know it yet, Adele. Don't let him in your head. He doesn't deserve to be there." Agent Renee stared off now, as if not quite seeing her, lost, for a moment, in his own thoughts.

It gave her a headache to consider all the ways she might be emotionally devastated. All the ways she was putting other people in danger. She pulled her own phone out, scrolling through, and wondering if she ought to warn anyone.

The killer was injured, though. At least there was that. He would take time to recover. Maybe she had enough time. At least for a brief moment, to solve this case on the Danube, put things back in order, and then see to her own business.

She leaned back, feeling her stomach twist, gritting her teeth against the rampant emotions swirling through her. Sometimes it felt like she was always one step behind. And other times, it felt like she was on the wrong trail entirely.

CHAPTER SEVEN

Adele and John arrived at the docks in Vienna, approaching the riverboat with nearly a half hour to spare on their eight AM deadline. Already, Adele could see passengers queuing up by a rail, some of them with luggage and others brandishing tickets. One passenger was gesturing wildly with their ticket and pointing towards the concrete gangplank leading up to the boat. The passenger faced off with a young woman in a black uniform who was standing by the ramp and holding out a hand.

Adele could hear the words drifting on the breeze—speaking English, one of the staples of the more touristy attractions. "I'm sorry, sir, but no one is allowed to board yet."

Adele frowned, sharing a look with John before approaching the line as well. The young woman held up another her hand in their direction also, shaking her head in frustration, and raising her voice to say, "I'm afraid I can't let anyone on before eight. Please, go to the back of the line."

John and Adele, in practiced synchronization, flashed their badges.

The young woman froze, swallowing once while stuttering a quick apology. "Go right ahead," she muttered. She moved a cordoning rope and allowed John and Adele past her. A few of the gathered passengers grumbled in frustration, as Adele moved up towards the waiting boat. The large white and blue vessel had three decks. The sleek, angled prow looked more like it belonged on a luxury yacht than a riverboat. The design of the vessel leaned heavily on blue glass and windows as a focal point. The top deck, from what she could see, and parts of the second deck, boasted doors separated by twelve feet or more on either side.

"Guest rooms," Adele murmured, nodding.

John followed her gaze, and then stepped off the gangplank onto the boat. The moment his feet landed, someone cleared their throat, and a new voice called, "Excuse me, are you with the police?"

Adele turned to find a man with a sweaty face hurriedly approaching them. He was thin, and built like a cyclist, with thick legs, and a thin torso. His eyes, though, didn't have anything in the way of relaxation that came with consistent exercise. Rather, he was scowling so deeply Adele thought he might sprain something.

"DGSI," Adele replied. "I'm Agent Sharp, this is my partner Agent Renee."

The man with the sweaty face glanced between the two of them, seemingly unimpressed. He looked over the railing towards the gathering queue of passengers. One of the passengers who'd been gesticulating wildly, ripped up his ticket, flung the pieces at the poor woman behind the rope, and then marched away.

The sweaty man huffed in frustration, turning back to Adele. "You've kept us docked long enough. How much more?"

"We only just got here," Adele said, keeping her own emotions from the night before in check. She breathed slowly, inhaling the breeze and the water. "Are you the captain?"

The man stared at her, wrinkling his nose. "What? No. I represent the owner of the vessel."

"The owner?

"Yes," the man said quickly. "My name is Mr. Larsen; I work with a law firm that represents the interests of Sightseeing Incorporated."

"That's the owner of this boat?"

"Among others. What did you say your name was?"

"Agent Sharp."

"Well, Agent Sharp, like I said before, we can't afford to keep the boat docked for this long. As you can see below, we're already losing passengers. Plus, we have others waiting for us. They will have been notified about the delay, but unless we are expected to reimburse them, we need to get going, and soon."

Adele shook her head. "Where's the crime scene?"

The man set his teeth and gave an impatient little huff of breath. At last, though, seemingly deciding the sooner they got this over with, the sooner they could leave, he snapped, "Here, on the third floor. Follow me, please."

Adele gave John a long look, who shrugged back at her. She hadn't been expecting a guided tour by a blustering lawyer.

"Sightseeing Incorporated," Adele said, walking quickly to keep up with their guide, "is this the only boat they have?"

"Only? No. They run ten; the program started about three months ago. It's quite new. Which is why it's important we maintain a good reputation. This," he added, glancing sharply at Adele, "is killing us."

His feet seemed to ring louder, tapping against the deck as he marched up a set of stairs, leading them along a row of rooms with blue doors.

One of the doors was propped open, with a line of yellow caution tape looping from the handle to the railing and back. Two police officers stood out front, reclining against the doorway, staring out over the rail with bored expressions.

The moment they spotted the agents, though, they shifted to attention, clearing their throats and standing straight-backed.

John nodded to each of the officers in turn. "They take the body?" he asked in heavily accented English.

The officer on the left, a young man with a bright, orange beard, nodded quickly, also replying in broken English. "Two hours ago, sir. Are you with—"

"DGSI," John cut him off. "The coroner say how long she's been dead?"

"DGSI?" The man said, hesitantly. "Isn't that French?"

Adele cleared her throat. "Under the purview of an Interpol task force," she said, quietly. The man seemed to ease at this comment and nodded quickly.

The second officer, an older fellow, with no facial hair, coughed delicately. "Placed the time of death sometime yesterday evening," he said. "A porter found her in her room."

"A porter," John wrinkled his nose. He glanced at Adele. "Of course... a *porter...*" he repeated, quirking an eyebrow and waiting for her to fill in the blank.

Adele, who knew exactly what a porter was, and knew what John wanted, waited instead, watching him with mild amusement. The tall Frenchman's eyes narrowed. "What's a porter?" he finally muttered.

Mr. Larsen, the representative, rubbed at the bridge of his nose, muttering beneath his breath. "Agents, please," he said, a bit more insistently. "I'm pleading with you." He glanced at his watch—a golden Rolex. "We have to depart the port in the next twenty minutes or refund more than a hundred tickets."

Adele whistled softly. "A hundred?" she said. "This boat is popular, then."

"My clients," Mr. Larsen said, crisply, "have designed a unique, one-of-a-kind experience along the Danube. Both long-term passengers, and those who wish to embark at whatever point in the journey they like, are able to enjoy the journey."

"So it's like a bus," John grunted. "A floating bus."

The man looked like he wanted to rub his nose again, but instead he forced a smile. “A porter, good sir, is a bit like a busboy for a boat.”

“And this porter who found the body. His name?” Adele said.

Mr. Larsen looked at her now. “A Mr. Brand. He was quite distraught by the whole thing, I assure you.”

“Where is he now?” Adele said, standing before the open doorway.

“I imagine preparing for the day, and hoping, like I am, we are able to set out on *time.*”

Adele turned away from the lawyer, now, to look at where John was poking his head into the doorway. “She was found choked to death,” John murmured, glancing back at Adele. “Read the full file yet?”

“I read what there was,” she returned, stepping past Mr. Larsen, and lowering her voice. “Choked on her own wallet.”

John made a swallowing sound, wincing and shaking his head before ducking under the caution tape and stepping into the small room with a window facing the front of the boat. Adele followed closed behind. Her eyes darted, instantly, to the bathroom door, which was slightly ajar, and also towards a single book discarded on the bed.

“Minimal struggle,” Adele ventured after a moment. “She didn't stand much of a chance.”

“Think our killer was waiting for her? Waited for her to sleep?”

Adele glanced towards the bed again but shook her head. “Not sleeping. Book is on the bed. Maybe she was distracted, though.” Adele glanced through the door towards the officers. “Where was the body found, exactly?”

The man with the beard pointed towards the threshold of the door itself. “Right inside,” he said, softly. “She was nearly blocking the door when she was found.”

Adele turned back to the room, frowning even more deeply now. She paced over to the bed, staring at the discarded book and then took three long steps to reach the door again. “That's a long distance to cover,” she murmured, “if she was caught by surprise.”

John was now by the bathroom, peering into the small space. “So maybe not surprise. Maybe she saw him coming. Recognized him?”

“Doubtful. If she moved from the bed to the door... Either running or...”

“Answering the door? Maybe the killer muscled his way in. Then left the same way.”

“Maybe...”

Adele exhaled through her nose, glancing around the room. “If he did, without being seen," Adele said quietly, "then it suggests he at least knows *somewhat* the layout of this boat."

"And?" John prompted.

"You heard Mr. Larsen. It's a new boat. Only three months. How many people would be *that* familiar with it?"

John was reading his phone slowly, shaking his head. "Still waiting on more information about Anika Blythe," he said, softly. "She was only twenty-three."

Adele winced. "How old was the last victim."

John rubbed his chin. "Twenty-one," he muttered, a note of disgust to his tone.

"Well, there's at least that as a connection. But Zeynep Akbulut is well known and wealthy. Anika Blythe..." Adele glanced around the sparse room. "Doesn't seem to fit the same cloth." She shook her head. "Anyway... even if the killer did know the layout of the boat. It suggests perhaps he killed Zeynep, got off that boat, then onto this one."

Adele turned, glancing out the door again towards where Mr. Larsen was practically glued to his watch. "Excuse me," she said.

"Yes?" he snapped. "Can we go?"

"Not yet. It's possible our killer struck on another boat before coming to this one. Did you hear about—"

"Zeynep Akbulut? Yes, of course. Everyone did. Very sad. Very. I'm not sure what keeping us docked, though, can do about that."

Adele frowned. "Do you know who owned that other boat?"

Here, Mr. Larsen's cheeks went the color of the young officer's beard. He coughed delicately, sighed once, then glanced off. "Sightseeing Incorporated," he said, softly. "One of the smaller boats."

Adele's eyebrows flicked up. She heard John come to a halt behind her, his shadow falling over the lip of the doorway.

"The same company who owns this boat owned the other one, too?" Adele pressed.

"Just a coincidence. A very bad one. I'm sorry, agents, but we have to depart now. So, if you don't mind... This is a calamity as it is."

John began to grunt, muttering, "No wa—"

But Adele interjected. "You can leave. But we're staying until the next stop. This porter, the one who found the body. We'd like to speak with him."

Mr. Larsen gave a long, gusting sigh of relief. He quickly wagged his head, nodding, and turning to begin marching down the stairs. "Of course, of course!" he called over his shoulder. "There's a café on the second level, towards the prow. He'll meet you there! Thank you, Agent Sharp!" He paused for a moment, before disappearing down the stairs, his small, sweaty-face peering over the steps. "And look... this business. This other boat. It's just an unfortunate coincidence. I can assure you."

"Of course," said Adele.

"Of course," muttered John.

Then, they watched the small man leave, hurrying quickly down the steps to get the boat moving again.

"Think it's a good idea to allow them to embark?" John murmured beneath his breath.

"Can't hurt," Adele replied quietly. She gestured towards the crime scene. "Nothing there. Both victims were young women. Both choked to death with items lodged in their throat."

John winced, rubbing at his own throat. "I already hate this guy."

"Yeah, well, let's see if the porter has anything to add." Adele shrugged. "And the two boats, both owned by Mr. Larsen's clients. Coincidence, hmm?"

"Right," John muttered, stepping past Adele and moving towards the indicated café. "Definitely. Coincidence. When is it not? Let's stop talking to bureaucrats. They're useless. This porter is the one who found the body. He'll know something—they always do. Coincidence—bah!"

CHAPTER EIGHT

Adele regarded the porter who wore a dark, silk uniform and a nervous countenance. His fingers tapped abruptly against the back of the chair which he seemed reluctant to sit in. The small, little café at the prow of the riverboat was a quaint amalgam of silver tables and chairs, and a small café which seemed to occupy two spaces that might have originally been intended for rooms.

Soft, instrumental music and the odor of reheated coffee wafted from within the café, lingering on the air above the tables.

Adele cleared her throat delicately as she leaned back in her chair. John had opted to remain standing near the stairwell which led back up to the rooms.

"I'm sure it was very upsetting," Adele said, quietly in English for John's sake. "But anything you can tell us would be a great help."

"I don't know what you want," replied Mr. Brand, suited enough to the language himself, his fingers increasing their tempo against the back of the silver chair. He seemed to be keeping rhythm with the music wafting from the café, and every so often he would glance back towards one of the speakers hidden beneath a green and white umbrella spread as an awning over the small shop.

"I didn't even know who she was," he said. "I just spotted the door slightly ajar, when I was making my rounds. Sometimes the guests order room service, or have special requests lodged for amenities they might need."

"What does this mean? *Amenities,*" John asked.

The man glanced towards the tall Frenchman, and only seemed to grow more nervous, his fingers tapping even louder. "Just things they want. Look, I really didn't know who she was. I wish I hadn't found that body." He closed his eyes for a moment, staring at the back of his tapping fingers. "It was all so horrible."

Adele waited patiently, allowing the man to speak, before saying, softly, "Did you see anyone nearby? Anything strange at all?"

"You mean besides—"

"Yes, besides that."

"Nothing. I'm telling the truth. I didn't see anything. No one was moving about the deck. Most the passengers stayed near the café, or the lowest level, watching the water or the passing countryside. It's really a beautiful sight. It's why most people board."

"And yet you were upstairs," John insisted.

The porter squeaked, scratching at the back of his head, and shaking his head quickly. "It wasn't anything like that. You have to believe me. I didn't have anything to do with it."

Adele sighed. "Look, when you found her, what happened next?"

"I told Mr. Larsen. He's the coordinator. Represents the company, but also keep things moving. And he immediately called the police."

"I see," said Adele. "Mr. Larsen, he works for Sightseeing Incorporated, yes?"

Here, the porter seemed to grow rather nervous. The chair beneath his fingers shifted, and he glanced off past John, as if looking for something. His voice became quieter, and he murmured, "He does a good job. And the company pays well. I don't have any complaints with them."

"Were you aware there was another murder, on another boat owned by the same company?"

The porter's hands twisted on the back of the chair. "I heard something. I don't know anything about that. Really. I've been stuck here ever since I found her. Look, can I go? We have passengers coming."

Adele looked towards John, who shrugged back at her. Both of them emitted a soft little sigh at the same time.

"Go on," Adele said. "We'll be in touch if we need anything else. And if you remember anything—"

"I won't," he squeaked, and then hurried away from the table, sucking in his stomach as he slid past John and then took the stairs three at a time in his bid for freedom.

Beyond, along the rail, Adele could see passengers now moving towards the café, and she sighed softly, looking towards her tall partner.

"What do you think?"

"If they're murders on the same boats," John said, "it could very well be an employee. Maybe even that guy. Really twitchy."

"He was kept on the boat all night."

"It doesn't mean he couldn't have come from that other ship. Whoever it is, they're moving from one to another, killing people."

Adele bit her lower lip and shook her head. "You really think it's an employee?"

"Don't know. I'm curious why he's targeting these women though. You know how I feel when—"

"I know. I get it. Crimes of opportunity? Or maybe he just seeks them out once he's on the ship?"

"Possibly. If so, though, he got really lucky to hunt down the eldest daughter of the Akbulut family."

"You think he targeted her especially?"

"Maybe it's like a needle in a haystack. Kill a bunch of people, but really only target one. Pretty sure I saw a movie about that. If either of these two was the *real* target, it'd be Zeynep Akbulut."

"Maybe. One thing is certain..." Adele trailed off, her tone grim, her eyes narrowed. "There's no reason to believe the killer is finished; there could be another body tonight."

"I certainly hope not," said a new voice. Adele glanced past John to see Mr. Larsen scowling and moving up the final step to the second deck. He shook his head. "What makes you think that?" He spoke quietly, shooting a glance over his shoulder towards where some passengers were near a rail, shooting suspicious look towards John and Adele. A couple of others were still approaching the café but were taking their time about it.

"In my experience," Adele said, quietly, "serial killers don't usually stop at two."

"A coincidence," Mr. Larsen said, quickly. "Don't say otherwise too loudly. Please." He added this last word as an afterthought.

"Well, if you want my recommendation, sir, you should speak with your employers and get them to dock all their ships."

Mr. Larsen actually coughed as if choking on air. He paused, then stared at her, his face turning white. "Wait, you're serious? No, Agent Sharp, that's entirely impossible. Not a chance."

"If I'm right," Adele said, quietly, "whoever this is, they're not done. You might be worried about losing a day or two of ticket fees, but if we find out this killer is somehow tied to you, you could be facing serious liability."

The man narrowed his eyes. "Don't speak to me of liability. Do you have a court order?"

Adele held up her hands. "No order. Just some friendly advice."

"I'm afraid, Agent Sharp, if that's all we have to go on, I'm not going to be able to communicate your suggestion to my employers. They'd laugh me out of the room. There's no way we're docking all their boats."

"If someone dies—"

"That's your job," he snapped. "Don't put that on me. My job is to make sure these boats run, and our passengers get to their destinations. Your job is to catch lawbreakers. Don't confuse us. I'll say where the boats go, and you figure out who's doing this."

Adele felt her temper flare, and her eyes narrowed. "I thought you said it was just a coincidence."

Mr. Larsen just snorted, turning and brushing past John angrily, moving back up the deck. Once he was gone, Adele shared a long look with her partner, and slowly pushed out of the chair. She joined Renee by the rail, facing the stairs, and returned to French. "Financial trouble?"

"Who? Mr. Larsen?"

"Maybe the company. He seems pretty antsy about the idea of docking their ships for a couple of days."

John shrugged. "They're a new company. Maybe they just don't have the leeway."

"We could get a court order."

"Think that'll help?"

Adele sighed, her hand trailing against the railing as she began to take the stairs with soft clanging sounds. "Maybe not. At least not yet. We should go check out that other ship. The one with the first murder scene."

"I already checked the schedule. It's now in Regensburg," John said, grimly. "Let's take a taxi. I'm already seasick."

The tall Frenchman glanced over the railing at the water, his eyes narrowed in suspicion—John had never much liked water—and Adele moved in front of him, guiding the way back towards the first level and to the gangplank.

Perhaps they'd get luckier at the first crime scene. Though, if news had leaked, trying to investigate the death of Zeynep Akbulut, without raising eyebrows, was going to prove difficult.

CHAPTER NINE

He thought of himself as little more than a vapor. A breeze, or a tumbling leaf. He saw himself as ineluctable.

He saw them as far less.

The man leaned against the railing of the ship, humming softly to himself, and looking out over the water. He watched as the other passengers joined him, following up the gangplank. He'd boarded bright and early in Gremheim. Another boat. His third in the last few days. Another coastal town.

Also his third.

He watched as other passengers above him, who'd boarded earlier, chuckled or moved about, some of them moving inside to the small little restaurant on the second level. He already detected the odor of sesame seeds and some sort of honey.

He inhaled slowly, and pushed off the rail, watching the new passengers arrive. His eyes traced from one unknown face to another, darting along the row of arrivals.

And then, his eyes flicked back. He paused, staring down at the young woman in the bright red dress.

Almost as if she'd adorned herself to attract his attention. Red marking the target.

The young woman had curled brown hair and wore two earrings so bright he could even see them twinkling from where he leaned on the second level. For a moment, the young woman paused, standing on the gangplank and meeting his gaze. She hesitated, frowning briefly. She did a doubletake, as if wondering if she recognized him.

He smiled at her for a moment, giving a little fluttering wave with his fingers.

The woman in the red dress hesitated, glancing over her shoulder, but then back at him. She gave a hesitant, confused little wave in return, but then quickly ducked her head, breaking eye contact and moving with the passengers onto the first level.

The man turned, rolling his shoulders, and stretching his arms. He glanced down at one finger, frowning. He'd bruised it on the last boat. She'd tried to bite him.

He'd have to be more careful this time. What a pretty package she'd make in that little red dress. Of course, he'd keep his word to the first two.

And this one as well.

He'd tell their parents they missed them. He'd tell them just how much.

It was only fair, after all.

He glanced down at the little postcard he now held between his fingers, looking over it once more. He pulled out a pen from behind his ear, wetting it on his tongue, and then returned his attention to the little note.

It had taken him some time to think through what he might say. But now... he felt he'd mastered it. He'd handwritten it, of course. Such things needed a personal touch. There, in tight cursive, it read:

Mr. and Mrs. Akbulut. I am very sorry for your loss. We all feel it greatly. I'm sure Zeynep misses you just as much as you miss her. My sincerest condolences. Some things just can't be avoided, I suppose. My thoughts and prayers are with you.

-M-

P.S. Mr. and Mrs. Blythe. Your daughter, Anika, was a real gem. She misses you too.

He finished the postscript, then gave a little nod of satisfaction. It seemed fitting, somehow, that Anika's parents were only notified as an afterthought. Some people had a spotlight on them. Others tried to hide from it.

He moved, still whistling, down the walkway, already preparing in his mind for what came next. This would be the best one yet. He could feel it.

CHAPTER TEN

They'd nearly missed the riverboat in Regensburg, and Adele and John had been forced to purchase tickets on the fly, racing up the gangplank before the passenger boat left the dock and floated back out into the blue current.

Now, Adele's brow was slicked with sweat, and she breathed heavily from their subsequent pace up to the second level. Above, she could hear the sound of footsteps, and milling passengers. John had been forced to turn sideways, making way for a young couple heading down the stairs in the opposite direction, their footsteps clanging against the metal.

Adele frowned towards a portion of rail by which a young man in a black suit was standing. He had an easy air about him, smoking on a cigarette and puffing the acrid cloud up, watching it carried away by the breeze.

The moment his eyes landed on them, though, he flicked the cigarette over the edge of the rail and cleared his throat.

"Police?" the man asked, quietly in German.

Adele glanced from John to the man. "That obvious?"

"Mr. Larsen called ahead," the man said, softly. "My name is Pierre Gaston, I am one of the managers of the River Metro Two, this lovely vessel you now find yourselves acquainted with."

"Pierre Gaston? Do you speak French, for the sake of my companion here?"

The man shook his head. "Not conversationally, no. Don't let my name fool you, I was born in Berlin. Now, Mr. Larsen said you had some questions for me."

Adele crossed her arms, frowning. "You found Ms. Akbulut's body?"

Again, the man didn't seem put out at all. He gave a little shrug. "Indeed. Right here, in fact." He nodded towards his feet, next to the railing. "I spotted her arm dangling over from the lower deck. Just lying there." He gave a little shudder and coughed delicately. "A very upsetting sight, to be sure."

Adele frowned as a young couple moved down a staircase, chatting to each other, and stepping past the self-proclaimed manager and the patch of floor where he'd been standing.

"Where are the police?" she said.

The main raised an eyebrow. "You are? No?"

"We are DGSI task-forced with Interpol," Adele replied reflexively. "But why is the crime scene not contained?" She looked at John now, switching back to French and filling him in. "This is the man who found the body."

John wrinkled his nose. "Doesn't seem too broken up about it."

"He says he's standing where they found her."

John returned Adele's dark look. "Why isn't the crime scene cordoned?" He leaned over the railing, scanning the lower deck for a moment.

"Excuse me," the manager said, clearing his throat and holding up a finger. "Might I say, Mr. Larsen talked with some of the local law enforcement, and after photographing the scene, they decided it was in everyone's best interest to simply move on."

Adele crossed her arms. "Move on? What do you mean move on? This boat shouldn't even have been in use again—not until we cleared it. Who authorized this?"

The manager winced, holding his hands up in mock surrender. "I wish I knew how to help. I do believe, though, you must speak to the company's liaison for such things."

"Let me guess," Adele sighed softly. "Mr. Larsen?"

"Exactly. I can answer any questions you like. The scene wasn't much of a scene once they took the body. I just found her here. Dead."

Adele turned back to the man, her eyes tracing the cold metal deck beneath his feet and the rigid railing at his back. The wind brushed through, fluffing the young man's dark hair only mildly, suggesting he'd made use of some sort of hair product.

"You don't seem too upset about it," Adele said, softly. She considered the situation. Someone had authorized the boat to return to use within the forty-eight-hour window. Hardly protocol. But as she thought about it, she supposed it made some sense, given who the victim was. Foucault had made it clear that reporters would be swarming over the scene. The last thing they needed was to help the vultures with the gossip columns to find the location of the murder. She could picture now: tabloids, running visuals of caution tape or police photographers around the rail ad nauseam. Still, none of it sat well with her.

"It was quite alarming to find Ms. Akbulut like that," the manager murmured, still calm. He gave a little shrug. "But I'm afraid I wasn't very fond of her."

"Oh? How so?"

"She was a bit of a... how do I say it delicately... A brat."

Adele tucked a tongue inside her cheek. For a moment, from above, she thought she heard movement, followed by a couple of whispered voices. When she glanced up, though, she spotted nothing from the railing above. Adele glanced towards John, shooting him a significant look then moving her eyes upwards.

The tall Frenchman nodded slowly, and quietly began to move away, towards the circling metal stairwell that led to the top level of the vessel.

Adele returned her attention to the manager who watched John's lumbering form with mild interest.

"And noting her as a brat," Adele said, quietly, "you had first-hand experience with her?"

He sighed. "I'm afraid so. She yelled at one of my employees, making her cry, and then yelled at me when I tried to carry her luggage."

"Do you remember why she was so upset?"

"She didn't like the room she had. It was comped, too, I might say. She wanted to switch with a better room, also free, I imagine." He muttered beneath his breath, spitting over the edge of the rail and then reaching into his inside chest pocket, pulling out a pack of cigarettes and maneuvering with deft fingers for another one.

He lifted it to his lips, pulling a green lighter from another pocket. Before he lit, though, he said, "I do believe Ms. Akbulut was quite comfortable cashing in on her name. Not only that, she was wealthy in her own right. Media appearances, sponsorships. And..." he shrugged, "What with her mother's ill health, the tabloids suggest she was due for quite a nice inheritance too."

Adele's ears perked at this suggestion. She wasn't one to keep track of the celebrity gossip. But the word "inheritance" to a crime-solver's ears, often sounded much more like "motive."

Still, it was hard to piece it together. She gave another long look at the manager who was busy lighting his cigarette. He seemed distant, indifferent really. But callousness was hardly a motive. He was standing on the crime scene, but again, whoever had approved the departure of this riverboat was to blame for the unprofessional nature of the crime scene.

It was all quite puzzling. For one, Zeynep Akbulut was a German who came from wealth. Whereas Anika Blythe, judging by her quarters and possessions had been a poor Austrian. Though they were still struggling to locate Anika's information, which also raised some flags.

What was the connection between these two women besides the boats? Were they simply crimes of opportunity?

Adele glanced at the sky, watching the sun behind the clouds continue its descent from afternoon towards evening, and also, eventually, towards another murder.

“We need manifests,” Adele said at last. “For both this boat and the River Metro Three.”

The manager shrugged. “I can ask Mr. Larsen about that. He'd be the one to do it.”

“Go ahead, then,” Adele said, frowning and crossing her arms. “Ask him. I'll wait.”

Pierre coughed, and paused, puffing once more on his cigarette, before sighing and then reaching reluctantly into his suit to pull out a cellphone. He turned slightly, facing the other direction and shielding his mouth with his shoulder as he dialed a number and placed the phone to his ear.

Adele listened for a moment. A long pause, and then, finally. “Yes, sir. Still here.”

Adele leaned in.

“Looking for manifests. Yes. For both boats, sir...”

Adele cleared her throat, and the manager glanced back, wincing a bit. For a moment, Adele could hear the blaring sounds of someone shouting on the other end of the phone. The manager winced, holding the phone away from his ear and holding up a single finger as if to say, “one moment.”

Then, at last, he returned the phone and cocked an eyebrow at Adele.

“We need it within the hour,” Adele said, sternly. “Before evening falls.”

“They need it in the hour, sir,” The manager parroted into his phone. He winced against another apparent tirade, holding the phone away again. He sighed, looked up at the sky as if praying for strength and then said, “Mr. Larsen does not think this is possible.”

“Tell him it better be possible, or I'll ground the entire fleet *with* a court order this time,” Adele said, scowling.

“I... would you like to speak? I have tinnitus already.” The German named Pierre began to hand his phone towards her.

At that moment, though, a loud yelp echoed from the upper floor.

Adele whirled, staring up as a man's head dangled over the railing. She heard a desperate series of shouting, followed by a cry of fear as the man tipped even further over the railing.

For a moment, Adele just stared, stunned, trying to make sense of the scene. But then, she heard the deep, growling voice of Agent John Renee.

Her eyebrows shot up, and she cursed, breaking into a sprint towards the stairwell, and taking the metal stairs three at a time.

CHAPTER ELEVEN

"John, what are you doing!" Adele yelled, emerging on the top of the boat. John, though, had one hand gripping a man by the collar, while dangling him over the railing, and the other pointed towards a woman standing off to the side with a camera in her hands, pointed at Renee.

A couple of other passengers, on the far end of the rail were glancing over in curiosity, but John's attention seemed fixated on the woman with the camera, and the precariously balanced fellow who was still cursing and flailing his hands as if to catch his balance. The woman had a beak-like nose, like a bird of prey, and hair the color of crow feathers. The man was bald with a baby-face.

"Give it here," John growled. "Both of you."

"Let me go!" The man yelled in stuttered French. "Stop! Are you insane!"

"Give it to me—now!" John howled.

"This is public property! We are allowed, you giant thug!"

The woman was still standing, edged against the side of the boat, aiming her camera at John and recording. Adele noted a second camera in the man's hand, which he kept up and out of reach of Renee, despite the large man's fingers tight around his collar.

"John!" Adele yelled.

He looked at her, and only frowned deeper. "Paparazzi," John said. "They were videoing our conversation below. Eavesdropping."

"John—let him go," Adele cautioned.

"Are you sure?"

"Wait—no. Hang on, John. Pull him back, then let him go."

Renee growled briefly. With a sigh, he brought the man back in and sent him stumbling towards the woman with the second camera. Before they could retreat, though, John moved in, hands outstretched. "Cameras. Give!"

"No!" The woman howled. "How *dare* you!"

"It's an active crime scene," John retorted. "You two skulking about up here, whispering and hiding, recording people without them realizing. Skeevy pervs! Give it here!"

"No!" The man yelped. "Freedom of press! You hound!"

John, seeming to take the hound comment as a compliment, reached in, snagged the man's camera from his hand and ripped it away with a triumphant yell.

Adele just watched in horror. John seemed to have a thing about reporters... Especially the more low brow sort. "John," she said, desperately, "this isn't keeping a low profile. This isn't what Foucault meant! Don't do anything rash!"

John gave another triumphant yell, though, as he snagged the second camera from the woman who had nowhere further to retreat.

"You ape!" she screamed. "I'll have your job! You too, bitch!" she said, turning on Adele, and screaming shrilly.

Adele blinked, then frowned. She hated how often John dragged her into these messes.

"The public deserves to know!" The woman said, swatting towards her camera to try and get it back. "Who was Zeynep Akbulut here to sleep with? We all know she was a whore! Who? Was it you?" she said, looking at John. Her eyes narrowed. "I bet it was. Yes! I can see the frontpage headline now! Fashion slut screws ugly cop! Scandal!" She wagged her head, and then lunged for the cameras, but John held them back, aloft and out of reach.

"Get a real job," John snapped, pointing one thick finger from the woman to the man who was clutching at his throat and hyperventilating. "I think I have whiplash," the man said, his voice trembling. "I'm feeling faint. You saw it, didn't you? Injured on the job. Someone has to pay!"

Adele resisted the urge to roll her eyes. She took another step towards her large partner, murmuring quietly. "John, let's not do anything hasty, okay? Foucault is going to hear about this. You know he is. How about we just go ahead and give back the cameras to the nice papara—"

"Shut up bitch!" the woman screamed. "Give me back my camera!"

John had paused for a moment, as if listening to Adele. He seemed to be doing his best to do this more ever since they'd gone on their date. The moment the woman shrieked though, his eyes hardened like flint.

Adele felt her stomach sink. She knew what was coming before it happened. "No!" she protested, desperately. "Don't—"

John tossed both cameras over the railing. He flashed a satisfied smirk towards the two paparazzi and winked. "She *was* here to sleep with me," John said, grinning. "We've been sleeping together for years!

Her mother too!"

Then, he spat off to the side and turned.

The two paparazzi were both staring, slack-jawed at where their equipment had plopped into the river. Adele winced, staring over the railing at two expanding rings of white against the blue. The riverboat continued away, distancing from them.

"Psychopath!" The woman screamed. "Tyrannical fascist!"

John winked at her. "Prove it." Then, he turned, his expression darkening as he marched towards Adele.

"John..." Adele said, slowly. "You can't—"

"What's done is done," he snapped. "Come on. Let's go."

"John!" she protested.

"No. We go."

Adele sighed at the top of the stairs, leaning back and tilting her head to stare forlorn at the blue sky. She closed her eyes for a moment. "Absolutely insane," she muttered beneath her breath. "John!" she yelled, turning. "John, come back!"

The two paparazzi were leaning against the railing. The man no longer seemed to be rubbing his neck, but his face was screwed up like a child on the verge of tantrum, his eyes red. He shook his head, blubbering, "We have to call someone! The police! The press! Someone! How dare—how *dare—"*

"I knew that little slut was sleeping around," the woman was muttering, seemingly taking the drowning of her camera in stride. "I knew it. Hang on Henry, I'm calling the office. New front page headline."

Adele seemed forgotten now in the face of a new story.

She sighed beneath her breath, and then turned, moving back down the stairs quickly after John.

The tall Frenchman was standing next to the manager whose phone was still in his hand. John shrugged and pointed towards the manager. Adele approached, glaring at Renee.

"Whoops," he said, beneath his breath.

She jammed her elbow into his ribs. "Whoops my ass," she muttered. "You're lucky if we don't end up fired for that."

"No evidence," John muttered.

"Yeah? If they ask me about it, I'm going to sell you out," Adele returned. "What is it with you and chucking cameras off of some place high?"

John scratched his chin. He shrugged. "Bad childhood?"

"Shut up."

"Nervous tic?"

"I said shut up. What?" she demanded, rounding on the manager. She switched back to German seamlessly, "Those manifests?"

"Yes... umm... should I ask about that commotion, hmm?"

"Just a misunderstanding," Adele muttered.

The manager gave a weary sigh, clearly tired of all the excitement. "I see. Well, Mr. Larsen said he'll send the manifests to you in the time frame you requested. Just so long as you don't park the boats."

"Fine, whatever. Give me the phone—I'll tell him where."

She heard the sound of angry footsteps against the stairwell behind her and winced. "John, head downstairs. I'll meet you there."

"And what am I supposed to do?"

"How about you avoid throwing anything overboard for a little bit? Call it a personal growth moment."

"I mean seriously. What should I do?"

Adele rubbed at her forehead for a moment, wincing and closing her eyes. Why was she dating this man again? Some things were beyond mysterious. Still, now wasn't the time to berate her partner. A couple of furious paparazzi aside, they still had bigger fish to fry. Or, in John's case, to bean with a chucked Canon.

"The boats," she said at last. Eventually, Foucault would come calling. The moment he heard what John had done, shit would hit the fan. But in the meantime, in the words of Renee, what was done was done. She couldn't dwell on it—not now. Reasoning with John was like trying to break through a brick wall with gelatin. No, best to just solve the case. Foucault could handle the rest. She swallowed back any further berating and refocused. "Look, I need you to figure out which ones are still on the water. The ones that belong to Sightseeing Incorporated."

"The boats?" John said.

"Yes, the boats." Adele was now pushing her partner towards the stairs. She could hear the clang of footsteps reaching their level from behind. She winced, leading John hurriedly down the stairs in a hasty retreat. After him, she called, "Find which ones have been active and will be active this week. If the killer is going to strike again, it will be on one of those. Now *move!"*

CHAPTER TWELVE

Adele found herself at the back of the riverboat on the lowest level, leaning against a metal post with a thick, wet rope tied around it. She winced against a spray of water, glancing once more at her phone. Still no manifests.

She glanced over her shoulder, along the more crowded portion of the boat. Nearly thirty passengers lined the lowest railing, some of them tossing breadcrumbs to seabirds, and others taking video of the passing countryside and other watercraft. Many were smiling, speckled with spray and damp.

Adele breathed heavily, grateful for the small crowd blocking her from view. The paparazzi hadn't yet found her again, but she knew once they did, things wouldn't be pretty.

She returned her attention to her phone. Again, no message. No documents of the manifest—like she'd requested. No call from Foucault—at least this part was good news.

She winced, anticipating the call. What would he do when he found out what John had done?

Renee's career was like a cat. It had nine lives. But even the most feline folk ran out of luck eventually. The crazy thing was, this wasn't the first time John had thrown a reporter's camera. Then again, to call those two *reporters* was a severe disrespect to the profession.

Adele leaned back, listening to the swish of the water against the hull, inhaling the breeze. She checked her phone again. Still no messages.

Was Mr. Larsen going to stiff her on the info? The man had sounded angry enough when she'd threatened to dock his boats. He'd promised to send the manifests along within the hour...

He only had fifteen minutes left.

For a moment, she considered calling John. The tall Frenchman was hiding out in the victim's vacant room, thanks to the Pierre, the manager.

John hadn't admitted anything, but Pierre had seemed a sharp fellow. He'd snickered when offering to show John a place he could make some calls and made a comment about "raining cameras." John had giggled in return which had only soured Adele's mood further.

No, best not to call him either. John was still busy trying to track the various boats owned by Sightseeing Incorporated. She wondered if he was faring any better.

Adele sighed, lifting her phone a third time. Still no messages, good or bad.

She cycled back to the case files in her email, opening the documents for the two victims. She'd already been through them. Zeynep Akbulut's information was nearly six pages long, most of it detailing what they already knew about her family's connections and fortune. Anika Blythe, on the other hand, barely had half a page. Her information didn't start until two years ago.

Nothing before that. Some tentative suggestion she was a student, but even the university where she studied seemed unconfirmed.

Strange. A name change? False papers?

Adele frowned, her eyes on the small photograph of the young woman in question. She had dark hair and kind eyes, and even in the license photo she was smiling at the camera.

Adele felt a flash of anger shoot through her. What a waste. She exhaled slowly, nostrils flaring. Anika Blythe... Perhaps no official record...

But what about unofficial?

Adele cycled in her phone to the internet client, typing in Anika's name and then searching through the most common social media engines.

She scrolled past one, then another. She clicked on a link, cycling to the profile pictures in question. The photos didn't match.

Adele refined the search on the profile, typing in the name and then "Vienna."

It took a moment, but as the results displayed, Adele's nose wrinkled... None of them matched the driver's license photo. She clicked to the second page... Then the third.

None of the photographs matched—

She stopped, staring, eyes fixed on a photo at the bottom of the screen.

Not a picture of Anika Blythe, but one of Anika B.

Adele clicked on the photo, cycling to the profile. It was sparse, nearly empty, as if everything had been hastily deleted. Only the profile picture remained. Adele clicked on the photo, frowning as another gust of wind and river spray speckled her cheeks and dappled her phone.

She wiped her sleeve over the phone, accidentally zooming in on the picture.

It was the second victim, alright, and Anika B wasn't alone. She sat next to a young man with a wide, sparkling smile. A handsome man, with blonde hair and a rugby-player chin. His ears were also bumped and bruised—cauliflower ears. Either a fighter or someone involved in contact sports.

Adele frowned at the photo, zooming out again. "Hello there," she murmured quietly. "Does our mystery beau have a name..."

She moved to the description of the photo. It had Anika's name and a simple caption. First, a small little red heart. Then the text, "w/ Emile."

The name "Emile" was hyperlinked. She noticed the photo had been uploaded nearly three years ago. It was clearly the same girl from the driver's license, but her last name on the media profile was missing, and other than the one picture, everything seemed to have been scorch-earthed.

Adele waited as the site loaded with her mobile data. The link to Emile's name led to another profile—this one far more active beneath the blue and white heading.

She cycled down, scrolling slowly, and then she stiffened.

Emile Hemler was still active on the site. In fact, he'd posted only a week ago. And there, in the picture was a group of young men and women, out at some sort of bar or party, it seemed. The text above the photo simply read, "*#clout.*"

Adele's eyes narrowed, but then stopped.

There, next to the handsome blonde man, with cauliflower ears, she spotted a picture of the victim. Except, it wasn't Anika Blythe. Rather, there in the picture, taken against the bumper of a Lamborghini, Zeynep Akbulut stood with one arm wrapped around Emile's shoulder.

Both of them were beaming at the camera, surrounded by other good-looking, young men and women.

"Hello there," Adele murmured softly, staring at the picture and then taking a screenshot. "Emile Hemler," she murmured. "And where might you be from..."

What were the odds? The same young man, three years ago in Anika's picture. Now, three years later, in a picture—posted only last week—with Zeynep Akbulut. Both clearly romantically involved once upon a time. And both women now ended up dead.

She moved back to Emile's profile information and then paused, staring. The young man was from Ingolstadt. She glanced up from her phone, along the river. Ingolstadt... wasn't that...

She shook her head slowly, trying to piece it together when a voice suddenly cleared behind her, and Adele nearly leapt out of her skin. She spun around, hand to her chest and glared at where John stood, watching her with a smirk.

"Don't sneak up on me like that!" she snapped.

A few passengers behind John looked over and then pretended they weren't watching.

"Sorry," John said, who clearly wasn't. "I got the information you wanted, though." He wiggled his phone in her direction.

"Stop smiling, I'm still mad at you. Has Foucault called you yet?"

John shook his head. "No evidence, no call. Trust me. I've done this before."

"That's not what I want to hear, John. Stop smiling. I'm—"

"Still mad at me. I heard you. But look, maybe this will help."

He turned the phone towards her, still, to her irritation, grinning.

"What am I looking at?"

John cycled through the picture, pointing at highlighted words in the far-right column. "The itinerary of each and every ship in the last week owned by Sightseeing Incorporated." Now, instead of happy, he looked mildly smug.

"They gave you all that?" Adele blinked.

"I hit it off with Pierre. He seems to like me."

"He's not going to send you very nice texts too, is he? Marshall and he should start a fan club."

"You sound annoyed, my dear. How's that manifest coming?"

"It's coming fine," Adele growled. "Give this to me." She cycled through the phone in John's hand, her expression still sour, before she paused, pulling up short. Her eyebrows inched up. She frowned, glancing back at her own phone, then turning to the itinerary a second time. "Shit," she muttered.

"What?" John asked, leaning in, eagerly.

"Ingolstadt is on here... A boat's leaving there this evening. In an hour."

"So?"

"So..." Adele said, looking up at John, "it means that city is on the Sightseeing Incorporated Route."

"And?"

"And, I found a young man by the name of Emile Hemler who was romantically involved with *both* of our victims."

"Let me guess," John said, his eyes fixed all of a sudden, his smirk turning to a look of cresting anticipation. "He lives in Ingolstadt."

"Yes. Exactly."

"And this boat?" John said, quickly. "Will it get us there?"

Adele glanced at the itinerary and winced. "No. It's not due to dock. Next stop is in Steinheim, thirty minutes from Ingolstadt."

John gripped the rail, his jaw tightening, his eyes fixed. "We need to get off this boat, then. If this fellow was involved with *both* victims, and also lives on the route for the riverboats, he had means and opportunity. And where romance is involved, there's always motive."

"Exactly. We need to get to Ingolstadt and catch him before he boards."

CHAPTER THIRTEEN

He gritted his teeth against the pain, though not too hard. He didn't want to crack a tooth. One hand gripped the forearm of his new apprentice, his lips close to her ear, hissing through flecks of spit and blood. "Where is your car, my dove?" he said in broken German, doing his best to enunciate in the dark. They walked hurriedly along a row of parked vehicles, moving across the broken and cracked sidewalk on the darker portion of the street. Two of the lights above them were out.

The young woman whose arm he gripped whimpered softly, shaking her head and muttering something too quickly for him to understand.

He tightened his grip, and with his free hand, jabbed his backup knife—which he'd kept in his rental car—against her spine. The rental was gone, already picked apart by police, no doubt. Bridges and airports would be watched. Hospitals too.

He winced at the thought, limping and feeling the warmth from his injuries, especially the glass along his face and chest.

He let out a rasping little puff of air and jabbed his knife again. "Car! Now!"

It had taken nearly thirty minutes to attract his apprentice. Playing possum by an old alley near a sandwich shop closed for the evening had proven difficult enough. His small size, though, especially at night, in the dark, often attracted good Samaritans, thinking he was a child.

His new apprentice had made cooing noises as she'd approached, murmuring, "Hello? Are you okay?"

And that was when their lovely little apprenticeship had started. He needed a car, but also a plan.

He guided his apprentice further, poking and prodding at her spine, enjoying her little squeals of pain and fear. "There," she managed to eke out, pointing with a trembling finger towards the end of the street. "There!" she repeated, fiercely as he poked at her back, even harder.

He liked the way their bodies contorted under pain. Liked the little gasps. Liked the sheer control of something so simple as sharpened steel. Her will was now his. Such an odd thing to conquer another human's autonomy.

He licked at the edge of his lip for a moment, panting softly and grinning in the night. Just as quickly as the pleasurable shiver had come, though, he felt a jolt of pain up his side, and along his cheek and he winced, scowling.

"Keys!" he snapped. "Now!"

"Please," she said, desperately. "Please—don't hurt me!"

"Keys," he barked. Damn it. What was the German word for 'hurry.' He sighed and poked at her back again, through her sweater. The woman stiffened, wincing. Across the street, a couple of customers were stepping out of a gas station. One of them glanced over, noticing the young woman and the small man accompanying her.

"Silence," the painter snapped. "Quiet!"

The woman whimpered, but obeyed, marching along the sidewalk, under the broken streetlights, away from the gas station, and away from witnesses.

They were nearing the green SUV the woman had indicated. Green. Not ideal. A color that stood out. He wrinkled his nose, but decided it was the best they could do on short notice.

He'd really screwed up. He should have killed the s Sergeant. He gritted his teeth, though not too tightly, and gave the woman another push along the sidewalk, sending her stumbling, but then reeling back due to his grip on her arm, like some sort of lure on a fishing line.

They approached the SUV, and he heard the jangling sound of keys in trembling fingers as she pulled them out, desperately trying to hand them over.

In the distance, he heard the sound of a siren. For a moment, he stiffened, watching blue and red lights, from streets over, reflect across the windows of the large apartment complex to their right.

"Please," the woman was blubbering now. Probably with snot bubbles and spit. All the nasty little fluids leaking from the orifices of his canvas.

"Shut up!" he snarled in French. "Open the door! Open it—now!"

He glanced back over his shoulder in the direction of the gas station, wincing once more against the pain in his neck, along his cheek. Damn it. He should have cut Joseph Sharp's neck. Should have killed him. Now he had too much heat.

Airports were out of the question. Bridges too. Even using a car... risky. Very risky. But he needed a place to lie low. Somewhere to hide for a bit until things cooled down. Leaving Germany by conventional means was out of the question...

He paused for a moment, frowning.

What about unconventional?

He watched as the keys were pressed and the lights to the SUV flashed as the automatic locks clicked. He watched the woman try to shove the keys towards him, desperately. She held out her hands as if in surrender, trying to step back. "Yours," she was saying. "Please. It's yours."

"No," he said, smiling for a moment. "Don't be silly, dear. You're coming with me. Go on now—go on. I'll be gentle." He jammed the knife against her back, even harder.

The woman tried to protest, her eyes flashing horribly, glancing back in the direction of the gas station. But the customers had returned to their own car and were pulling away in the opposite direction. Even the red and blue lights, and the distant sound of the siren had faded now.

They were alone, in the dark, with the SUV.

The painter paused, standing next to the canvas. She had a small little tattoo on her wrist—he could see it when she'd opened the car door, where she still gripped her keys trying to offer them to him like some sort of sacrifice to appease a god.

He frowned at the tattoo past her sleeve.

A marked canvas.

He could feel his temper rising, staring at the stupid little squiggle of ink. A *marked* canvas!

"Bitch!" he snarled, and slapped her, hard with an open hand.

She yelped, but didn't retreat, the knife still against her spine.

"Please," she sputtered. "Take it. Take the car. Yours."

She spoke in broken and stuttered German as people often did with foreigners, thinking that somehow, by dumbing down their speech they would make it easier to understand. He snorted, and took in a delicate, inhaling little breath, trying to think.

Well, that tattoo was just the icing on the cake, wasn't it? He was looking forward to a long night of stress-relief and creative expression, somewhere in a parking lot, hidden from sight, where the screams could be muffled.

But what was the point playing with an already marked canvas? Even now, hearing her whimpering, he wrinkled his nose.

Tempting, certainly tempting. But he was no hack. He wouldn't paint over another's work. Especially some sloppy, amateur.

No. This was the cherry on top of a shit sundae. Everything ruined.

Joseph Sharp alive. Police out in droves. He couldn't leave the country... And now the tattoo—even the pleasure he'd planned for the evening. Ruined.

He stood for a moment, considering his next step, one hand still pressing his blade to the woman's spine, the other gripping the keys she'd extended, relieving them from her grasp, and holding them tight in his fingers.

There would be roadblocks on bridges, at checkpoints. Even the car couldn't last long.

But if not a car, no airplanes, no trains...

He paused, frowning briefly. Then his brow, the shaved eyebrows no more than a prickle, arose.

What about a boat?

He'd heard of more than one cruising riverboat crossing into Austria and beyond via the Danube... How far to such a stop? Not too far, surely... Close enough. Certainly close enough.

He exhaled, nodding to himself and making up his mind. He needed out of this cursed country, this botched masterpiece. He needed out *now.*

"Thank you," he said, quietly.

And then, he jammed the knife into her spine, allowing her to fall. The blade twisted as she stumbled, like a puppet with snipped strings, yelping in pain as she did. He stared at where she lay, bleeding on the ground.

She might not die. For a moment, he just watched her writhe in agony. He leaned against the hood of the SUV, wiping his knife off on his sleeve, and hefting the car keys. She twisted and contorted in such lovely patterns. He could have just killed her outright, could have cut her deep... but where was the fun in that?

Someone had already marked this canvas. And now he'd ruined it.

Maybe, if he'd aimed properly, she'd recover the use of her legs... with some therapy. Maybe she'd be wheelchair bound. Maybe no one would find her, and she'd simply bleed out. She was whimpering now, increasing in volume.

He leaned down, patted her on the cheek, and murmured, "Thank you," again. He watched her writhe for a moment longer, for the sheer joy of it.

And then, he slid into his new vehicle, humming to himself, wincing against the shards in his cheek, and putting the vehicle in gear. He felt a momentary temptation to run over the woman where she lay, half on the sidewalk, half off.

But why put her out of her misery?

Misery was the point, after all.

And so, carefully, he avoided the form of the desperately mewling thing and pulled onto the road, driving slowly, carefully, and checking street signs. He needed to make his way to the river, and then onto one of the riverboats.

The clock was ticking. The noose was tightening.

But like always, they'd miss him again. They always did.

CHAPTER FOURTEEN

John and Adele reached Ingolstadt as night arrived and the clouds came with it. The city seemed separated between main portions of civilization, large swathes of farmland, and then residential islands of homes clumped together amidst the flat land. Adele gritted her teeth, glancing up at the sky as their taxi driver pulled into the parking lot outside the dock. She glanced at the small, red digital clock on the dash and shook her head. "Boat isn't leaving for another twenty minutes," she said, quickly.

John frowned, glancing towards the vessel sitting by the dock. A few passengers were handing tickets to a collector and being ushered up the ramp, but for now, the area was sparse under the darkening skies.

The tall Frenchman's eyes darted to the railing beneath the bridge, and he exhaled softly, pushing out of the taxi and stepping onto the sidewalk. Adele remained in the front, frowning and checking her phone. "Address came in," she said quickly.

John leaned against the window, ignoring the taxi driver who watched them both curiously.

"Emile Hemler's address?" John asked.

Adele bobbed her head, once, frowning from the boat to her phone. "He only lives ten minutes from here."

"He might not be getting on the boat," John said. "Maybe he's laying low."

"We still don't know it's him."

"He knew both victims—intimately."

"True. Still."

John scratched the back of his head, one forearm against the outside of the windowsill, his full frame half-bent. "Well? What now?"

Adele frowned in concentration, considering their options. She looked at the sky again as the clouds pulled in. A heavy rainfall might affect the riverboat schedules. On the other hand, the forecast only mentioned a drizzle.

"One of us needs to be with the boat," she murmured. "No choice. If Emile's the killer, he'll be on it. If not, we at least need someone on one of those things."

"There were ten boats owned by the company," John replied, softly. "If Emile isn't our guy—we have a ninety percent chance of choosing the wrong floater."

Adele leaned her head back, and she could feel the dark eyes of the taxi driver watching them even more curiously now. Again, she ignored the man, hoping that by speaking in French they were offered enough privacy.

They needed to find Emile. It was the only lead, and a strong connection between the two victims. On one hand, he very might well have been in transit, or heading to the boat now. For all she knew, he'd already boarded.

On the other hand, if he was at home, someone needed to find him before he could slip away.

"Think we have to split up," Adele muttered, feeling a sour taste in her mouth. "No, I know. I hate it too. But what other option? You need to go on the boat, I'll go to his house."

John sighed, pushing off the windowsill and crossing his arms over his large chest. "You sure? I could go with you. You might need backup. I've seen you shoot."

"Ha. Funny. But no. We need someone with the boat."

"*Merde*. Fine," John said, rubbing his jaw, and glancing up at the ever-darkening skies and the gathering clouds. "Looks like rain," he muttered.

"Forecast doesn't think so."

"Those guys are never right," John snorted. He turned back towards the boat, shaking his head. "I hate the water," he muttered beneath his breath.

Adele patted her partner through the window, fingers against his knuckles. "You'll be fine," she said. "Just avoid the wet part."

"Great. Thanks. Avoid the wet part—genius advice American Princess." He snorted, and began to move away, heading towards the boat and leaving Adele with the taxi driver and her phone—carrying Emile's address—resting on her lap.

Before he'd gotten far, though, John's phone began to ring. He paused, pulling it out and checking it. The blue light reflected off his features in the darkening night. After a moment, John stiffened, wincing.

"Who?" Adele asked.

John swallowed, and then clicked the phone to silent, stowing it back in his pocket. “No one,” he muttered.

“Who was it, John?” Adele said, eyes narrowed.

“No one,” he repeated.

“It was Foucault, wasn't it?”

“Dunno. It's fine. I've got it handled!” John waved over his shoulder and began to march towards the ticket queue to the boat again.

Adele pushed her head out the window, calling after him, “You can't dodge his call forever, John!”

He waved again, this time without looking back, hunching his shoulders against the cool breeze over the river, and marching with steady steps, like a man facing the gallows, towards the boat on the river.

Adele sighed, leaning back inside the cab and glancing towards the driver. She switched the German and, softly, murmured, “Here, please.” She pushed her phone, showing him the address for Emile Hemler.

Without comment, the driver nodded once, not even plugging the address into a GPS, suggesting he knew these streets by memory, and pulled out of the small, concrete lot behind the docks. He moved onto the street beneath the overcast skies, steadily picking up speed as he maneuvered through the outskirts of Ingolstadt between the farmland bridging the gap of suburban islands.

Adele's one arm rested against the frame of the open window, her bangs fluttering in her eyes, and she winced. Night was coming.

And with it, predators in the dark would start to hunt.

CHAPTER FIFTEEN

Adele thanked the taxi driver while sliding quickly out of her seat and pointing up the sidewalk. "Wait for me there, please. I shouldn't take long."

The driver frowned at her, but then sighed and nodded, gravel crunching quietly as he maneuvered up the street towards the indicated stretch of road. The small houses on the outskirts of Ingolstadt were only a ten-minute drive from the docks. Even here, she could smell the odor of river water and glimpse evidence of gulls and birds which had made their mark on the sidewalk and the occasional parked car on the old, worn streets.

She glanced at her phone again, double-checking the address, then frowned towards a small, worn white duplex. The windows on one side were shuttered, and one of the windows was boarded up, with indications of blue-green glass on the ground, suggesting it had been shattered from the inside.

Adele's eyes narrowed further as she moved slowly up the sidewalk, one hand darting to her firearm, caressing the grip.

Adele came to a halt in front of the door, next to the boarded-up window. She scraped some shards of glass off to the side with her shoe, momentarily thinking back to her father's house in Germany. She frowned, and glanced up, noticing a security camera facing the driveway. Her frown only deepened. The camera didn't have the door or the sidewalk in view. Rather, it angled off to the side of the house, as if keeping an eye on the small garage behind the condo. Adele tapped against the door, stepping back and placing her hand on her holster.

"Police!" She called, her voice filling the air.

She heard the sound of a smashing bottle further up the street, and what sounded like voices, drifting from an open window on the other side of the condo.

She waited, frowning, and then knocked again, louder. She tried the door handle. Locked.

"DGSI!" She said, louder now, her voice carrying in the night.

Again, no answer. Feeling a jolt of frustration, she open-palmed the door, banging hard. Her other hand gripped her firearm, her knuckles tight.

"Open up! Police!" She yelled.

Again, there was no answer.

Muttering to herself, Adele began to turn but just then, she heard what sounded like a million old men gargling their throats. It took her a moment to realize it was the noise of a sports car engine. She wrinkled her nose, glancing along the street, and watched as a spaceship pulled up the road, moving towards her. The thing looked like something out of a movie, with bright red paint, and even two little German flags fluttering from the mirrors. Someone had stenciled big, blocky, graffiti style letters over the hood. Along with the horrible engine sounds, loud, obnoxious music blared from the tinted windows. She stared, jaw unhinged, as the sports car pulled into the driveway of the condo, moving beneath the security camera pointed towards the garage, and then came to a purring halt.

The noise died, mercifully, and the music shut off a second later. The door slammed, and she heard the crunch of footsteps as someone moved around the side of the house, humming off key to complete the now silent song from the overpowering car stereo system.

A handsome, blonde man stepped around the side of the condo, flicking keys between his fingers, but then pulled up short, staring at her.

Adele met his gaze, frowning. "Emile?" she said, her voice gruff.

She recognized the man from the Facebook pictures. He had the jaw of some sort of athlete, and the physique to match. His pants were low, and his shirt untucked. The keys which had been circling his fingers came to a halt, and he hastily jammed them into his pocket. "Who are you?" he snapped, frowning. A second later, his eyes darted to her weapon, and he swallowed, taking a quick step back.

"Police," Adele said in German, deciding to avoid the alphabet soup conversation about all the different agencies she was associated with. "I need to speak with you."

The young man glanced shiftily off to the side and scratched at his chin. "Is this about Zeynep?"

Adele followed his gaze toward the expensive car parked in front of the garage. She looked up at the security camera facing the thing. "Yes. So you know what happened to her?"

The man crossed his arms, frowning. "Everyone knows," he said quietly.

"Mind stepping onto the porch, and keeping your hands where I can see them?"

For a moment, she thought he might refuse. This was the only connecting point between the two victims, so far. He lived within a ten-minute drive of the Danube. He'd clearly been romantically involved with the victims. Means. Motive. Opportunity.

But instead of retreating, the young man sighed and stepped onto the porch, moving towards the door, and leaning against it.

When he turned to face her though, Adele stared in surprise. The man was blinking tears from his eyes. He reached up, rubbing angrily at his face, sniffling, and then glancing off again. The silence stretched, now.

For a moment Adele stood there, rooted to the spot, feeling a jolt of discomfort and she stared at the young man doing everything in his power not to meet her gaze.

She adjusted, swallowing once, and then shifted track. "I'm sorry for your loss," she said slowly. "Do you know why I'm here?"

"You just said. Zeynep."

"And when did you hear she..." Adele trailed off.

"Was murdered? On the news. Like everyone else."

Adele felt a pang of guilt and pity. "I'm sorry you found out that way. I take it you two were close."

He shrugged, his chin jutting off to the side for a moment. "We were what we were," he said, growling. "We didn't put a label on it."

Adele looked past him towards the driveway again. "That car was a gift?"

He hesitated, looking like he wanted to deny it, but then, with an air of resignation, his eyes still damp, he nodded once. He glanced sheepishly at the busted window of his small condo. "Hardly something I could afford. She paid the insurance, too. I guess I'm gonna have to sell it now. Though I'd give it away it meant I could get her back."

It was a dramatic, romantic notion and yet it seemed authentic coming from his lips. The same lips were now trembling, as if he were trying to hold back further tears. Adele remained hesitant, her hand slowly leaving her holster. She wasn't sure what to do. Generally, she had a good read on people. And as far she could tell, Emile was exhibiting grief, not guilt. But killers were clever, too. She remained attentive, watchful, studying him.

"How did you know Zeynep?" Adele said, quietly.

He shrugged once shoulder, adjusting his low hanging pants. "We'd been hanging out for nearly a year. She liked me. Some people thought she could be a bit..." he hesitated, and then trailed off. "But she wasn't like that around me. It took some time for her to lower her guard is all. She was brought up different. But she tried really, really hard to make friends. The reason she cared so much about what everyone thought of her was because she wanted people to like her. And sometimes, without realizing it," he shook his head, "she could annoy people with how hard she tried." He smiled softly. And shrugged. "I'm not that sensitive though. I kind of liked it when she got like that. It was cute."

He sniffed again, leaning against the door and banging his head softly against the wood. He closed his eyes. "Why are you here? Did you find who did it?" He looked at her, earnest.

Adele didn't reply at first, her lips feeling dry all of a sudden. She considered her options. Her instincts were whispering one thing, but the facts suggested another thing entirely. Slowly, still careful, Adele said, "Did you know a young woman by the name of Anika? You were in an online photo from three years ago."

The man frowned. "Three years... Oh, yes. Anika? I... a while ago, yeah. What about her?"

"Did you know that she was murdered yesterday?"

It was as if he'd been shot. The man gaped, and then doubled over, sliding down to the porch. He made a wheezing, gasping sound, and then looked up at her, his eyes desperate. "You're joking," he said.

"I'm afraid not," Adele murmured. "She was found yesterday. You know anything about it?"

The man's fingers were trembling, and he shook his head wildly side to side. "I'm cursed," he murmured. "I'm cursed. I can't believe it. Annie too? When? How?"

Adele watched him, trying not to be too cold, but also refusing to be drawn in with the emotional outburst. One could never tell with psychopaths. They often practiced enough to blend in. But another part of her, a softer part went out to Emile. As far as she could tell, he was in genuine pain. The tears alone seemed real enough.

"I'm very sorry for your loss. I have to ask, though, it's strange how both of them were romantically involved with you."

He looked at her as if he'd been slapped, staring unblinking with tear-filled eyes. "Y-you think *I* did this?"

"We're following all leads. I don't think anything. It is strange that you live in Germany, and Anika was from France, yet somehow you two were still connected."

At this, though, he snorted. "No, she wasn't."

"Excuse me?"

"Anika Everett? Right? The one in that picture online. That's the Anika I know."

"No. not Everett. Anika Blythe," Adele said, slowly.

Here, though, Emile just snorted, some of the grief lifting for a brief moment as he shook his head in disbelief. "Her name wasn't Blythe! That's just what she told people. Her last name was Everett. We went to the same school. That's how I met both her and Zeynep. I was lucky to get in. Pure scholarships." He shrugged. "I don't have much money, but I'm good at math."

"You met them at university?"

"Yes. Anika changed her name. Her last name. She's from here. I can show you her house. Only a twenty-minute drive." He glanced sheepishly to the side. "It's in a much nicer neighborhood. Much," he said, emphasizing the word.

Adele could feel her brow furrow, could feel her heartbeat pestering her chest. "You're telling me Anika's last name isn't Blythe?

"No. It's Everett. She changed it when her parents kicked her out."

Adele paused, and then her eyes widened. "Wait, Everett? As in Everett Motors?"

The young man tapped his nose and pointed at her. He gave a soft little sigh, staring at his fingers, and closing his eyes. "She was a good girl," he said, softly. "Didn't respect her father's business practices. Thought he was making his money through exploitation. It led to this huge fight. And so she left. They cut her off. She had to switch schools. Go to a cheaper place. She moved to Vienna. I think she wanted a new start. I was sad to see her go. But I haven't seen her in a while." His voice trembled like a child's. "You're sure she's the one who died?"

Adele paused, but then gave a brief, quiet nod, frowning, her own mind racing. She stared at Emile, and then said, softly, "Where were you last night?"

At this, he snorted. "The same place I am every night, every week. Up at the library at the school. We have to check in online. Hang on. Let me show you."

He fished out his phone, and quickly scrolled through; a second later he lifted it, showing the device to her. It was a page for a school library with signatures on a screen. She peered in at the check-in times. He flipped to another page, and Adele frowned.

"Four-thirty until midnight?" she said. "You do that every night?"

He shrugged. "Like I said, I don't come from money. I have to keep the scholarships up. Besides, why would I kill them? I liked them. Zeynep brought me that car. I'm not able to keep it without her. Maintenance alone will bankrupt me."

Adele glanced back at the phone. "Would you have been recognized at the library?"

"Yes," he said, emphatically, wagging his thick chin, his blonde hair swishing. "I bring coffee to the librarian every night when I arrive. Besides, the school is like an hour from here. I hear Zeynep was killed on a boat. There's no way I could've been there."

"This librarian, she would've seen you arrive and leave?"

He shrugged. "You can ask her. Most likely. Others would've seen me too. The janitor is usually the one that chases me out of the fireside study room so he can lock up. Sometimes he lets me stay longer. You can ask them. I don't know their numbers. But I'm sure the school website has them."

Adele could feel her stomach sinking. Of course, the online sign-in sheet wouldn't be enough. She would have to check his alibi. But her instincts were starting to override the inference of the facts... Emile didn't act like a guilty man. She had a slow, cresting prickle along her back, coupled with an inkling of a suspicion that Emile's alibi would check out.

Shit.

She shook her head slowly, and said, "I need you to stick around. Just so long as I confirm your story. Again, I'm sorry for your loss. Truly."

The young man watched her and gave a soft little sad sigh.

Adele turned, shaking her head. What more could she do? It wasn't like she thought it was him anymore. Now, though, the connection seemed clear. It wasn't Emile. It wasn't some boyfriend in Germany.

No, rather, it seemed obvious enough.

Akbulut came from wealth. An heiress to a fashion empire. And Everett Motors was also a household name among anyone associated with the elites of the elites. Another young woman attached to wealth.

Both of them rich. Both of them heiresses to empires, and now both of them dead.

That would be the connection.

She gritted her teeth, heading quickly towards the taxi and waving for it to approach. She needed to tell John.

CHAPTER SIXTEEN

Agent Renee stretched his legs, stalking up the metal stairs towards the bridge. He needed to see if they could delay the boat. So far, no sign of the young man in Adele's picture.

He paused for a moment on the second deck, staring down towards the passengers below. He watched them, his eyes flicking, trying to spot their suspect.

"Come on," he murmured softly. "Where are you?"

As his eyes darted around, though, there was no sign of Emile Hemler. John glanced down at his phone, scrolling towards the pictures again, to double check. The wind was picking up over the river, and the horn for the riverboat blared—a final warning for passengers.

John cursed, glancing towards the bridge. Through the tinted and slanted windows, he could see the captain behind the controls. Maybe he should stop the thing. His fingers moved towards his identification, and his jaw set in a determined line.

Just then, though, something caught his eye. John frowned, staring across the deck, towards a row of doors for quarters. A young woman hurried along the rail, heading towards the back of the boat.

A second later, as the woman clutched at her purse and moved quickly, John watched a dark figure fall into step behind her. The man was moving slow, carefully, stepping lightly. He even glanced over his shoulder with a nervous posture. He continued in the direction of the young woman, still moving slowly, on the balls of his feet.

John frowned, his attention diverted from the bridge.

He watched the fellow approach the young woman and could feel his heartbeat skipping. The two of them disappeared around the side of the boat. The young woman didn't seem to notice the man sneaking up behind her.

John growled, listening as the final warning from the riverboat blared in the sky. The clouds were even thicker above, threatening rain. John picked up the pace, hastening along the rail, along the side of the deck, in the direction where the two figures had disappeared from sight.

***

She looked so vulnerable, just standing there, leaning against the railing and wearing that pretty red dress. Her blonde curls were caught by the breeze, beneath the overcast skies. He glanced up, looking against the night-time horizon.

Rain was coming. Soon, the skies would weep. Good. Grief was the proper response. He held a rose in one hand, twisting and twirling it. His fingers rubbed against the thorns, and he glanced towards the small note card he'd taped to the stem of the ruby rose.

He looked up again, watching as she moved along the rail, heading around the side of the ship, her red dress fluttering.

He smiled to himself, but then glanced back over his shoulder. A tall man was moving towards him. He frowned, watching the tall man duck under the stairwell, and continue in his direction.

He gritted his teeth, feeling the cold in his chest spread to his stomach. He jammed one hand into his pocket, ducking his head as if against the breeze, but also shielding his face from sight. He held the rose and felt a prick of one of the thorns against his thumb. He winced, dropping the rose and the card. His finger leapt to his mouth, on instinct alone, and he sucked at the blood.

He cursed, and bent over, reaching slowly for the rose again. He paused, kneeling against the cold metal, glancing along the edge of the boat in the direction where she had disappeared.

He could no longer hear her footsteps. Had she gone below deck again? Shit.

Behind him, he could hear the clang of footsteps on the metal. The tall man was drawing nearer, the shadows stretching before him. A horn blared in the air, warning the passengers the boat was about to embark.

Before he had fully plucked the rose off the ground, large fingers reached past him, grabbing the rose then picking it up. A gruff voice murmured, "You dropped this."

He hesitated, still staring at the ground, not wanting to be seen near the second deck; he muttered a hasty apology and accepted the red flower. Hunched and refusing to make eye contact, he began to stroll, as if aimlessly, along the deck. He couldn't pick up his pace. Not yet. It would be too suspicious. He couldn't do anything memorable. He needed to be forgotten, unseen. A ghost. Expendable at his very core. Just like it had all started.

He held the rose, his thumb streaked with blood. He winced, and continued to move, slowly, listening for the sound of footsteps behind him. He could feel the tall man watching him. He'd come too far to back out now, though. He gritted his teeth. If he had to take down two birds with one stone, then so be it.

***

John's frown only deepened in the night as he followed the suspicious man who continued to walk slowly on the balls of his feet after the young woman. As he rounded the back of the riverboat, he spotted as the woman paused, bending over to tie her shoe. The man behind her kept moving quietly, but picked up pace, sneaking from behind.

No other witnesses; they were in a dark, secluded corner of the second deck. His hand reached for his pocket—a flash of something silver. A knife?

“Hey!” John shouted. No time for his gun—she would be in the line of fire.

He broke into a sprint, covering the distance between them with rapid footfalls, a feral snarl ripping from his lips. “Bastard!” he yelled and lunged.

The man whirled around, the woman screamed, and John slammed into the stalker, sending both of them careening into the thick, metal rail.

John gasped heavily, his hand tight against the scruff of the man's neck and collar. He shoved the man's face towards the ground, shouting, "Don't move! Don't move!"

The man beneath him struggled, kicking, trying to rise. He sent an elbow backwards, striking John in the jaw.

The woman was screaming something in German.

John grit his teeth, wishing Adele had come with him. He always ended up needing a translator in situations like these.

Gasping heavily, John got to his feet, keeping a knee against the man and lodging him against the railing. His hand went to his holster, pulling his gun and pointing it at the fellow's head.

"Stay on the ground!" he snapped.

The man looked up at him, wide-eyed, wary. His hands, which had been scrambling towards John's leg to push it off, froze at the sight of the gun.

The woman screamed even louder now, her voice screeching towards the night sky.

John held out a cautioning hand towards her. "You're safe now," he said, firmly. He breathed, his chest rising and falling slowly.

The woman, though, stared at the gun, swallowed, but then hurried over, summoning some inner courage. She tried to tug at John's leg, muttering something beneath her breath and shaking her head.

John frowned, staring at where her small, pale hands tugged at him. The stalker was glaring, but as the woman drew near, he looked up, a tender but simultaneously sheepish look in his eyes.

John felt a jolt of confusion. Something was off. Slowly, he extricated himself from the stalker, glancing to the woman's hands, and at the expression on the man's face. Still hesitant, careful, John took a cautious step back, his gun lowering to his hip.

"No," the woman was saying, shaking her head and her finger at John. "No, please."

"I don't understand you," John retorted in French. "Police. *Polizia!*" what was the German word again. "BKA," he said, quickly, remembering Agent Marshall. Impersonating a German fed probably was a big no-no. But as far as John was concerned, everything was game in matters of translation.

At this, the woman's eyebrows shot up, and the man on the ground stiffened, wide-eyed, and shaking his head wildly. The woman rattled off a question in German, and the man replied just as hurriedly. Now that John's knee had removed, and his gun was lowered, the woman was reaching towards the man as if to help him. They both stared warily where John's weapon pointed at the ground.

John was even more confused. He swallowed, staring over the railing, then back. The woman was acting like she knew the man. And the man, now, up close, was holding a bag of crisps in one hand.

The man pointed at the bag, then the woman, and mimed a popping motion with his hands.

The woman frowned at this and tweaked the man's nose. Again, they both looked up, hesitant, cautious. The lowering of the gun seemed to strike them as good news, but the tall, muscular Frenchman over them still left them wary.

John closed his eyes for a moment, and when he opened them, he saw the woman holding the man's hand, trying to help him to his feet, both of them still careful, murmuring softly in German as if trying to appease a wild dog.

They were together. The man had been slinking up behind her to pop his chips, or surprise her. John had tackled an innocent man with his girlfriend. Perhaps wife. Maybe sister, he thought, hopefully. She was really quite pretty.

Inwardly though, he kicked himself. He was a taken man now. No point in such thoughts. He looked away, shaking his head and wincing once more. He held up an apologetic hand, holstered his gun, and then hurried away, growling to himself, and wondering where on earth Adele was.

***

He didn't think of himself as a killer.

And yet, perhaps, that was what he was. There was no sense denying the plain truth. He watched as the tall man moved off, heading behind the railing, and disappearing towards one of the rooms on the top of the ship. He breathed a soft little sigh of relief. He wasn't being followed. That had been close. He could still feel his heart hammering in his chest. He winced at his thumb, glancing down at where the thorn had pierced him. He made sure he rubbed his blood off on his shirt, leaving no sign. And then, he moved along the edge of the ship, around the railing.

A door slowly swung shut. An edge of a red dress fluttering out of sight within.

The bathroom. The door continued to slowly close, carried by a spring-loaded arm at the top. The man grunted and took three quick steps forward, his hand shooting out, catching the door before it shut completely. He slipped through the door, following after the woman, and then allowed the door to *click* behind him.

He looked around the small bathroom.

The woman hadn't seen him yet, now humming to herself and adjusting her dress in the mirror.

She wrinkled her nose as she glanced around the public toilets, and immediately went for the soap dispenser above the sink.

The man glanced towards the two stalls. Empty as far as he could tell. He looked back, reached out, and clicked the lock.

The sound alerted the woman. She spun around, sharply. The moment her eyes landed on him, she gasped. He held a finger to his lips and lifted the rose with the note.

"I have a letter for you," he said, quietly.

The woman breathed, her chest rising and falling against the red dress, her eyes wide. Her lovely curls framed her now pale face, and one hand braced against the sink, as if looking for something to throw.

"You have to understand," he said, quietly, "this isn't about you. Perhaps it is. But it shouldn't be. Not everything is about your kind. Though you live as if it is."

He wasn't sure why he was talking. The last two times he'd snuck up behind them, fast. Now, though, in a locked room, with no witnesses, it almost felt cathartic to get some of these words off his chest. How often had he wanted to talk with one of them? To tell them his piece?

She glanced uncomfortably around the bathroom, her eyes moving to the stalls now as well. But where he had been looking for witnesses, she was looking for aid. Neither of them found anything. "The letter?" she said, carefully. "For me? Please, I'll talk to you outside." She spoke confidently, firmly. The voice of the woman who'd been trained to be in charge.

Unearned authority, of course. Authority bought, and authority paid for.

He spat to the side, feeling his temper flare, his teeth set together.

"I'm lying," he said, growling and taking a step into the room. "This isn't for you. It's for someone else. Someone like you. I made a promise, and I keep my promises."

The woman was shaking her head, one of her hands still lathered with soap, the faucet still running, with a quiet swishing sound. The boat was moving now, and he could feel the quiet rumble of the engines through the vessel. A faint, quiet tremor.

But sometimes, even the softest of motions could have the greatest impact.

He took another step towards her, and now she held out her hands, shouting. "Leave me alone!"

Loud. Too loud. He couldn't let her scream. He darted forward, fast. She tried to yell. The sound died on her lips.

He tossed the rose and the note against the faucet, grabbing at her neck. He squeezed, and she slapped at his wrists. Long nails gouged against his arm. But he slammed his hand against her wrist, breaking her grip.

"Stop!" he commanded. "I'll tell your parents you miss them. I'll tell them how much you mean to them. Don't worry. Everything's going to be okay."

She tried to gasp, struggling where his hand wrapped around her throat. She whimpered, shaking her head, her curls shifting against the bathroom wall. He held her firm, though, like a butterfly pinned to a page. So pretty, so useless, so defenseless. Given beauty at birth, her wings rising from the cocoon that she had never built. A cocoon she didn't deserve. And yet compared to the moth, how much more appreciated?

And he held her there, tearing at her red dress. He reached down, ripping at the hem, and she screamed again, but the sound was muffled by his hand.

"Don't be dramatic," he sneered. "I don't want that."

He ripped part of the fabric of her dress, and as she tried to struggle, he held her fast with one hand. His other jammed the piece of her dress against her lips. But she closed her mouth, seemingly sensing what he intended.

She locked her teeth. And he snapped, "Open your mouth! Open!"

Desperately, she jutted her chin forward, but he squeezed hard against her throat and finally she opened, gasping, and he jammed the fabric past her teeth.

She tried to bite him, but he was expecting it, and jerked his fingers back. He squeezed on either side of her mouth now, releasing her throat with his other hand, and he shoved a piece of her own dress down the back of her throat until she started gagging.

It wasn't a pleasant sound. He could remember, though, that very sound for hours, weeks, months. He could remember the noise echoing in the small room, off the white walls. Could remember her eyes fluttering. The gagging, the choking, the desperation. And what had any of them done?

He growled towards the sink, and then shoved her to the ground. She was no longer struggling, his hand against her lips, the choking sound switching to a horrible, gagging noise.

Sometimes they threw up, choking on their own vomit. Other times the item did it entirely.

He held her there until the sounds stopped completely, and then, he stood up, breathing heavily. He wiped a hand across his forehead, his pricked thumb throbbing. A small streak of blood trailed over his cheek, and he stared into the mirror, breathing heavily.

He didn't consider himself a killer. But perhaps what he thought didn't matter. With shaking fingers, he reached for the soap, lathered his hands, washed them, and then reached for the card and the rose. He lowered them, placing them on the crumpled woman on the bathroom floor.

Then, wiping his hands off on his shirt, he moved towards the door, clicked the locks, glanced up and down, and froze.

Two eyes were looking at him. "Sorry," said the person. An older woman, maybe in her fifties. "Is this one out of order?"

He could feel his heart pounding. He blocked the slit in the door with his body, preventing her from looking beyond. He nodded once. "Sorry, maintenance. You'll have to use the one on the lower deck."

The older woman was already shaking her head and grumbling to herself, moving away, down the stairs.

He scowled, watching her leave, and then turned, shutting the door with a *click*. Hastily, he stepped away, moving as quickly as he could without drawing attention.

She'd seen his face. Not good. Would she remember, though?

Unlikely. It depended. It depended when the body was found.

He moved even faster now, his footsteps loud against the deck. Whatever the case, this would all be over soon.

He moved down the stairs, amidst the gathering passengers on the lower deck, blending in, disappearing, once more, into the crowd.

CHAPTER SEVENTEEN

Adele raced from the taxi, the red brake lights illuminating the concrete in front of her rapid footfalls. Her eyes fixed on the large riverboat, the sound of the horn blaring in the air as the mooring ropes were lowered.

Adele cursed, hissing beneath her breath as she raced across the tarmac, angling towards the boat. Her phone pressed to her ear, and she muttered beneath her breath. “Come on... Come on!”

But Renee wasn't picking up; likely his phone was still on silent while ducking Executive Foucault's calls.

Adele growled, yanking her Interpol identification from her pocket and folding her wallet so it was front and center as she hastened towards the departing ship. A ticket collector standing by the raised, concrete ramp was frowning as she neared, one of his hands braced against a boarding rail. He began to shake his head, holding out a halting hand. “Sorry,” the man said in German, “you're too late!”

“Out of my way,” Adele said, firmly, flashing her credentials.

The ticket collector paused for a moment, frowning at her wallet, but a second later, his thick, woolly eyebrows inched up, and he stepped hastily to the side, allowing her access to the ramp. A couple of passengers on the lower deck peered over the railing, watching her with curiosity etched across their countenances, but Adele was already hastening forward, moving towards the white rail. The small entry gate was already latched and the boat—now free of its bonds—began to drift away from the rubber bumpers, moving back out onto the swishing waters. The gap began to widen between the rail and the dock, and Adele knew if she waited a second longer, it'd be too late.

“Careful!” the ticket collector called in warning behind her, but she was already cautious enough.

She took one giant step, her fingers scrambling, her wallet tumbling, nearly falling into the churning water beneath her. The overcast skies above only further darkened the already gloomy nighttime river.

Adele swallowed once, hanging onto the closed latch-gate, and exhaling slowly, her hands gripping the rail. She paused, on the exact wrong side of the gate, her back to the water as the boat continued to pull away. With one foot, she carefully reached down, edging her wallet back beneath the rail, and onto the dry deck.

A few of the passengers were still watching her curiously. One older couple were shaking their heads in disapproval. A young woman was snickering behind her hand, watching the scene in fascination.

Adele frowned, throwing one leg over the gate, and only taking a moment to inhale once both her feet were safely on the deck. She bent over, picking up her wallet and jamming it in her pocket before fixing all the looky-loos with an intense glare as if daring any of them to make something of it.

"You," she said, firmly, pointing at the snickering young woman. "Have you seen a tall Frenchman around? Probably avoiding the water. He's scared of it."

Before the woman could reply, a voice cleared behind her. "Not sure that last part needed mentioning," John muttered.

Adele whirled around, her gaze fixed on the tall Frenchman. He shot a look uncomfortably up at the second level, but then turned his attention back towards her, flashing an uneasy smile. "Everything okay?" he said, gesturing towards the railing. "Didn't know you were trying out for hurdles."

"Har-har. Come here," Adele said, quickly, gesturing at her partner and stepping off into a less crowded portion of the deck beneath the curling metal stairs.

John came closer, again shooting an uncomfortable look up the stairs, but just as quickly returning his attention to Adele.

She hesitated, her own news on the tip of her tongue, but at his hurried glances and shifting posture, she felt a sudden tinge of unease. "What?" she said, slowly. "What did you do?"

John cleared his throat, glancing towards the nearest passengers who, it seemed, had grown bored with the French agents and were staring across the river at the nighttime countryside. "Do? Nothing. Why?"

"You look guilty."

John shot another look towards the stairs, wincing. A young couple suddenly passed by, heading in the other direction and John ducked his head, coughing into his hand and bending over a bit.

Adele sighed even more loudly now. "You didn't run in to any more paparazzi, did you?"

John watched the young couple who were murmuring to each other and sharing a pack of chips. He winced, watching them move hurriedly in the other direction, gesturing towards one of the attendants in a black uniform at the far end of the rail. He turned his back now, his features cast in shadow from the staircase above. "No. No paparazzi," he said, quickly.

"Foucault call you yet?"

"Umm. No."

"Is your phone off."

He scratched at the corner of his chin and winced.

"John!" Adele said, gritting her teeth. "I was trying to reach you, you goon. I need you to keep your phone on!"

"Sorry," he muttered quickly, wincing. "It's fine. Look. I'm turning it on. Battery was running low." He pulled his phone out, pressing at one of the buttons on the side with a thick, calloused trigger finger.

"Right. Battery, fine," Adele said, still frowning.

"What's got you in a bad mood?"

"You mean besides the *murder* case we're working?"

"Yes, besides that."

She crossed her arms, and for a faint moment, as a breeze picked up, she thought she felt the light dappling of moisture against her cheek. She winced, glancing at the overcast skies and wondering if it was the first sign of rain.

"Emile isn't our guy."

John blinked. "You found him?"

"He was at home. It's not him. He had an alibi for both nights. I called the school and they connected me to the librarian who confirmed his story. He was in a study room until midnight on both nights. The school is an hour from here."

John frowned, shaking his head. "But he *was* connected to both victims?"

"Yeah. Apparently they met at school. But get this, Anika Blythe? That's not her name."

John's eyebrows went the way of steam.

"It's actually Anika Everett."

"Umm. Who?"

"Everett. As in Everett Motors? They're a huge deal in Germany."

"Not all of us keep track of German motor companies, Adele. How huge of a deal?"

"As in Akbulut huge," Adele countered. "Wealthy—very, very wealthy."

Now, John looked intrigued, watching Adele carefully. "Oh."

"Exactly. Oh. Two young women, both of them heiresses to massive fortunes—slated to receive an inheritance to rival most powerball lotteries."

"Holy shit. You're serious? That's the connection then," John said, excitedly, shifting from one foot to the other. "Someone's hunting heiresses. But why?"

"That's the million-dollar question."

"More like billion-dollar," John snickered. At Adele's expression, he quickly coughed into his hand and said, "So why did she change her name?"

"Falling out with the family, apparently. Anika objected to some of her father's business practices. Didn't seem to think they were ethical—at least, that's how our friend Emile sees it."

"Reliable?"

"Don't know. He did seem broken up about the girls."

"At least there's that. So if Anika was estranged from her family, maybe money has nothing to do with it. Would seem odd to target someone who has severed ties from their fortune if the point is wealth." John frowned, crossing his large arms over his equally massive chest. His sleeves strained against his forearms, and his brow furrowed in thought as he reached up, scratching at his burn mark beneath his chin and along his neck. "You don't think they were botched kidnapping attempts, do you? Maybe our killer didn't know about the estrangement? Maybe he was after their family fortunes."

"If so, he's not a very good kidnapper," Adele returned. "Besides, the murders weren't done with a gun or a knife. He used..." She winced. "Zeynep's own necklace and Anika's wallet. Choking them of all things. I mean, who does that?"

John watched her for a moment, his expression softening in the shadows of the curling stairs above them. Now, Adele could definitely feel flecks of moisture against her cheek and forearm. A light drizzle rising over the river as they moved into night, moved further into the domain of the killer. When would he strike again?

Adele shivered, meeting John's searching gaze.

"Are you alright?" He murmured, softly, reaching out a tentative hand, and taking her hand cautiously in his. His large, calloused fingers felt rough, like whittled sticks. Everything about John Renee seemed tough, calloused—everything except his eyes. Normally, those too, would be like granite—especially when killers were involved.

But not when he looked at her. Not when his guard lowered—as rare an occasion as that was. And for now, in the shadow, on the riverboat beneath overcast skies at night, John's eyes were searching hers, as if looking for anything he might be able to do. Any way he could help.

Sometimes it was hard to remember exactly why she'd agreed to start seeing the man. Other times, it was nearly impossible to forget.

She sighed, and leaned in for a moment, resting her head against John's chest and inhaling softly. He smelled like soap and aftershave. She closed her eyes and felt his hand move over her shoulders, his large arm holding her close, gentle and sturdy at the same time.

She needed to think—needed to find another angle. The killer wasn't after money, that seemed clear enough. Why was he targeting these women, though? The family fortunes couldn't be a coincidence. But how did that help? What sort of psycho went after power, influence, and wealth? It was just begging to get caught.

Unless the killer didn't care if he was caught.

Or worse, unless he expected it.

She winced, frowning. If the killer was looking to get nabbed, then they were in bigger trouble than she'd first anticipated. There was no telling what someone that desperate might do.

As she leaned against John, in the shadow of the stairs, inhaling softly, she felt her pocket begin to vibrate.

"John," she said, slowly. "Are you—"

"Not me," he said, quickly. "Phones. Mine's ringing too."

Frowning, they both extricated, glancing down at their devices. Adele answered hers first, while John watched his with suspicion. She raised the phone, pressing it tightly to her ear. "Hello?" she said, quickly. "Who is this?"

"Am I speaking to Agent Sharp?" said a voice on the other end.

It took her a moment, but then she recognized Mr. Larsen—the lawyer for Sightseeing Incorporated. "This is she."

There was a long sigh on the other end, then an awkward pause. "I—I know how this looks," Mr. Larsen said, slowly, clearing his throat. "I know that you said—well, you said a lot of things. Perhaps I should have listened. You have to understand, though, Agent Sharp, that it's my job to—"

"Larsen," she said, cutting him off, frowning now. "What happened?"

The liaison sighed on the other end of the line. And for a moment, the wind seemed to pick up, carrying the first few droplets of drizzling water scattering across the deck. Then, Mr. Larsen muttered, so quietly Adele winced, struggling to hear.

"A third victim," she managed to make out. "We have a third body. It's on River Metro Seven. Currently docked at Steinheim."

Adele swallowed once, but then her spine tingled. "Have the passengers disembarked yet?"

"I—what, no. Not yet. But they're looking for—"

"Larsen, whatever you do, keep those passengers on that boat. We're on our way."

CHAPTER EIGHTEEN

The skies seemed in indecision. Clouds rolled, lumbering with rain, but only flecks and pulses of the occasional drizzle dispersed from the heavens. The night stretched deeper beneath scarce moonlight as Adele and John marched towards a slew of flashing blue and red strobes. More than ten police cars and SUVS lined the docks, the glare and glow of the lights reflecting off the white paint and tinted glass of the riverboat docked there.

Adele glimpsed passengers against the railings, watching the six police officers and three squad cars preventing entry or exit from the large ship.

Adele picked up her pace, feeling flecks of rain droplets dappling her cheeks as she marched towards the stalled ship.

"Think he's still on board?" John asked in a low voice, following after her.

"Larsen said no one had a chance to disembark yet," Adele replied, firmly, her hands bunched at her side. "The killer is still on board. He has to be."

The riverboat itself was in port, waiting on the side of the river, and for a moment it seemed as if everything were hanging in the balance, waiting for something, hovering on the crest of action. Adele, even from where she strode towards the gangplank, could hear the disgruntled murmurings of the waterlogged passengers.

She could glimpse the frowns, and the fierce, whispered conversations. A few eyes fell from the railing above, fixating on Adele and John as they moved nearer.

"Foucault reach you yet?" Adele muttered beneath her breath.

"No. I, er, keep missing him."

"Right. I bet you do. John, we have a lot of witnesses here. Please don't do anything stupid."

"Yes, American Princess. Though, if you ask me, getting on a hunk of floating metal in the middle of a river is pretty dumb to begin with."

A couple of the police officers nodded as Adele and John flashed credentials and ducked under caution tape, moving up the ramp towards the riverboat. The small gateway was opened by a porter in a black suit, who gestured at them, wincing as he did.

"Are you with BKA?" the man said, quickly.

"Interpol," Adele replied reflexively. "Mr. Larsen call ahead?"

The porter bobbed his head, waving a hand towards the second deck. "Come, come," he jabbered. "There are already police up there."

They took the metal stairs, ignoring the fixated glares of the waiting passengers around them, and as they reached the long deck at the top, like an alleyway with one side overlooking a sharp drop, Adele noticed a long section of the deck had been cleared. The doors, here, lining the ship were opened, where breeze and small droplets of rain could enter with a swirl. At the far end of the deck, though, next to another, wider, taller door, there stood five police officers gathered. Some of them seemed to be moving around with evidence bags. One was speaking to a man who looked like the coroner. And two others were keeping a watchful eye on the surrounding passengers.

Adele gave a soft, shuddering sigh, but swallowed it back and turned to regard their guide. "Anything you can tell me about that room?" She nodded towards where most the caution tape had been used.

"It's a bathroom," the man replied, reflexively, his arms and legs straight like some sort of military personnel as he marched them along the rail in the direction of the crime scene.

"A bathroom?"

"Yes, ma'am."

"And this bathroom was available to the public?"

"It is, yes. But it isn't used as much as the ones on the lower deck, where most of the passengers linger."

"I see. And when was the body found?"

"I—I don't know. I wasn't the one who found it. But we rerouted the ship about three hours ago."

Adele glanced at her watch and gave a little sigh. That would mean the killer had struck no earlier than five PM. It was now eight.

She provided a quick nod of gratitude to their guide as they reached the open door surrounded by police, and, after showing her ID again, she moved into the crime scene with John behind her.

Three other officers were examining the bathroom, two of them canvasing the sink, and one standing near the main object of attraction beneath a hand dryer.

Adele paused, frowning at the body.

Once a young woman with golden curls, her red dress now wilted around her. She lay motionless, one of her eyes open, as if staring accusingly at Adele.

A second later, Adele heard John mutter a series of oaths behind her, and she felt the tall Frenchman brush past her as he approached the body, his shoulders hunched as if against a sudden blast of chill wind.

"Christ," John said, muttering darkly beneath his breath. "How did she die?" He shot this question towards one of the officers standing nearest the body.

The man winced, and, also in English, said, "Choked on a piece of red dress. We have it bagged." He added, in a faint murmur, "And cleaned up some of the vomit."

Adele wrinkled her nose, feeling a jolt of grief accompanying the rage burbling inside her chest. She hated this killer. Whoever he was, whatever his motives, he seemed to be targeting defenseless young women. Isolating them and attacking when they were helpless.

"Did anyone see anything?" she asked.

The officer's eyes bounced from John to her. "We still have people questioning the passengers, but so far nothing. Apparently, this portion of the deck wasn't well traversed."

Adele sighed, nodded, glancing at the sink, and towards the soap dispenser.

The police officer cleared his throat. "One of the faucets was running when she was found. If that means anything."

"Probably means the killer struck when she was washing her hands," Adele said, softly. "I'm not sure that helps us though."

John turned his back on the victim, wincing, as if he couldn't quite take the sight. He raised up one finger, "A young woman. Just like the other two. Choked to death on something from her person." He held up a second finger. "Also like the others."

"Do we know her name yet?" Adele said shooting the question towards the officer. The man nodded, and with a knowing tone and tilt of his eyebrows, said, "Abigail Havertz. The daughter of that famous TV chef. The one who owns that restaurant chain."

Adele frowned, shaking her head. "I don't know it."

To her surprise, it was John who interjected, "You don't know the Havertz restaurant chain? I'm surprised, Adele."

She looked at him. "How do *you*?"

John coughed. "The commercials are very," he coughed delicately, "interesting."

The police behind John snickered, and said, "You mean that one actress who plays the hostess? She should do movies."

Adele rolled her eyes. "All right, forget I asked." Her tone went somber, regarding John with a long, meaningful look. "So we have another heiress, then. A wealthy, young woman killed by choking on one of these riverboats owned by Sightseeing Incorporated. Is that about the gist of it?"

John shook his head, rubbing his jaw. "How is he targeting these people? He definitely seems to have a knowledge of the boats. He knew this bathroom would be empty. He knew he would have privacy to do what he wanted."

"We need those manifests." Adele glanced back at her phone and felt her temper rise. Mr. Larsen had been hardly forthcoming about sending the crew or passenger information. He'd said he get them to her three hours ago.

"Think we should go a legal route?" John asked.

Adele gnawed on the corner of her lip. "Maybe Foucault knows a judge who'd be willing to do a favor on short notice."

John crossed his arms. "Do you think the killer is still on board?"

"The boat makes a few stops," Adele said, quietly. "But on the other hand, if the killer knows the scope of these boats, maybe he's an employee or an overnighter; it's worth a shot. We need to keep the passengers on the boat. And we need to contact the executive to figure out a way to make Sightseeing Incorporated cough up those manifests."

At that moment, there was a flurry of voices from outside, and Adele frowned, turning towards the door. John shifted next to her as well. A second later, a man with a bicycler's physique, and a visible temper, was standing in the door, the hand of a police officer at his shoulder, trying to pull him back.

"I represent this boat," the man was snarling, "get your monkey paws off me." The moment his eyes landed on Adele and John, though, the man hesitated. He coughed delicately, wincing once, and then tapped a finger to his ear. "I'm sorry," said Mr. Larsen, the liaison for Sightseeing Incorporated. "I couldn't help but hear you talking about getting a judge involved."

Adele frowned, approaching the man in the door, giving a little nod towards the police officer who lowered his hand. "You promised me those manifests hours ago. Where are they?"

Larsen winced, and tugged at his collar, shifting uncomfortably beneath Adele's glare. "Things like that take time. I had to jump through some hoops myself. They're coming your way."

"Let me be clear," Adele said, "you're either going to send those to me within the next five minutes, for all three of these ships, or I'm going to get a judge to shut down your entire business for a month while we investigate. Understand?"

The man winced uncomfortably, and he looked like he wanted to protest further, but his eyes slid from Adele's face, and landed on the body of Abigail Havertz in the back of the bathroom. The moment he did, his eyes widened like saucers, and he froze in place, his face going pale all of a sudden. He let out a soft little squeak, and then massaged the bridge of his nose. "All right," he said, shakily. "I'll get those to you."

"Five minutes," Adele said, firmly. "I mean it."

Mr. Larsen give a little wave of his hand. "Fine, done. Like I said, I needed to jump through some hoops. But I got the permissions I needed. Look, I know this looks bad... But we can't keep the passengers locked on the boat like this... Imagine what they'll think!" In a smaller, more pitiable voice, he added, beneath his breath, "Imagine the reviews... If we could just let them leave—"

"No," Adele said, cutting him off and shaking her head simply. "We're doing things my way now. You, for the sake of your own ass better get out of the way and sit down. I told you to dock these boats. And now because of you, she's dead. Get a good look." Adele stepped aside, like a presenter, revealing a prize. She glared at the side of Mr. Larsen face. "Take it in. That's you're doing. Get me those manifests. The passengers are staying on board until we sort out who's who. All of this could have been avoided if you would have just listened to me."

Mr. Larsen looks like he wanted to protest, but Adele spoke first, iron in her voice, "Four minutes."

He cursed softly, and turned on his heel, fishing his phone out of his pocket, and shouldering roughly past one of the police officers, muttering darkly as he did. Adele watched him retreat to the rail and begin to jabber away into his phone. They needed those manifests to check the passengers on each of the ships. Three victims, three different ships. The killer was moving fast. He knew the scope and lay of the boats. He seemed to know the routes traveled. The killer was targeting young women, all of them from wealth. But why?

"Adele," John said suddenly.

She turned, frowning; she watched as John bent over the corpse and delicately extracted something from behind the woman's head, which had been trapped, out of sight in the shadows of the sink and the air dryer.

"What is it?"

In answer, John just lifted and turned the thing in his hand. A rose, with a note taped to the stem.

Adele blinked. "He left something? He didn't leave anything before..."

John just shrugged and pulled the note from where it was taped to the rose. He tossed the flower into the sink, but then held up the note, and, slowly, began to read, in English:

Mr. and Mrs. Akbulut. I am very sorry for your loss. We all feel it greatly. I'm sure Zeynep misses you just as much as you miss her. My sincerest condolences. Some things just can't be avoided, I suppose. My thoughts and prayers are with you.

-M-

P.S. Mr. and Mrs. Blythe. Your daughter, Anika, was a real gem. She misses you too.

As the words fell still, so did everyone else in the room, as if poised.

Adele shifted uncomfortabl, and shook her head. "He wrote a letter to the other two victims... I don't understand. Is he taunting them? Mocking the parents?"

John nodded slowly. "Must be. Why?"

"Do you think he's targeting the parents? Maybe he's killing the girls in order to make the parents suffer. Maybe this isn't even about the young women themselves."

At the same time she said it, Adele felt a flash of guilt, realizing how callous the words sounded standing so close to the body of Ms. Havertz. She winced, glancing in the direction of the young woman, then looked away again, regarding the note card in John's fingers.

"Well," she said, softly, "our killer knows English. Maybe he just wanted to guarantee all the victims' families could read it."

"So he's educated then, or a native speaker—tourist?" John said. "He's taunting the parents, the survivors. The rose is just another mockery."

Adele shivered, shaking her head. Her phone buzzed. She glanced down, and her eyebrows went up.

"What?" John said, sharply.

"Don't worry," she muttered. "It's not Foucault. I just got three of the ship manifests."

John whistled. "That little guy moves fast when he's motivated."

Adele glanced towards the doorway that led back out onto the deck. Mr. Larsen was no longer within sight. She rocked back and forth on her heels, then turned away from the body, away from the crime scene, and moved back out to the open door. She needed some fresh air. "I'll send you the manifests," she said, quickly. "There's going to be a connection. Pay close attention to crew and employees. Also, keep an eye on any customers that stayed overnight. Anything that stands out, any connecting point, that's going to be our killer." She paused for a moment, one foot out onto the deck, the other still in the bathroom. She felt a little chill, but it had nothing to do with the breeze or the few droplets of rain.

"What?" John said, softly.

Adele gave a shake of her head. She winced. "I-I can't help but feel that he almost wants to be caught. This all feels desperate. This note, the taunting. It feels like he has an end in sight." Adele winced, shivered again, and then stepped onto the deck. "We need to catch him soon."

CHAPTER NINETEEN

Adele and John both stood by the railing, their postures bowed, their phones precariously balanced over the edge, angled towards the waters below as they scrolled through the manifests with glazed eyes, the glowing screens like moonlight in the darkening night. Below them, John and Adele could see the many passengers gathered on the first deck. Adele felt her eyes drawn, every couple of moments, from the manifest, towards the crowd below. As she read the names, comparing them between the three boats, she wondered which names belonged to which people. Many eyes, many faces, looked up at her, regarding her with interest. John was scrolling through the manifests as well, though he seemed to be growing bored.

The documents were opened as PDF files on her cell phone screen, and Adele's eyes traced through the names. There were over a hundred passengers below, on the deck, but on the manifests, only twenty employees. She compiled the list, moving all the names into the same spreadsheet. One at a time, she eliminated them, checking all the names in one row against the others. At last, she looked up, glancing at John, and feeling her pulse quickening.

"I've got two," she said.

John glanced at her, eyes widening. "Two names?"

"Two employees."

John quickly stowed his phone, "I also got two names. What were yours?"

Adele pointed. “Guy Vierra and Pierre Manet," she said, slowly. "Look, Manet was a porter. Vierra is a chef. Both of them have been on all three ships during the times of the murders. In the case of the porter, it was a narrow squeeze, but he arrived just in time on River Metro Two to kill Zeynep."

John nodded, glancing at the other name. "And Vierra?"

"The chef. He's had ample time on all of the boats to commit the crime.”

At that moment, Adele heard a softly clearing voice, and she glanced over to see Mr. Larsen standing at the top of the stairwell, watching them, with a speculative look. "*Guy* Vierra?" He said.

Adele stared at Mr. Larsen, unsure how she felt about the man eavesdropping. But then, deciding to not make anything of it, she spoke curtly, in English, “Hello, Mr. Larsen. I appreciate the cooperation.”

“Mhmm,” he grunted. “Whatever. Look, you mentioned Vierra's name, right? He's worked for the company in different ventures for nearly ten years. Only recently did we move him to the riverboats when this part of the business started a couple of months ago. You think it's him?"

"Is Mr. Vierra still on the ship?"

"You haven't let anyone leave," he said in manner of reply.

"Good. Take us to him." It wasn't a request. She didn't say it politely. With men like Mr. Larsen, an inch always became a mile. And so she couldn't give so much as a millimeter.

The liaison for Sightseeing Incorporated gave her a long look from his reddened face. The lights from the ship, embedded in ceiling, glowed, reflecting off the rail, and illuminating his eyes. The raindrops still continued to come sparse and scattered, cool and chill against Adele's skin. But it wasn't anything compared to the cold look Mr. Larsen gave her. At last, though, he turned stiffly, and grumbling, said, beneath his breath, "Follow me. I'll show you to the kitchens."

The kitchen was on the third deck, behind the bridge. As she pushed through a door marked, *Employees Only* and followed after Mr. Larsen, she watched men and women in black outfits moving about a small kitchen, preparing food for the rooms, or, likely, for the café below.

“Chef Vierra!” Mr. Larsen shouted, suddenly, his voice carrying through the kitchens. A lull fell over the activities. Adele watched as a grease fire started, and it took the chef a second to notice. The man in question cursed, then smothered the fire. Then, shooting uneasy glances towards them, the same chef slowly extricated his fingers from the handle of the frying pan, cleared his throat and said, "Er, yes, Mr. Larsen?"

The chef's face had gone pale, and a thin bead of sweat glazed his upper lip. He didn't wear one of those white hats, but he did wear an apron, black like the outfits of the rest of the employees. He took a timid step forward, rubbing nervously at his thigh. The man was wire thin—not at all what Adele would have thought for a chef. She could see his bones pressing against his cheeks, and even the top of his collarbone beneath his shirt.

The man's fingers were long, and twiggy, and he rolled them uncomfortably against his thigh, leaving streaks of grease.

"Come here," snapped Mr. Larsen, wiggling his hand like a master calling its puppy.

The chef seemed reluctant, and the others in the kitchen were all watching, curiously.

"Get back to work!" Larsen snapped, waving a hand at the rest of them.

This small, wild tempered man seemed to run a tight ship. The crew immediately began to work on their dishes again, pretending like they weren't paying close attention to what was transpiring with their chef.

The skinny, bony man in his greasy apron came to a halt, a few paces further back than convention might have suggested. He was even more nervous now. And the sweat across his upper lip seemed to have spread to his forehead as well. The man wiped at his head, and then rubbed his hand off on his apron. "Yes, sir?" He said, hesitantly.

"They have a couple of questions for you," Larsen said, bluntly. Then, with a growl in his voice, he said, “it's about the murders."

Adele resisted the urge to roll her eyes or reach out and slap the liaison. The last thing they needed before starting an interrogation was to get the subject defensive. Already, though, he seemed cagey enough. The sweat didn't seem just from the heat of the stoves, but also from firing nerves, visible across the twitching of his brow, and the tightening of his pronounced cheekbones.

"Murders?" He said. "Oh, dear God." He shook his head wildly, and nearly fell, reaching out to brace his hand against a metal rack full of porcelain dishes. "I knew it. Those three women. The ships I was on. I *knew* it," he said, his voice high-pitched and strained. The man looked ready to faint, and John took a quick step forward, as if to catch the guy. But this motion only caused the chef to squeak and throw out a hand reflexively, banging his knuckles painfully against a dangling cooking pan.

Adele blinked at the man's reaction, clearing her throat delicately. "So you admit you were on those other boats?"

The man didn't even hesitate. Instead, he wagged his head wildly, starting to cry now. Sniffling, tears dripping down his cheeks. "Oh, dear God. *Yes*. I was. I knew this was going to come. I knew you would come for me!"

Adele blinked. "Are you confessing, sir?"

At this, though, it looked like he'd been punched in the gut. His one hand against the metal shelf gripped the pole so tightly his knuckles went white. His face was the same color, but the tears stopped, and the sweat stayed, and his mouth unhinged in horror. "Did I...are you—what? No! Not at all. That's not what I'm saying. I knew I was being framed! What were the odds? Each of the ships I worked at, someone was murdered. I knew how it would look. Someone is trying to frame me! You have to believe me!"

Adele frowned, crossing her own arms, and glancing back towards the door, wondering if they should find someplace more private for this discussion. She shared a look with John, who shrugged back in her direction.

She said, "So you're saying you didn't have anything to do with the deaths."

"No! I'm clearly being framed. It's a set up. One of you wants my job," he yelled, whirling about and pointing his twiggy finger at the rest of the workers and employees in the kitchen.

Mr. Larsen sighed, rubbing his nose. He leaned in next to Adele, and in a fierce whisper, as if she were somehow his confidant, he said, "He has no alibi. It's clearly him. Arrest him, and then we can move on with disembarking the passengers."

Adele though turned away from the liaison, her voice rising, "Mr. Vierra, do you have an alibi or not?"

The chef shook his head. "I don't know when she was killed. Why was she killed. I'm sure I have some alibi."

"Around five," Adele said. "Nearly four hours ago."

The chef's arm sprang out, expressively and he declared, "Aha!" He wagged his bony face up and down, his chin like a pointing finger. "Yes. Yes. Yes, yes. I *do* have an alibi. I was here." He pointed another finger towards the kitchen stoves. "I started a grease fire," he declared triumphantly. He paused, though, and then coughed delicately. "It was a very small fire," he added, glancing towards Mr. Larsen.

A couple of the other cooks were snickering where they were chopping vegetables.

Adele raised her voice, facing the two female chefs. "Is this true? Was he here around five?"

It took them a moment to realize they were being addressed, but then the soft chopping sounds faded, and both women looked up from where they were working. One of them glanced at the other and nodded quickly. "Yes. He's worked since three. He hasn't taken a break. He doesn't usually. You didn't kill anyone, did you Mr. Vierra?" She addressed this question towards the tall man, who hung his head, massaging the bridge of his pronounced nose.

Adele frowned at the woman. “So you're saying there's no way he could've slipped away?"

Both cooks shook their heads adamantly. "Guy doesn't allow any of us to do anything without micromanagement," one said reluctantly, as if aware she was both complaining about her boss and providing his alibi at the same time. She shrugged. "He was here the entire time. We would have noticed if he left."

"It would've been a relief," the other one muttered, seemingly emboldened by her boss' tears and twitchy nature.

Adele exhaled, but nodded slowly, returning her attention to the chef. "I'm sorry for bothering you Mr. Vierra. But as you say, you were on all three ships. You didn't happen to see anything did you?"

The chef was already shaking his head though, between shooting dirty looks at his two coworkers. For a moment, Adele considered asking him to calm down, and think through his answer. But the man clearly wasn't in the frame of mind to do either of these things. So she nodded once, and then said, "I still need you to stay on the ship while we check your alibi on the other two."

His words exploded like a confetti cannon. "I can provide a detailed schedule. The others, my kitchen staff, would be able to tell you when I was there or not!" The chef still sweated profusely and twisted at the edge of his apron with nervous fingers.

Adele looked to John, and turned, moving towards the door.

"Hang on," Mr. Larsen declared. "Arrest him. You need to arrest him! We need to get the passengers off the ship."

Adele didn't reply, continuing.

The liaison frowned, and then hastened after them as they stepped back out onto the deck, leaving the kitchen, and allowing the door marked *Employees Only,* to slowly swing shut.

Larsen reached out as if to tug at Adele's arm, but John growled, and the lawyer lowered his hand as if he'd touched something hot. "You don't know,” the lawyer weaseled, a whine to his voice. “Maybe the chef's alibi is just a cover. Maybe *they're* lying for him. You should ask them. They're not above taking bribes, trust me." Then, as if adding a key piece of evidence, he said, “Plus, things have been stolen from the passengers recently. We think an employee has been stealing—if they'd steal, why not lie? See what I mean?”

Adele sighed, turning sharply, and fixing Mr. Larsen with a piercing glare. "I'm afraid I don't. But, either way, *he* has an alibi, and on top of that, he's a recognizable figure. No one seems to have seen anything like this killer. But not only that, look at his fingers; they're long, brittle. The man who killed these women was strong, blunt, and rough. He choked them to death; do you know how difficult that is? He forced them to swallow a wallet, a necklace, and a piece of fabric. It's not the chef."

Mr. Larsen was muttering darkly now, shaking his head as if deeply aggrieved.

Adele turned away though, bowing her head as if in prayer to focus. "One more shot. The porter." She looked at Mr. Larsen. “You know anything about him?"

CHAPTER TWENTY

"What was his name again?" Larsen said, standing on the deck, some of his grumbling replaced by a note of hope at the prospect of arresting someone after all. Adele glimpsed excitement in his eyes.

"Manet," she said, simply. "He was on all three ships. What deck does he work on?"

The liaison winced, pausing and thinking through the employees for a moment. Then, he clicked his tongue. "Ah, yes, Pierre. I remember hiring him. He's supposed to be helping passengers settle in their rooms, but that would be on the deck with the crime scene. We had that cleared out. At your orders," he added, significantly.

"Alright, so where is he now?"

"Employee break room, probably. Hang on." Mr. Larsen reached to his belt, but instead of drawing a phone, he pulled a small walkie-talkie. He paused for a moment, pressed a button, and then said, "Hello, this is Larsen, I'm looking for Manet. Where is he?"

There was a pause, a staticky voice, and then a crackle that said, "Pierre's not here."

Larsen snorted. "Was he there recently?"

A long pause. Some muttering voices and more static. Then, "No. We haven't seen him."

Mr. Larsen shook his head in frustration, then glanced up towards the bridge. He pressed the speaker again. "Hello, this is Larsen. Is Pierre Manet there?"

A longer pause, this time, but then, another static-filled voice replied, "The porter, sir? No sign of him here. Sir, do we have any idea when we're going to be allowed to—"

Larsen clicked off the walkie-talkie. He rubbed at the back of his head, frowning. "I guess he's not accounted for."

Adele shared a long look with John. "Is there anywhere else the porters might gather? Take a smoke break or something?"

"Smoking is expressly prohibited in front of passengers," said Larsen, as if from a rehearsed cue card. "No, I can't think of anywhere. Maybe he's on the first deck."

Adele tapped her teeth with a finger, considering their options. Only one name remained connecting all three ships. The same name that was now mysteriously missing. Hiding, perhaps? Escaped? She felt a jolt of adrenaline, and found her heartbeat rising. "All right," she said, trying to remain focused, "we need to find Mr. Manet. John, can you get a couple of the police from the crime scene to come help us look. I'll start on the first deck and start moving through the passengers."

Mr. Larsen sighed briefly, but then said, "I'll ask some of the crew to help out as well. Maybe it will raise morale to give them something to do. Really, though, is this necessary to keep the passengers—"

"Just help us find the porter. We'll take things one step at a time, Mr. Larsen."

The small, hot-tempered lawyer looked like he wanted to protest, but then he just shrugged, biting his lip and began to move, walkie-talkie rising to his lips as he took the stairs down to the lower level, already issuing instructions for the crew in the break room to start looking for the porter.

John began to move towards a different stairwell, further back, which would lead to the second deck where the crime scene was. Adele, for her part, followed Mr. Larsen, hastily, taking the metal stairs three at a time, as she moved back towards the first deck.

The porter was missing. He had been on all three ships. All three crime scenes. The chef was cleared. He didn't have the countenance, the physique, and he also had an alibi. Which meant there was only one option remaining. Process of elimination ended with a giant, pointing finger directed exactly at the porter.

"Where are you hiding?" she murmured to herself.

For a brief, horrible, moment, Adele wondered if perhaps the porter had already disembarked somewhere else. But according to the manifest he was supposed to work through the night.

She picked up her pace, moving down to the final deck, where the passengers were gathered. As her hand slid along the railing, and she could hear Larsen behind her, now, where she had passed him on the stairs, still jabbering into his walkie-talkie, and answering to the responding static, she stared across the faces. The passengers were leaning against the deck, or gripping the railing, many of them edging towards where the ramp was, complaining to a few police officers blocking their way.

Adele heard the sound of thumping footsteps above, suggesting John had wrangled some of the police to help their search. She watched as a couple of other porters, who didn't match the photo of Pierre

Manet, stepped out from a room at the back of the ship, and began to move through the passengers, looking about, curiously. Adele's own eyes swept the crowds, from her slightly elevated purchase on the fifth step. She frowned, still looking.

"Manet!" she called out, suddenly.

A few eyes looked towards her, curious, but then glanced away again.

Adele took a step down, lower, still scanning the heads, the faces, the grumbling, the dark countenances. "Manet!" she called, louder.

Again, no response. She watched us two of Larsen's employees moved through the crowd, glancing at people. Her own eyes went from the light clothing to the darker ones matching the suits the porters wore.

John and three police officers emerged at a stairwell next to the break room on the opposite side of the ship. With her and Larsen on one side, the two employees in the middle, and the police at the back, they were like a net, closing. Or a noose, constricting.

"Pierre Manet!" she said, even louder now.

She saw movement towards one of the railings, closest to the exit ramp.

Her eyes shifted. The man in question ducked his head, trying to move away from John and the police officers. But as he did, she realized, though he was no longer wearing his work clothing, the man's face was pockmarked, and he had a thin, scruffy yellow beard. The same face she recognized from Manet's picture on the manifest.

"John," Adele said, sharply, pointing.

John looked over at the same time as the man looked up. His eyes landed on Adele, and then he muttered darkly and bolted, sprinting in the opposite direction of the police, and towards where Adele and Mr. Larsen were waiting. Adele hastened down the steps, hand moving to her firearm. But the man was moving quickly, and he shoved into an old couple, sending them careening towards Adele.

"Stop!" she yelled.

But the man was still moving.

John and the three police spotted the commotion and were shouldering their way roughly through the crowd to reach them. Adele, making sure the couple was okay, extricated herself, and then broke into a sprint, racing towards the back of the boat, towards a clearer, more shadowed section of the deck.

The frightened porter, wearing street clothes, froze at the back, near a railing twice as high as he was tall.

Adele's weapon was in her hand now, pointing. "Stop!" she demanded, firmly. "Don't move.”

The man gave her a long look, breathing heavily, one hand jammed into his pocket, the other making a fist.

"Wait right there, Manet!" she said, firmly. "Don't do anything rash."

The man's eyes twitched, flickering with fear. He seemed to be gauging his options, his tongue tucked in one cheek. Just then, John arrived with loping strides, the three police officers flanking him. “Stop!” John snarled, moving towards the man wedged against the tall wall.

The sight of the giant, musclebound Frenchman drawing nearer seemed to decide it for the porter.

Manet cursed, his pockmarked, stubble-covered face stretching into a furious glare. And then, he spun around and began to clamber up the rail.

"Don't," Adele said sharply.

But he kept going, his back muscles stretched against the thin fabric of his street clothing.

"John, grab him!"

The tall Frenchman, though, was already moving, sprinting. The police officers were a second slower, but they also began to move.

Adele could hear Mr. Larsen, dangling over the stair rail behind them, screaming instructions, pleading things like, "It's all okay folks. Just a small misunderstanding."

Adele ignored him, though, and broke into a sprint behind John as well. By now, Manet had reached the top of the rail. He straddled it, one leg dangling over towards where John tried to snag it by jumping.

The man yelped and yanked his leg up just in time like someone jerking a chicken tender out of the reach of ravenous dogs.

"Get down!” John snapped.

The man looked around, his eyes twitching, shifting, then, he looked over the rail, and gave a resigned sigh.

"He's going to," Adele began.

The porter jumped.

"Jump!" she finished, in frustration. The man plummeted over the rail, and out of sight. There was a sudden splash.

John was already halfway up the rail, but Adele yelled. “No, this way! John, come!” she said, sternly. The tall man turned, blinked, but at her gesturing, his eyes widened and he nodded. Instead of clambering up the railing at the back, he followed Adele, who was cursing, and the two of them raced back in the direction of the police officers blocking the passengers.

"Out of my way," Adele yelled. The police officers blinked, recognizing her, but then spotting her gun, and immediately stepping away. John and Adele took the ramp, down to the dock.

They sprinted along the concrete barriers, staring towards the back of the boat. Adele spotted white streaks in the blue water and heard splashing. They watched the man desperately trying to claw his way through the water towards the opposite shore.

"John," Adele said, quietly.

"Fat chance, American Princess. This one is all yours."

"Damn it. All right, hold my phone." She handed it to John, and then began to sprint forward, racing towards the edge of the dock. The passengers were all watching now, curious. A few youngsters were cheering, as if rooting for some sports team. Adele growled, and yelled, "Stop swimming!"

She stood at the edge of the dock, bracing herself, preparing to dive in. But John held out a hand momentarily. He spread his large arms wide, and then slammed them together with a loud *clap!* He did it twice more. Then, in English, he shouted, "You just missed him. Here, let me aim. I bet I can hit his head from here!" Enjoying himself, John slammed his hands together again, the acoustics of the metal hull and the water, carrying the noise.

The man in the water cursed, ducking suddenly. Then, two hands suddenly broke out of the water, raised up in surrender. John smirked at Adele and winked, rubbing his hands off on his shirt. Adele just shook her head, watching as the suspect, hands still raised, dipped below the surface. He clawed at the water, scrambling back up, but just as quickly raised his hands again, and began to panic.

"Come towards the dock, and I won't shoot!" Adele demanded, firmly.

The man, treading water behind the ship, seemed caught in indecision, but the echoing, reverberation of the *claps* like gunshots still seemed to linger, and then, with a series of cursing and spluttering, he turned, scooping water with reluctant, dreading motions back towards the dock. He was a poor swimmer, but when he reached the edge of the dock, towards one of the mooring posts, covered in a rubber guard, John reached down, and snagged the man by the collar, lifting him bodily from the water and dragging him, scrambling and gasping up onto the dock.

The sodden, dripping man was shaking his head, trying to protest and curse, but Adele kept her weapon on him. “Hands up, put them behind your head. Stay on the ground! John, check for a weapon.”

But the tall man was already frisking their waterlogged porter.

"This is a mistake," the porter was saying. "I can't believe you shot at me! I didn't hear you. It was just a misunderstanding."

At that moment, though, John grunted, and his hands emerged with a silver watch, pulling it from the porter's pocket. A second later, John snorted and pulled out a long strand of pearls. Other small trinkets and jewels emerged from the man's pockets as John frisked him.

The porter began to shake his head, spluttering, but Adele cut him off.

"Be quiet," Adele commanded. "Mr. Manet, I have questions for you."

CHAPTER TWENTY ONE

Adele was glad the employee break room had been cleared, but it still smelled vaguely of smoke, though the porthole window was open above a round, felted table next to a large vending machine only half stocked with protein bars.

John had refused to use his own handcuffs on the porter, citing the potential for rust. So now the man sat, with his arms behind him, thrown over a spindle-backed wooden chair. The porter's pockmarked features twisted, and he had a wincing, ducking way about him as his eyes twitched around the break room. For a moment, he paused, peering towards the door which led back out onto the deck.

Adele knew they wouldn't be disturbed, however, as two uniforms were now posted outside. Mr. Larsen had tried to enter, most likely to sit in on the interrogation. But though he was a lawyer and a liaison for the company, he didn't represent Mr. Manet, and Adele had denied him entry.

Now, she studied the porter, frowning to herself slightly. A grey Tupperware, which they'd taken from the kitchen, sat in front of her. And her fingers rested over the lip, hovering above the glittering items in the tray.

John stood off to the side, behind the man for no other reason than to cast his long shadow over the fellow and put him off guard.

"I can explain..." The porter said, breaking the long silence. He spoke French well enough, hoping, it seemed, to get into their good graces by using their country of origin. His tongue darted out, like a gecko's, dabbed at his lip, then retreated as he gave another long puff of air.

"Explain why you ran?" Adele said, softly, "Or why we found stolen jewelry on your person." Her fingers now probed into the grey Tupperware, swirling a necklace of pearls about, and tapping a finger against a silver wristwatch, two of the larger items among an ensemble of earrings, necklaces, and rings.

"I... I can explain," he said, hurriedly.

"You keep saying that, but don't ever get to the part where you do so. I'm waiting."

The porter sighed again, shaking his head and tilting back so he was staring at the ceiling for a moment as if gathering himself. He continued to twitch, his eyes darting nervously about even when focused on nothing more than the painted beams.

"I knew about the murders," he said, quickly, clipped, his words starting then stalling in a rhythm like a failing engine. "I did—I knew... But..." he winced. "I didn't... I mean to say, I knew how it would look."

"How what would look," Adele pressed, deadeyed.

"You know..." he tried to move his hands, but then winced as they strained against her cuffs. "This... being on those boats, telling no one. I just knew it'd look fishy."

"That doesn't explain why you ran."

The man snorted and dipped his sandy-blonde hair towards the grey tray with the jewelry. He twisted his head side to side as if balancing a scale. "That does."

"The stolen jewelry."

"I never said it was stolen."

"Passengers have been reporting missing items."

"Coincidental."

"You seem to be involved with a lot of coincidences," Adele replied, frowning more deeply now. The man, she'd determined, was clearly a thief. Athletic, too, given how he'd climbed the rail and dove into the river. But at the same time, he seemed adamant about his innocence.

Then again, most criminals were.

Still... That rose, that strange note, the taunting of the parents of the victims... Adele had felt certain the killer *wanted* somehow to be caught. A reckless killer, a desperate one. But Mr. Manet...

Her eyes moved from his chin to his narrowed eyes. He seemed caught in a cycle of self-preservation. Desperate only when threatened. The sort of sneak thief that preferred shadows to limelight. But a killer?

"This jewelry," Adele said, softly, "would have come from wealthy patrons, no doubt."

"I mean. It's mine. I was trying to sell it, is all," he said quickly. "Bought it off a friend. He runs an online store, see. Wanted to make a quick buck by having me sell it to passengers. No luck so far," he added quickly, shaking his head in sympathy with his own plight. "But I'm a trooper. I don't believe in quitting. Never give up, that's what I say. And, besides, my friend was nice enough to offer a ten percent commission on sales."

The words came quick, rapidly. All of it complete bullshit, Adele knew without batting an eyelid. But impressive at how rapidly the lie reached his lips.

"Let's say I don't believe you," Adele said, softly. "At all. And let's say you *did* steal these items." The plastic container rattled as she tapped against the pearls again and a couple of rings went sliding.

The man tried to protest, but Adele cut him off. "Hear me out, Mr. Manet. Let's say you are a thief. And let's say, to get items like these ones we found in your pockets, you'd have to find wealthy targets."

"I... I see where you're going. But I had nothing to do with their deaths."

"You do insist on your innocence, I give you that. But the evidence," another rattle, "seems to disagree." Adele leaned in now, breathing slowly through her nose, unblinking and watching Pierre's face. "Did you kill them? Were you trying to steal from them? And when they caught you, did you silence them? Is that what this is all about? Some stupid jewelry?"

Mr. Manet squeaked, shaking his head and wagging his face side to side. "I—no, what—never! You have to believe me!"

"That's the problem with being a thief and a liar, Mr. Manet. I don't believe you."

Adele got to her feet, shaking her head. She looked towards the closed door to the employee break room and called out, "We're done!"

A second passed and then the door opened as two uniformed officers entered. "Take him into custody," Adele said, quietly. "And get him out of here."

The policemen nodded, moving quickly over to Mr. Manet and gripping him by the arm. The small man continued to protest, shaking his head frantically, but Adele looked away now, ignoring him completely. She'd heard enough.

As Mr. Manet was led away, John cleared his throat, and in French said, "We're giving him to the locals?"

"Yeah. Think so."

"You don't think it's him?"

Adele looked John square in the eyes, then glanced back down at the jewelry in the Tupperware. "I don't know, John. I can't tell. He's clearly a thief. And he was on all three boats. And he probably targeted wealthy patrons. But... I don't know..."

"Seems like a rat. A coward. Not a killer."

Adele shrugged. "Maybe that's what I'm picking up on. I... I'm worried it's not our guy." She paused. "The first victim was killed with a strand of pearls... Does that sound like the sort of thing a thief might do? Throw away perfectly good jewelry?"

John crossed his arms, his frown so deep, his eyes were now cast in shadow. "What now then?" he murmured.

Adele spread her arms, indicating the break room. She nodded her head towards the vending machine. "Grab a protein bar. We've got this place to ourselves, for at least a bit. I'd like to go over those manifests one last time.

CHAPTER TWENTY TWO

Adele's head drooped over her phone, and her back ached from the bowed position in the spindle-backed chair facing the break room table. John's head was in his arms, snoring across from her, a pile of protein bar wrappers scattered around his side of the table.

Adele blinked blearily, running through the manifest a final time. She closed her eyes, holding them shut a moment, before opening them wide, hoping by that simple gesture to stave off her rising caffeine headache, and desperate need for sleep.

A second later, a quiet knocking resounded on the door.

"Yes?" she called, blearily.

The door opened, allowing a shaft of morning light to come as well. Adele winced, glancing at her phone and feeling a jolt of frustration. Dawn already. They'd allowed some of the passengers, the ones without rooms, to disembark earlier, once they'd provided and verified their IDs and addresses.

The overnight passengers, though, and the rest of the crew had been kept on board. Adele knew they couldn't maintain this, but she could feel time threatening to slip by, could feel her frustration mounting.

A head poked in the now open break room door. A throat cleared. "Agent Sharp?" said a policeman.

"What?" she said, a bit more crankily than she'd intended.

"That's it for the passengers," the officer replied, also blinking against sleep and rubbing at his salt and pepper temples. "Did you have anyone else on the list?"

Adele glanced at the door, pausing for a moment. She'd interview another three passengers and two employees who'd been on *two* of the boats. None of them, though, fit the bill. Her eyes glazed as they returned to the manifest on her phone.

No connections she could find. No common links between all three boats. Besides the porter—who was in local custody and clamming up—and the chef, who's alibi cleared on two of the boats, they had nothing left to go on.

"Any news on that court order?" Adele asked, looking to the local.

The policeman shook his head. "Couldn't reach the judge. He's still sleeping. I'm sorry, Agent Sharp."

She waved him away, and blearily closed her eyes. They needed to get the boats off the water until the killer was caught, but the cruise line—and Mr. Larsen especially—was raising a ruckus and flat-out refusing. Despite what had happened, he still considered it Adele's job to find the killer, while it was his job, in his words, to run the prospects of Sightseeing Incorporated.

She imagined the bad press was already costing them. Grounding the fleet would only make things worse.

But three women were already dead...

She shook her head in frustration, closing a fist in front of her.

At that moment, though, the policeman cleared his throat where he stood in the doorway, and she looked blearily over, raising an eyebrow above a likely bloodshot eye.

"I... We do have someone who wishes to speak with you."

"Oh?"

"Yes," said the officer. "We have him on the dock for now. Wanted to see if you were available." The man glanced towards where John was still snoring into his arms. One of the protein bar rappers seemed to catch a gust of the tall Frenchman's breath and skittered across the able, before tumbling out of sight into shadow.

"Who is it?" Adele said.

"Mr. Klose," The police officer replied, with an apologetic wince. "The husband to Abigail Havertz."

Adele sighed softly. The third victim's husband wanted to speak. That hardly boded well. Still, she was out of leads as it was. It couldn't make things worse, especially not with John sleeping. The Frenchman wouldn't be able to assault any more reporters while unconscious. At least, so she hoped.

"Fine," Adele said.

"Should I bring him in?"

"No, I'll come out. I need the air." Adele pushed to her feet, trying not to loose the groaning sound threatening her lips.

She followed the policeman out on the first level of the riverboat. The rails were now clear. Most the passengers either sleeping in their rooms or returned home with names and addresses logged. It was a risk to send the part-time passengers home. But Adele decided that if the killer was still on board, he most likely would be one of the overnighters or an employee for such familiarity with the layout of the vessels. As it was, she felt stuck.

She followed the police officer past two posted guards, whose heads were also nodding, despite the steaming cups of coffee clutched in each of their hands and moved towards the concrete dock.

Amidst the police cars, she spotted a single white sedan with a fancy-looking spoiler on the back. She didn't know anything about cars, but the thing looked like the sort of vehicle John would drool over.

Standing against the hood of this car, his arms crossed, was a man in a soft sweater, wearing a somber expression as he stared at the boat. The man in the sweater had pleasant, handsome features, in a prep-school sort of way. He couldn't have been much out of his early twenties.

When he spotted the policeman and Adele approaching, he uncrossed his arms, wiping his hands against his pants in a sort of nervous tic, before straightening up and watching them near.

As Adele stepped over a concrete barrier, she winced, blinked, and, beneath first sunlight, came to a halt in front of the third victim's husband.

"Mr. Havertz," she said, quietly.

"Are you the agent in charge?" he asked in German, his voice high-pitched and soft. Not quite lisping, but near enough. A soft man, in a soft sweater, with soft features. His eyes were ringed red, suggesting he'd been crying, and his posture was now stooped as she addressed him, pulling in on himself, defensive and guarded. He blinked off to the side for a moment, his voice hoarse, but he swallowed and tried again, "Please, are you in charge?"

"Yes," Adele said, reflexively. "My partner and I. How can I help you, Mr. Havertz. I'm very sorry for your loss."

He gave a weary little nod and closed his eyes. For a moment, he didn't open them, simply standing there, eyes closed, beneath the sun.

"She liked the sunrise, you know," he murmured. "We would often go on the porch to watch it together." he smiled, his eyes still closed. "I'm going to miss that."

"Like I said, I really am sorry." Adele felt a lance of shame and frustration. If she had managed to dock the boats, this man's wife would still be alive. Then again, she knew how the world worked. Perhaps, how it *had to* work. The lives of the many wouldn't be put forever on pause for the few. No, the concerns of the few always seemed to end up on her desk, usually too late.

The soft man in the soft sweater gave another little, high-pitched sigh. "We were only recently married, you know."

Adele nodded if only to provide some sort of reaction. She still wasn't sure what the man wanted with her. He'd already been notified of his wife's death. The police would've taken care of that. It wasn't like she could provide any new information. Still, perhaps it wasn't about a solution, or really *doing* anything. Maybe she just needed to listen.

"How recently?" she said, her reflexively inquisitive nature taking over from her sleep deprived state.

"Only a couple of months. Or, well, not even that. More like five weeks." He sighed. "I keep track, because it's hard to forget when you became the luckiest man in the world. Five weeks ago. That's when it happened for me. When she said *I do*. And now," he shrugged, his eyes open once more, but seemingly wishing they were closed, "all this. It just doesn't seem right."

"It never does, sir," Adele said quietly. "Your wife, she was very wealthy."

He snorted, waving a hand. "I didn't care about any of that, but I suppose you're right, she would've been. If she hadn't married me."

Adele frowned, blinking in the sun, and said, "What do you mean?"

"Ah, well. She had to give that up. When I found out, I told her not to. I wasn't worth all of that. But she was adamant. I couldn't change her mind." He shifted again, his arms crossing once more. "Her family didn't approve of me. I..." he said, hesitantly, tapping a finger against his dark skin, "I wasn't exactly the right shade or creed, if you catch my meaning."

Adele didn't react, though she wanted to wince. She nodded. "So her family cut her off?"

"Yes. Or, well, they threatened to. I'm sure they were about to. I don't really know. We cut ties with them before they could with us." He laughed but the sound died just as quickly. He stared off now. "Agent, I don't mean to take your time. But do you know who did this? It wasn't her family, was it?" His voice cracked now, and tears slipped down his cheek. "I didn't cause this, did I? If she hadn't married me. If she'd only—"

"—sir, it's not worth thinking like that. And no, it isn't because of you. And I doubt it was her family. We have a serial killer. It's not something we're spreading widely right now. But I'm sure you've read about the deaths on the other boats."

He gave a shuddering sob but nodded once.

"I hate to say it, sir, there's nothing you could've done. Others failed; others neglected. And the killer, at the end of the day, is the only one to blame. I will catch him. I don't think that will help. But maybe."

"Maybe."

Adele began to turn, but then she paused momentarily. "Your wife," she said, "we identified her because of her driver's license. But on her ticket she was going under a different name. Adlon. Is that your last name?"

The man paused for a moment, his face creasing in tear-stained smile. He even chuckled, briefly, and shook his head. "No. That's a joke. It's from one of our favorite books. We found it was easier to avoid being tracked down by her family."

"They would track you down?"

"To harass us. They once hired a private investigator because they thought I was from bad stock."

Adele winced, nodding sympathetically, but at the same time, like the sun rising above, the heat against her cheeks, she felt a slow, dawning sense of realization.

It was so simple. Obvious even.

Fake names. These were boats, not airplanes. Entry was little better than concert tickets—the killer was using a fake name to travel from boat to boat. He had to be. She shook her head slowly, gave another apologetic nod towards the widower, and turned, walking away, mulling this over.

Mr. Havertz wouldn't benefit by her staying. He wouldn't benefit by her going. There was really nothing that she could do to help. But maybe, just maybe, if she caught this guy, it could give some measure of peace.

As she moved, she quickened, picking up her pace, heading back towards the boat.

The killer was using fake names. That would explain why she couldn't find a commonality on the manifest. But not only that, this was the second victim who wouldn't have inherited their family fortune. Anika had been cut off. And now, it turned out, so had Abigail. Did the killer know that? Was this envy over status and wealth? Over beauty?

Or was something else going on here?

Adele felt a little shiver. She thought back to that rose, that note taped to the stem.

This was personal, but clinical.

Deeply connected, and yet sanitized.

Something was going on here that she wasn't picking up on. Something that was costing young women their lives. She needed to go back and look over the evidence once more.

CHAPTER TWENTY THREE

He reclined lazily at the café table, overlooking the swishing blue-grey waters beneath the dawning sunlight. He'd already been up for a while, listening, watching, like a gargoyle perched on a cathedral, keeping track off all within its domain.

He watched the police cars around the dock, and also watched the two agents—one of them tall, the other shorter, with blonde hair. The woman seemed to be in charge, though the tall agent, with a scar under the side of his chin, seemed a mulish, stubborn fellow.

Just his luck they had locked the boat down before he could get off. He'd tried to leave with some of the short-term passengers, but they'd been checking identifications against ticket names, and so he'd been forced to double back and remain behind with the overnighters and the crew.

Now, sitting at the café table, feeling the cool metal slowly warming in the sunlight where his fingers tapped, he simply watched and waited.

He also listened.

Two tables over, a group of young friends—likely college-aged—were muttering to each other. One of the young men was saying, "They can't keep us here, can they?" He spoke in English, with a London accent. "It's not right! Hear me!" the young man's voice rose, and he directed the shout towards where a police officer was stationed by the café window, keeping an eye on the passengers.

The officer cleared his throat and glanced uncomfortably off to the side.

Another one of the college-aged tourists was shaking her head firmly. She had short-cut, purple-dyed hair, and sniffed in frustration. She spoke to the officer in German, her accent quite heavy, but decipherable. "When can we leave?" she demanded, growling.

A couple of other passengers, sitting at another table, nursing small coffees and teas were frowning as well, wagging their heads in agreement—a sure sign things had grown serious when locals and tourists agreed on anything.

The police officer shifted uncomfortably again, but the girl yelled at him in German once more and he shrugged his shoulders, adjusting his uniform once. The officer in question had salt-and-pepper hair, and bags under his eyes, suggesting he hadn't slept well the previous night.

The man at the café table, on the other hand, had slept like a babe. Three down. One to go. Everything had to end at some point. He'd thought by starting this all, some of the rage, the pent-up fury would have dissipated, like pus leaving a wound.

But the more he killed, he'd found his anger only to rise. The memories came too. The gagging, choking sounds reminded him of... *her.* He frowned now, his fingers no longer drumming against the metal table, his eyes narrowed beneath the rising sun over the boat. The stirring of the morning had prompted vehicles and pedestrians to begin moving along the river walks. A small group of looky-loos had gathered at the entrance to the dock, watching the ship. He'd spotted cameras and reporters among them. He'd even seen a couple of reporters try to sneak over one of the chain-link fences before being caught by the police and dragged off.

Now, though, as he watched the college tourists lambaste the police officer, he felt a flicker of frustration.

The officer was just trying to do his job. No sleep, poor pay, little appreciation, and no respect. That's how it often went with such folk.

"I'm sorry," the officer said, shaking his head helplessly. "Nothing I can do until I'm given the word. It shouldn't be much longer."

This only prompted a further outcry from the two other tables with customers. The overnight passengers were now scowling in synchronization, all trying to express their displeasure at once. The officer now clammed up, shrugging and staring off over the heads of the gathered onlookers.

The man at the café table just watched, quietly, silently. He didn't raise his voice; he didn't shake his fist. If anything, his only annoyed glance was spared for the disrespectful children. They didn't understand the way of the world. Didn't understand the amount of shit an officer like that, a beat cop, had to go through. If he'd been so unfortunate as to have been stuck babysitting the passengers, it meant he was a low man on the totem pole.

Fingers started tapping on the metal surface once more. The man sighed, watching the scene through hooded eyes, his expression docile, careful, calm. No reason to fear. Not now. Not yet.

She would be with him soon.

The fourth.

It was all coming together. They didn't have a clue who he was. They didn't have a clue what he wanted.

Perfect. He wondered what his next postcard would say. Should he tell them why? Should he tell them what he was going to do after?

He smiled, faintly, but then erased the expression, folding his hands on the table in front of him. Such unusual things, hands. Interesting what they could accomplish. So many uses in those ten fingers.

He studied his folded hands for a moment, his neat, expensive suit sleeves pressed against the table. The hands were his, calloused and rough. The hands of a menial worker—the hands of a man who knew an honest day's labor. The suit didn't match the hands. But his past didn't match his future, either.

Some things simply couldn't be explained. Strange what fate would give and then subsequently take back.

If he could trade it all... suits and everything for one more day with her...

He swallowed now, glancing off over the railing and watching a seabird circle...

He'd do it in a heartbeat.

But alas, that wasn't an option.

She was gone. And so they would pay. They had refused to before. Then, they'd paid later. But now, they'd pay the ultimate price.

Just one left.

He remained quiet, calm, listening to the grumblings, the mutterings, the protests. Little more than the bleating of a flock behind wooden fences. Bleating meant nothing.

Action was everything.

Soon.

CHAPTER TWENTY FOUR

One dead, two dead, three, four? They needed to find a lead... Something clear, something certain and concrete. Adele gritted her teeth at the thought. She stood on the dock for a moment, watching the white sports car idle in the parking lot. Abigail's husband wasn't leaving, contenting himself, it seemed, to remained parked under police surveillance, staring up at the large boat where his wife had died.

Adele hated leaving him there, untended, unaided. But there was nothing she could do.

She glanced back, up towards the boat. Towards where the porter had been taken into custody. The locals would be booking him soon enough, no doubt. They'd keep him overnight, at the very least—and he'd be serving time for the jewelry he'd stolen.

But was he a killer?

"Unlikely," she murmured, softly, answering her own question.

She stood on the dock, on the very edge, her toes practically poking over the dappled concrete, towards the waters below. The water was oddly still, today. No rising wind, no droplets of rain. The wake of boats and watercraft hadn't disturbed the flowing river, yet.

Rather, it was like watching a trail of sheer glass extend beneath reflective sunlight.

She sighed slowly, staring at where her feet jutted over the concrete edge. For a moment, she wondered how cool the water was. The sun was starting to bake, and the back of her neck often burned faster than the rest of her. She reached up, rubbing at her warm neck and then pushed her bangs out of her eyes, frowning to herself.

The deadest of ends.

The porter was in custody, but she knew it wasn't him. Knew it in her bones. Pierre Manet wasn't the sort of man to write a note, leave a rose. He was an unctuous, slimy weasel of a man. He wasn't a killer. He was a thief. He wasn't bold, he was someone who preferred the shadows. He didn't have the will to do this.

She knew a coward when she saw one. And while killers were monsters, heinous, they weren't always cowards. They put action to their evil thoughts.

Muttering to herself and choosing a few special insults, she felt her phone begin to buzz in her pocket. Adele swallowed, wincing, and then lifted the device. She stared at the number, and then went cold.

Foucault.

Damn it.

She glanced over her shoulder, looking for John, but he was likely still napping in the break room on his bed made of protein bar wrappers.

Double damn it.

For one, wild moment, she considered letting it go to voicemail. At this point, though, they were bordering on insubordination. Besides, John had been the one to throw the equipment off the boat, not Adele. It wasn't her job to duck and hide. Her career wasn't in jeopardy. Besides, John's stint with the DGSI had nine lives. She was curious, like a cat, to wonder how on earth the tall Frenchman was going to escape punishment this time.

So she answered.

"Foucault?" Adele said, her voice sounding far too high-pitched to her own ears.

"Adele?" The Executive's voice replied, just as stern and firm as she'd dreaded.

"I... yes sir?"

"You sent in a request for us to ground ten water boats."

She blinked. Not about John, then? "Oh, yes, sir." She shifted uncomfortably, watching the white sports car absentmindedly, her own mind whirring. "I didn't want to bother you, so I didn't send it across your desk, sir."

"Yes, well, Paige sent it my way."

"Of course she did," Adele said. "Sir," she added.

"I'm afraid it's bad news, Adele. Sightseeing Incorporated is putting up a fight. Judge Diel woke to six lawyers at his office first thing this morning. Ten missed phone calls, apparently. He called it harassment and blamed our department."

"I—I'm sorry, sir. Could Ms. Jayne, perhaps—"

"No, you're Interpol correspondent is no help either, I'm afraid. Look, Adele, I'm sorry, but we can't ground those boats, not yet."

Adele hissed slowly, loosing air like steam from a kettle. At least the call wasn't about John. But somehow, now, she realized, this was far worse.

Without grounding all the ships, there was no way to track down the killer. For all she knew, the bastard had slipped the boat long before they'd even arrived. She had no clue where to go from here, other than a wild goose chase on some other boat. She couldn't waste time skipping from ship to ship hoping that luck would help her save another life.

She stared at the idling, white sports car. Winced against the sunlight. Winced, even more, against Mr. Havertz' words about his wife. She'd liked sunrises apparently. She'd loved him more than her family's wealth.

Someone like that didn't deserve to die, did they?

Adele considered it for a moment. Perhaps *deserve* was the wrong word. No one was solely their highlights. Most people were a mixture and hid their flaws well enough.

But this killer, this predator, he'd allowed his worst nature to take the reigns. And she was kicking against a wall, unable to find entry into even the simplest lead.

"Sir, I beg you to reconsider. Is the judge willing to take a phone call? If you'd give me his—"

"Ha! Absolutely not. Out of the question, Agent Sharp."

"Sir, really, we're running—"

"I get it. But no. Ships won't be grounded, Sharp. That's final."

Adele huffed a breath but nodded slowly. "Alright, sir. Anything else?" As she said it, she winced, staring off and resisting the urge to cross her fingers.

"One other thing."

"Oh?"

"I'm having reports that Agent Renee had an altercation with two violent civilians."

"I—er, what?"

Foucault cleared his throat. "Are you alright?"

"Am I—excuse me, sir?"

"They attacked, you, yes? John said they tried to push you overboard. Renee's report includes a description of you trying to escape but being outnumbered." She heard what sounded like rustling paper and then a flipping page. "I see one of them tried to kiss you. Apparently, he was drunk—is there anything you'd like to add?"

Adele just stared, her mouth unhinged. She felt something like ice and sheer outrage fall across her shoulders. "Tried... tried to *kiss* me, sir?"

"Yes. We've confirmed their identities. A couple of low-life paparazzi scum. Looks like they filed a report with locals. Something about cameras being damaged." He cleared his throat delicately. "Renee's report said they were taking photos of you in indecent postures."

"I... They were... so... Renee's not in trouble?"

"Renee? As far as the report goes, he was only protecting his partner. That's what we're going with in communication with the Germans. Why, do you have something else to add to the report?"

Adele stared at the sky for a moment, considering her words. The initial jolt of outrage cycled through her, whirling again and again.

A bald-faced lie. A lie directly to the executive.

Then again, John was the same agent who used federal money to lease sports cars. He'd once tackled a man into a river and parked a helicopter on a mountain during a snowstorm. She could picture, in her mind's eye, John snickering as he wrote the report.

Damn nine lives... More like nine hundred.

"I... I don't remember things the same way, sir."

"Well, if you want to add anything, file a report. Adele, I need you focused on this. All three of these victims had high profiles. The stories are starting to seep out in local channels. It's only a matter of time before we have more cameras on us."

"I understand, sir. I won't be filing a report." She gritted her teeth. "But John may be adjusting his."

"I see."

"Yes, sir. Is that all?"

"Focus, Agent Sharp. Catch this bastard before I'm swimming in red tape. Hear?"

Adele sighed, but then nodded. She realized a second later, he couldn't see her. "Yes, sir. Of course, sir. No red tape."

"And Adele, I'm sorry about those reporters. If you'd like to press charges..."

"No, sir," she said, reflexively. "I... I don't quite remember it like Renee, sir."

"So you said. Alright, good day, Agent Sharp. Report back with anything. On the case. And try not to get kissed by any more paparazzi."

Adele heard the line go dead, and she stood on the edge of the dock, seething, folding her fingers into a fist and glaring across the water.

"I'm going to kill him," she muttered to herself. "*Kill.* Him."

She could picture the shit-eating grin on John's face when she confronted him. One of these days, she knew his antics would catch up with him. With *them.* Did she really want to be around when the pied piper came calling?

John wasn't by the book. He wasn't always honest. He was a damn fine shot, though, and reliable and loyal. Still... sometimes it felt like trying to train a toddler not to bite other children.

She found her fingers reflexively moving back to her phone. She lifted the device, scrolling through until she found the contact she wanted.

The Sergeant.

And then dialed.

If there had ever been polar opposites in their approach to their careers, John and the Sergeant were it.

Adele wasn't sure why she was calling, until the voice answered after the second ring.

A grunt, then, "What? I'm busy."

"Nice to hear from you too, Dad," she said, resisting the urge to roll her eyes.

"You can't visit me. I'm fine."

"I'm not calling about that."

"I don't need you checking up on me either," the Sergeant said, gruff as ever.

"I'm not checking up on you. I have a question."

Compared to John's unprofessionalism, and the chaotic nature of moving from boat to boat, Adele supposed she simply wanted to tether herself to something reliable and consistent. Her father was the consummate professional. He was gruff, blunt, and had the affectionate bandwidth of a pet rock, but he had been good at his job. And consistent. He'd been a Sergeant for longer than she'd been with the FBI. Besides, it wasn't like she had leads coming from any other source.

"Dad, I'm not calling about that."

"Good. What do you want, then?" He cleared his throat. "I mean, how are you?"

"I'm fine, Dad. Are you still at the hospital?"

"Course not. I'm back home."

Adele felt her temper surge. "Dad," she said, sternly. "The asshole who attacked you is still out there!"

"Are you tracking the case? How do you know he's still out there."

"Of course I'm tracking it. The guy who attacked you is in the wind,

Dad. You should be at the hospital, or somewhere safe."

"I am safe. Besides, the hospital food was awful. I missed my mushroom soup."

For a moment, in the background, Adele thought she heard the sound of voices. Of course, her father didn't have friends. So she assumed he was now watching TV while eating soup. Again, predictable. Professional. And unceasingly frustrating.

"Dad, do they at least have a police car outside?"

"I told them not to. But they wouldn't listen." He sounded angry.

But his frustration brought her some relief. At least the German police force was keeping an eye on one of their own. She sighed, shaking her head. "And you're feeling okay?"

"I thought you weren't calling to check up on me."

She gritted her teeth, biting back a retort. But then, she sighed, swallowing her pride, and, still standing on the dock, facing the water, and occasionally glancing back towards the white sports car, she said, "I need your help."

"My help?" Her father made a slurping sound, suggesting he'd taken a spoonful of soup. "I'm not leaving Germany."

"Well, I happen to be on the Danube. But I'm not asking you to come here. Look, I'm just trying to figure out my next step. I'm stuck." It was a vulnerable thing to say to her father. He was the sort of man who gauged someone's character based on their success. And yet, instead of jumping on the admission, there was a long pause, and then her father said, "What's the problem?"

Adele felt a little flutter of relief. She wasn't sure why, but those words, from this source, cut through the layers of defense, frustration, habits, and allowed her to feel a small weight lift from her shoulders.

"I have a killer. He's on a river, moving from boat to boat, taking out wealthy young women."

"Sounds awful. You catch him?"

"If I caught him, I wouldn't be calling you."

"Well, you should catch him."

"Thanks Dad. I'll write that one down."

"No need to be sarcastic. What's the problem? Why can't you find this guy?"

"Because I don't understand how he's tracking these women."

"You said they're rich?"

"Definitely."

"Was he targeting them specifically?"

"It looks like it."

"What's the timeframe between the kills?"

"Three days," Adele replied. He's killing one every night. And we haven't found anything conclusive."

"So you're telling me, over a period of three days, this killers' targets just so happened to all decide to take a river cruise?"

Adele blinked. She hadn't been thinking of it from this angle. But when she considered it, she realized her father was right. It was one thing if he was targeting them randomly. But there was something personal about this case. Something intentional. It wasn't random. But then how on earth had all three of the victims managed to end up on the same cruise line in the same week?

"You're right," she said, slowly. "Maybe it is random then."

"How would he have known they were on those boats?"

She considered it, but then frowned. "He wouldn't have. It took me nearly a day to get those manifests. And that's after three murders, and a lot of pressure. There's no way he would've had the access to that, unless he worked with the cruise line."

"Well, you can't rule that out."

"But if the targets *aren't* random," she said, trailing off, "there's no way. It would've been a million to one odds that all three of these heiresses would've chosen to be on these boats within days of each other. That doesn't make any sense, does it?

"Maybe it *is* random then."

Adele thought to the rose, thought to the postcard, thought to the personal, intimate way of murder, having them choke on their own items. All of them symbols of wealth. A necklace, a wallet, and an expensive, designer dress. The killer was lashing out, and it was personal. He been taunting the parents with that note. So it wasn't random. She didn't believe it. Which meant he'd chosen, handpicking these victims.

"Dad, you're a genius. You should go back to the hospital."

"If I'm a genius, then I know best."

"You always did," she said with a sigh. "Look, thanks. I'm going to talk to someone really quick. Let me know if you need anything."

"Goodbye, Adele."

Adele hung up first and began stalking towards where the white car waited in the parking lot outside the dock.

It wasn't random. He'd chosen those victims intentionally. So how on earth had the killer managed to get all three of these wealthy, young women onto the boats within the time frame he needed? She picked up her pace, marching towards the parked vehicle.

CHAPTER TWENTY FIVE

Adele's knuckles rapped against the window of the white sports car. There was a pause, the sound of music fading as a volume knob was adjusted, and then the window rolled down. She stared into the car, and Mr. Havertz looked up at her, tears in his eyes, which he hastily wiped away with the back of his sweater sleeve.

"Agent," the man said quickly, "can I help you? Did you find him?"

Adele considered her next words carefully, watching the man. Slowly, she shook her head and said, "Sorry. Not yet. But maybe you can help with that. I have a question. I wish I'd thought to ask it sooner." She paused, considering the angles, but then nodded, cementing her determination. She said, "What made your wife decide to take this boat trip? Without you."

"Oh... well, the ticket was only for one."

Adele blinked.

He hesitated, and then said, "We didn't have enough to afford a second one. They didn't comp both."

"Excuse me? What do you mean *comp*?"

He frowned. "I-I thought you knew. The company, the ones that own these boats, some sort of Sights corporation or something..."

"Sightseeing Incorporated?" Adele said, stiffly.

"Yes, them." Mr. Havertz gripped his steering wheel, though the car was motionless, and the engine was off. "They comped the ticket. She was under stress at work and frustrated with her family cutting her off. She was looking into getting a real job. We didn't have the money for things like that. We probably wouldn't have for a long time after. We both thought it was a good idea."

Here, his voice shook, and he let out a little sob. "In fact, I encouraged her to do it. I told her it would help her unwind, to remove some stress. Three days paid vacation, moving up and down the Danube River? It sounded perfect. But if I'd known—" his voice cracked.

"You didn't know," Adele said, sternly. "This isn't your fault. But please, you're telling me that the company that owns the boats paid for your wife's ticket?"

"Yes. We got the ticket in the post. Along with a note welcoming her to try the tour." He shrugged. "It's not unusual for someone from my wife's family. A lot of times companies will approach to try to get the wealthy and influential to use their product or business. It helps to raise their own notoriety."

Adele shook her head. "But I thought your wife was cut off."

"It's not exactly public information."

Adele stared, her mind spinning. "Do you happen to have that letter?"

Here, his face fell. "No, I'm sorry." He pressed his head back against the seat rest, staring at the felt ceiling of his luxurious car interior. "I wish I'd kept it. But we didn't think to at the time. All we needed was the ticket according to the letter."

"You threw it away?"

"Nearly a week ago. I'm sorry. Is that important?" Before Adele could reply, feeling her stomach plummet, Mr. Havertz suddenly snapped his fingers against the steering wheel. His eyes were wide, and his other hand darted to his pocket, fishing around. He pulled out his phone, tapping his finger in a sort of excited motion against the wheel. "Hang on," he said, quickly. "I don't have the original envelope, but my wife was the one who got the letter. She was so excited that she sent me a screenshot when I was at work."

Adele felt her mouth go dry as the phone was turned towards her. Mr. Havertz cycled through the images on his phone until he ended up at one. He clicked it, and the image blew to full size. A hand was holding an open letter. Adele leaned in, practically in the cabin of the car now, staring at the small screen.

The logo on top of the letter in the image was for Sightseeing Inc. It had the company's name in the masthead. The type was simple. Only two lines.

Congratulations, you've been chosen for a free trip on the Danube River. Tickets are enclosed, and further information can be found at www.sightseeinginc.co.uk.

Adele stared. "Can you go to that site?"

Mr. Havertz nodded quickly, seemingly grateful to have a role to play besides that of grieving husband. He opened his browser and tried to cycle to the website, but then frowned. "It doesn't go to anything. It's just a dead page."

Adele pulled her own phone out, and tried the same address, twice.

Both times she went to a dead page.

"Dammit," she said, firmly. "That's not the company's website. They don't operate in the UK. It's a fake, I'd bet anything."

The man stared at her, stunned.

"You've been more than helpful, but could you text that picture to me, please?"

Mr. Havertz hesitated, but then nodded quickly. "What do you mean it's fake? Are you saying someone else sent those tickets?" His eyes widened. "Are you saying it was the killer?"

"I'm saying that I need you to send that to me. Please. Here's my number. Hurry."

***

Adele studied her phone as she marched to the second level where most of the overnight rooms on the boat were located. She zeroed in on the first door, closest to the prow and raised a hand, knocking loudly, and said, "Mr. Larsen, we need to speak!"

It took a moment, and she knocked again, even more loudly. For a moment, there was no answer. A sudden anxiety swarmed Adele's mind, and she began to reach for her holster, but just then, the door swung open with a creak. A man, wincing, his face practically bruised on one side as if he'd been sleeping against a hard pillow stared out at her. Sleepy, and wearing pajamas, Mr. Larsen didn't seem so much like a toady lawyer, but more like a supply teacher who'd slept in. He blinked against the light over Adele's shoulder.

"Yes?" He said, gritting his teeth. "I'm sorry, Agent Sharp, but I've already spoken with the board. We're not willing to ground the ships. You should've heard from a judge by now."

She replied, tight-lipped and rapid. "Not here about that. Though you *should* ground the ships. Look, tell me, what's this?"

She rotated the phone, shoving it up and close to Mr. Larsen's face. He winced, then with a resigned sigh stared as he read the screenshot of the letter. Then he frowned. "That's not from us."

"You're sure?"

"Positive. I'm involved with all promotional efforts. We don't send out things like that. Our market research showed that people found it manipulative."

"You wouldn't want to be manipulative."

If he caught the note of sarcasm, he ignored it. "What *is* that? Some sort of joke?"

"No, Mr. Larsen. A counterfeit. It was used to lure Abigail to this boat. And I suspect our other two victims were given them as well."

Adele turned as Mr. Larsen spluttered in his doorway, still half asleep. She began to march down the stairs, ignoring his calls after her. Dawn was beginning to reach morning, and she needed to speak with John. She felt a jolt of frustration, remembering Foucault's comments about his report.

"I got you," she muttered beneath her breath.

This letter was from the killer. It wasn't the company. It couldn't be. They wouldn't have any interest in the second victim. Anika didn't have money anymore. She'd been cut off from her family and wasn't even using their last name. No, the killer had sent these letters. Would the other two have them as well? There was no time to check, but she assumed so. Her father was right; how else would all three of the targets have been on the boats within the same three days? Who else, then, had received a similar letter?"

"Adele," a voice suddenly called out.

She spun around, and spotted John standing on a portion of the deck near the café at the front of the lowest level. He was looking up at her, where her hand trailed along the railing.

"John," she said, frowning. "I have something."

He winced. "Erm, I hear you spoke with the executive." He gave a playful little chuckle, but it came across as more nervous than anything.

She paused, frowning at his handsome features, down to the scar along his chin, down to the nervous, twitching way he shifted back and forth. "John, if we're going to go out, you can't involve me in your lies."

He blinked, winced. "I thought it was sort of funny."

"I know you did. I don't. I care about my career."

He blinked. "And you're saying I don't?"

Adele shrugged. "I'm not looking for a fight. I'm just telling you, if we're going to go out, you can't involve me in your lies. You need to tell the executive the truth. If you don't, I will."

The words came quick and firm. For a moment, she thought John might lash out, or double down. But instead, the tall Frenchman scratched at his chin, then sighed, nodding once. "I panicked. I'm sorry."

She blinked in surprise, but then reached out and patted the large Frenchman on his muscular arm.

"You have to tell the executive the truth. Take back that report. Or

I'm going to. I don't want to be involved." She spoke matter-of-factly, firmly, almost robotically. Perhaps she wasn't that different from her father after all. But then, as John sighed and began to nod in acquiescence, she said, excitement flaring again, "But not now. Look, I have a lead."

John leaned against the wall nearest the café. Behind him, at two of the tables, passengers were sitting and muttering to each other. She saw a police officer near the café, looking uncomfortable, and staring in any direction except for the nearest table with a group of college students.

Adele looked away now, pointing the phone towards John and tapping the picture Abigail's husband had sent her.

"What is this?"

"A counterfeit."

"I don't understand."

"This," Adele said, firmly, "was not sent by the company."

A couple of the college kids were looking over now, watching. And Adele lowered her voice, and moved away now, heading down towards a cleared portion of the deck near the rail. John followed.

"What do you mean?"

"I mean," she said, slowly, "our killer sent this to the third victim. That's how he was luring them onto the boats. He was representing himself as a member of the company. He even had a website set up and everything."

"A website?"

"It's down now. I checked. But yes, he had a website. He was trying to get them to get on board, thinking they were being comped because of their wealth and their family names."

"I thought two of the victims were practically cut off."

"Yes, that's right. Wait, how did you know about the second one?"

"Anika?"

"No, the third one. Sorry. Abigail?"

"I talked to the officer that took you to her husband. He was listening to your conversation. Why? Is that an issue?"

"No. But look, we don't have confirmation the other two had the same letters. But they must have. And so, if the website is down, that means he's already lured everyone he wants to. We don't know who's on these boats, or how many victims he has in mind."

John winced but nodded in slow realization. "But if he has more, then he's already set them up."

"Exactly. But look, he sent this letter anonymously. He pretended to be part of the company."

"So?"

"It got me thinking." Adele nodded, firmly, feeling her pulse quicken, her mind spinning. She'd been mulling this over and realized it had to be true. There were no other options. The manifests hadn't turned up anything. All the employees were accounted for, their names in the system. The overnight passengers had already been checked, and their names were tied to their rooms.

"What are you thinking?"

"What if our killer wasn't just anonymous on these letters to lure our victims. What if he was anonymous on the boats too?"

"Come again?"

"John, I'm saying what if the killer's name isn't on the manifest? What if he didn't even buy a ticket?"

John stared. "Anonymous."

"Anonymous," Adele said, “Exactly. We need to find out who is on this boat that shouldn't be."

CHAPTER TWENTY SIX

After the two of them split up to cover more ground, John circled the spiral staircase towards the first level. "Stupid paparazzi," John muttered to himself as he stomped down the stairs, doing his best not to look at the water. "Stupid Foucault," he muttered... "stupid Ad—"

He caught himself and frowned. No. Not Adele's fault. His own damn fault. And that temper of his. And now, he'd gone and pissed Adele off.

She hadn't sounded angry; she'd simply drawn a boundary. But in a way, that was almost worse. And now she wanted him to come clean to Foucault. Embellishing a couple of details in a report about scumbag reporters—who cared?

She did. Which was one of the reasons he liked her. Adele held herself to a higher standard than most. She seemed to think John was the only one who cut corners at the DGSI, but she wasn't paying close enough attention. It wasn't him who was different, it was her. And he admired her for it.

He sighed... One way or another, he supposed he'd have to get back on her good side.

He scowled at the thought, but then continued his march towards the crew break room. Adele seemed to think the killer was anonymous on the boat. What better way to get back in her graces than to catch the murderer?

He could tell this case was starting to eat at her, especially given the distraction of what had happened to her father in his own home.

John's hand clenched into a fist at his side, and his eyes narrowed.

Maybe he had been behaving like a child. John hated the thought of Adele being further burdened by his own dumb actions.

He rubbed a hand along his chin, tracing his scar, and then flexing his fingers. One thing at a time, though.

He couldn't split his attention.

Catch a killer—Adele would thank him then. John burst into the break room, inhaling the faint odor of cigarette smoke, apparent most near a haze by the porthole window in the back of the room, near the vending machine.

A couple of employees were sitting at the felt table he'd been sleeping at earlier. They looked up in surprise as he neared, staring.

John fixated his eyes on a silver-haired man wearing glasses and a black suit with golden buttons. “You,” John said, pointing. “What's your name, sir?”

The man shared a look with his coworker. A younger, blonde woman, with a very plain face, but a fidgety mouth, her lips bunched up on one side, creased with dimples.

The man paused, then, hesitantly, spoke in German, wincing and tapping his ear. John sighed in frustration but tried English now. “English? Either of you?”

The young woman cleared her throat. “Yes,” she said. “My father doesn't, but I do.”

John looked at the girl now, eyes up. “Your father? You both work here?”

The dimpled girl nodded quickly. “Yes. You—you're with the police, no?”

“Mhmm. Look,” John said, crossing his arms and frowning. “I need to know if there might be any way to get on this boat without paying a fare. Any friends of employees, or relatives,” he said, slowly, glancing knowingly at her father.

The girl's eyes went wide, though, and she instantly shook her head. “No!” she protested. “Definitely not. Never.”

Her father frowned, speaking in German, and she replied quickly, translating. Her father's silver eyebrows dipped now, low, and he scowled at John.

“Come on,” John pressed, crossing his arms. “I won't mention it to the higher-ups. We all know how they can get,” he gave a nonchalant shrug in a would-be commiserating way.

The daughter and father duo didn't bite. Instead, they just stared at him, still frowning, and beginning to look uncomfortable.

John sighed. “Alright, I'm sure neither of *you* do any of that. Of course not! But... *but...* maybe you know someone. Another employee, someone on the crew—someone who likes to just occasionally sneak a friend or two on board free of charge. Couldn't blame them, could you? It's a really nice boat.”

He ended by trying to flash a schmoozing smile.

The girl looked mildly indigested, and she winced as if contemplating his words. “No, sir,” she said quickly. “Mr. Larsen would never allow it. We need this job. My father—he has bills. Please, don't say to anyone we do this."

"I wasn't saying *you* did; I was asking—"

"No!" she protested. "Sorry, but our break is over. Goodbye." Quickly, the young girl tugged at her father's arm and hastily beat a retreat, tugging him past John and towards the break room door.

A second later, the door clicked shut, leaving John alone across from the vending machine.

He massaged the bridge of his nose and sighed, slamming one fist into the felt of the table. "Damn it," he muttered. He'd never been much of the schmoozing sort. People didn't tend to lower their guard when he was around. Adele had once told him he looked like a James Bond villain. He'd objected to the characterization, but others didn't seem to.

Where was that stupid Italian agent of Adele's when needed? Lenny? Loni? Whatever his name was. People always seemed to like Leonard.

Focus, John thought to himself. He waited for a moment, considering his options.

Anonymous. That's what Adele thought. Someone was on the boat anonymously. But the way the crew reacted made it clear that Mr. Larsen and his company ran a tight ship. Would an employee really risk it, just to smuggle a friend or acquaintance on board? It would have to be more than one employee, since the only connection between the three boats was already accounted for.

It didn't seem likely...

So if not one of the porters or crew...

What about someone higher up?

John's eyebrows inched up in the break room, and he could feel the warmth of sunlight through the port hole window against the back of his neck.

Someone influential might not be so worried about Larsen's heavy-handed tactics. On top of that, someone higher up wouldn't have nearly as hard a time riding fare-free. No ticket, no paper trail.

But who would know of someone like that? John wasn't familiar with all the positions of authority on a boat, or all the people involved in keeping such things floating.

He considered his next move for a moment, and then a small smile tugged at the corner of his lips.

Perhaps...

Yes.

He needed someone who'd speak. Someone who was antsy enough, worried enough about their own skin, they might gab just to deflect.

John had just the candidate in mind.

***

"I don't know anything!" The tall, bony chef protested from where John had cornered him in the walk-in refrigerator. "I swear." The man shook his head, trembling, no longer sweating in the cold of the refrigerator compartment. A row of vegetables and pre-cut meats rested on metal shelves behind the man. A plastic, dangling curtain, cut into strips blocked the entryway behind them, along with a large metal door which was now ajar.

John crossed his arms, not quite blocking the exit, but standing in such a way that it would make it difficult for the chef to leave without brushing past him.

"Is that how you want to play it?" John replied, in equally accented English. "Hmm? You might have an alibi, but that doesn't mean we won't reconsider you as a suspect. The best way to help yourself is to help me."

The chef's sharp cheekbones stood out against his pale skin, which had taken on a sickly sheen the moment John had followed him into the fridge. The small basket of bread rolls, which he'd been carrying, now hung drooping from one hand, one of the rolls having fallen and landed on the ground, unnoticed near the chef's foot.

The nervous man adjusted his overalls, glanced past John for a moment, and then puffed a breath, a plume of fog rising from his lips in the cold compartment.

"I can't," he said, his voice nearly a whimper.

"Come on," John pressed, frowning and crossing his arms in a way that made his biceps bulge. "Prison wouldn't suit you, sir. The food is horrible."

The tall chef squeaked, but then, after shooting another look past John to make sure no one was looking, he said, quietly, "It's nothing—not really... But, you want to know who would be able to get a guest on without a fare?"

"Absolutely."

"The captain, of course."

John nodded, slowly. "Makes sense. But do you have anything besides conjecture?"

The chef sighed, and his arms seemed to go even more slack under the weight of the stress. Another bread roll went tumbling, rolling beneath the metal shelves next to a plastic container of sliced peppers.

"Look," he said, in such a soft whisper, John had to lean in to hear. "We had to prepare a special meal two evenings ago."

"The night before this most recent murder?"

The chef shuddered and wagged his head. "Yes, yes. Then. The captain has a special diet. But this time, he requested food he couldn't eat. Enough food for *two.*"

John frowned. "I-I see."

"The captain was dining with someone. It doesn't mean anything, but Captain Schultz doesn't normally associate with the guests."

John's eyebrows ratcheted up. "Ah—so you think he has a special invitee on board with him?"

"No, I don't think that. I'm just saying what I know. Look, I—I need to get back to work. Are we done here?" The man's fingers tightened nervously around the handle of the bread-basket, but John was already moving, turning towards the plastic strands of curtain, and the metal door.

"Don't worry, I won't bring your name up," John said, over his shoulder. "You've been a *big* help."

The chef waited, watching John leave, but as the door began to swing shut to the fridge, as an afterthought, chef called, "Be careful. Captain Schultz is not a gentle man. He used to serve in the navy."

John looked back, frowning through the slowly closing gap in the door. The chef just stood there, wincing and waiting, more bread rolls at his feet, unnoticed.

John paused, wondering if the chef had anything more to add, but the man didn't follow him, preferring, it seemed, the frigid refrigerator as opposed to John's company.

He wasn't sure what that said about his charm.

But that didn't matter now.

He had a lead.

The captain, of all people, a navy man apparently, had a guest for dinner two nights ago. One day before the murder of the third victim. The captain clearly couldn't have been the guest smuggler on *all* the boats. What sort of person could have a connection with the captain, and enough of a connection with other employees at the other victim-sites to gain access there as well? Someone with influence, no doubt. Another employee? A woman?

If anyone could invite an anonymous person on board with no paper trail, it would be the captain of the boat itself. Perhaps the other captains on the other boats had done the same.

John picked up his pace, moving from the kitchen and heading directly towards the bridge.

CHAPTER TWENTY SEVEN

Captain Schultz was standing by the controls with a scowl to match even the most frightening sculptures of stone. The man was shorter than John, but had taught muscles from labor rather than barbells, and a chin the size of a concrete block.

Another crew member was standing next to John, wincing and trying to keep himself between Renee and the captain. "Sorry, sir," the small crew member was saying, shaking his head. "He wouldn't take no for an answer. Says he's police."

The captain finally looked over from his grey and blue console of controls, buttons, dials, and gauges.

Captain Schultz examined John with a long look, then the very upper corner of his lip twitched in a sort of sneer.

"You're not police," Schultz said, returning his attention to the control panel, and frowning towards a flashing orange light. He adjusted something and then shook his head, muttering darkly beneath his breath in German, but switching back to English, likely for John's sake. "Damn thing isn't meant to just linger like this," the captain said. "Not with the way we were running her last week. Needed maintenance six hours ago." He scowled now. "And you say you're police? You're one of the people keeping us stuck here, hmm?"

John blinked at this reversal of terms. Normally, when confronted by a law enforcement officer, people put on their best behavior, or went defensive.

This man chose aggression instead. It might have just been John's imagination, but the captain was even doing Renee's own patented crossed-arm-and-bicep trick.

John frowned and, reflexively, crossed his own arms.

"I'm not police. I'm DGSI."

"French?"

"Yes."

"You're not only that, though, are you?" The captain, with the wild, jetting eyebrows said. Despite his white hair, and stark features, and wrinkles like dried mud, his physique was that of a twenty-year-old athlete.

"No, sir," John replied. "I served too."

"Not navy. Special forces, right? You all have the same look."

"Could say the same thing about you sea monsters," John returned, feeling an old sensation of nausea swirl through his stomach. Partly due to the memories of time at sea on more than one mission, and also due to his interactions with most navy crew. He'd never much gotten along with them. Not enough time with their legs on solid ground, in John's assessment.

The captain's sneer only became more pronounced.

"You're big. Too big. Liability on a boat. Might tip the thing."

John blinked at the direct insult. "You *are* Captain Schultz, yes?"

"That's what they call me, Goliath."

"My name is Agent Renee."

"Goliath it is. What do you want, Goliath?"

John wasn't sure which direction to take the conversation now. Chef Vierra had warned him the captain would be aggressive, but John hadn't realized how much. The man was scowling full, making no effort to hide his obvious disgruntlement. Granted, they *had* docked the man's boat and sequestered him for nearly a day, now.

Still, Schultz didn't seem interested in making it easy for anyone involved.

"I'm here about a guest of yours," John said, deciding to keep his cool. The last time he'd lost it, cameras had been tossed. He didn't need Adele to have another mess of his to clean up. So, he bit back any scathing retort and pressed on, calmly. "You had dinner with them two nights ago."

The captain's eyes narrowed. He glanced towards the crew member behind John, but the smaller man just winced and shook his head rapidly.

"He didn't tell me," John said, quickly. "I have eyes and ears everywhere. Something you navy folk wouldn't understand."

"Alright—so what? I had dinner. What about it? You're not asking me out, are you, Goliath?"

John felt a finger twitch. He felt a pulsing in his temple and gritted his teeth against the simmering anger rising in his chest. For a moment, he paused, considering how much trouble he might get in if he punched a boat captain. Navy once, Schultz was a civilian now, after all. Not a very *good* captain, John thought, bitterly, if the man had left the service only to end up a commercial vessel.

Focus! He thought to himself. Anger, rudeness could be tells.

Distractions attempting to camouflage the truth. *Stay on point.*

"So you admit you had dinner with someone two evenings ago?"

"Yes, but like I said. So what?"

"*So*, I'd like you to tell me who it was."

The captain shot another look towards the crew member behind John. This time, though, it wasn't an accusing, or suspicious glare. Rather, it seemed... if anything... nervous.

John frowned at the characterization, but the captain recovered quick enough. His brow twitching back into a frown of annoyance, and he spoke quickly. "No one. Just a friend."

"What was this friend's name?"

"Like I said, no one." The captain turned away from the flashing orange light now, straight-backed, straight postured, as if he had a spine made from a titanium rod.

John's frown deepened, and he found himself inhaling slowly, then exhaling. "I see," he said. "And what if I were to tell you your secret dinner guest is a suspect in a murder investigation, hmm? Would you be so glib then? I wonder, as a man who has spent his life at sea, how much you'd enjoy the inside of a jail cell."

The captain stared at John now, his posture still motionless, like a statue's, but his eyes fixed as if frozen unblinking.

"Your guest," John continued, pressing his advantage. "Was his name on the manifest? Hmm? It was a *him,* wasn't it?"

The captain coughed delicately, now, cracks appearing in his cold facade. The nerves from earlier returned, and the man shifted, tugging at one ear. "I can assure you," he said, delicately, "my *guest* didn't have anything to do with—"

"I'll decide that. And if you're wrong, and you keep holding out, that's going to make you an accomplice." John's eyes narrowed.

"Look, Agent Renee, this is a misunderstanding," the captain said, his voice firm once more, but his eyes betrayed his thoughts. Gone was the teasing, gone was *Goliath.* Clearly, the man was spooked. But why was he holding out?

John felt a flash of frustration. He wasn't sure how chain of command worked on a civilian's pleasure craft. He doubted the captain held anywhere near the same sway as one might on a military vessel. But even there, one could always find a bigger fish up the food chain.

And the captain was acting like someone caught between a rock and a hard place.

"Who was it?" John said, even more insistently. He began to reach for his handcuffs, still frowning until the captain finally relented with a sigh.

"Look, I guarantee—and tell him I said it—he had *nothing* to do with the murders."

"*Who?*"

"Eicke Rohm."

The crew member next to John shifted uncomfortably. The captain nodded once as if emphasizing the words. For his part, though, John just frowned. "Who?"

The captain's eyes flashed in frustration. He glanced over John's shoulder, eyes through the open door. But to his credit, he didn't lower his voice, or try and shrink back on his word. He stated the name, slowly, enunciating this time, "Eicke Rohm."

"Never heard of him. Who is that?"

The captain passed a hand through his silver hair, closing his eyes in his leathery face for a moment, before turning with a grunt of disgust to face the console again. The blinking orange light reflected off his skin, illuminating the more shadowy portions of the bridge.

"That," the captain said, still enunciating, "is the CEO of Sightseeing Incorporated. He owns this bloody boat. So of course his name isn't on a damn manifest. He enjoys sailing on the ships—gets room and meals free. Is that all? I've got work to do."

John stared at the side of the captain's face. "The CEO?" he said, resisting the urge to stutter as he collected his thoughts.

"That's what I said."

"Where is he?"

The captain grunted. "Damn if I know. He was on the ship last night, though, when you locked down. Probably in his rooms."

Here, the crew member coughed, though, and raised a hand. "Actually," the man said, quietly, "the rooms the boss was using are empty. I talked with one of the porters. Mr. Rohm wasn't there last night."

John felt a chill beginning to creep up his spine.

For his part, though, the captain seemed indifferent all of a sudden. He grunted and shrugged again, now fixated on the glowing orange light, and tapping a calloused finger against one of the dials with a small, flicking red needle.

"The CEO was here, but you don't know where he is now?" John said, turning to look the crew member dead in the eyes.

The small man had a stiffer spine than John thought he might at first. Instead of quailing, or squeaking at the sudden attention, the man simply nodded once. “I'm afraid not. Truly, though, the captain is a busy man. If you don't mind...” He extended a hand towards the door.

But John was already moving. “Show me to the room he was using,” John said. “And I'll get out of your hair. We need to find him. If he's still on the ship, I need to know where. *Now.*”

CHAPTER TWENTY EIGHT

"I'm serious," Adele said, pointing her finger at the small, toady man for emphasis, "if you know anything, you need to tell me."

Mr. Larsen had now donned his suit in place of pajamas. His hair was combed again, but his cheeks were tinged, as ever, with a faint red flush. He stood across from Adele on the second deck, towards the back of the boat, refusing to budge an inch. Behind him, the sunlight reflected off the water, and birds flew over the churning liquid, moving near the boat and then retreating, as if searching for food.

"Like I said, I don't know of anyone smuggled aboard," the liaison insisted. "And *you* need to listen to *me*." He returned her finger jab. "Let the passengers off the boat. You've kept them overnight. Some of our crew have already been working for two days. They're exhausted. We don't have enough rooms for everyone. This isn't right!"

Adele lowered her hand, but felt it bunch into a fist. After all her admonishing of John's temper, she could understand why he operated the way he did. Still, she knew causing a scene wouldn't help anything. She couldn't resist, however, from allowing an edge into her voice. "You don't lecture me about what's *right*. It's your fault that third woman died to begin with!"

The man didn't look convinced by this argument. His eyes flashed. "Maybe it's *your* fault? Maybe if you were better at your job, we wouldn't be in this situation. Regardless, you can't keep—"

Before he could finish, his phone began to ring.

Tempers were rising, but at the sound, it was like a bell at the end of a boxing round. Both Adele and Mr. Larsen loosed soft little sighs as if to gather themselves. Larsen pressed the phone to his ear. "What?" he snapped.

Adele watched him as he listened. Then, a smile began to twist his lips. He looked at Adele, and the smile became a taunting grin.

"What is it?" she snapped.

He lowered his phone, still smirking. "I think you're going to be getting a call soon."

No sooner had the words left his lips, then Adele's phone buzzed. It wasn't a call. But a message. From the executive. She glanced down, read it, and her expression took on the opposite form of Mr. Larsen's. She scowled as deeply as he leered.

Agent Sharp, let the passengers off the boat. Judge's orders.

She tried to hide her frustration, but it was difficult in the face of Mr. Larsen's glee. "You're going to cost people their lives," Adele said through pressed teeth.

"And you are costing people their jobs, their time, their resources, and sleep," Mr. Larsen returned just as zealously. He moved over to the railing, glancing down, and waving a hand. "Looks like the police got the good news as well. Finally."

Adele watched in frustration as what looked like a sergeant approached the police blocking the exit to the ship, and talked with them in low voices. The passengers, nearest the exit, with bags and purses and overnight cases, watched hopefully. A moment later, an exchange passed between the passengers and the sergeant, and a collective sigh of relief arose from the pedestrians. One by one, they began to move past the police officers, heading down the gangplank onto the dock.

Adele clenched a fist, watching one man, then another, and a couple, and then a family, and then two more passengers as they moved off the ship.

Soon, word would make the rounds, and everyone, crew, employees, and passengers would find a way off.

There was nothing she could do about it. She glanced back at the message from the executive and considered calling him. But what would that help? If the judge had given an order, there was nothing she could do.

"Well, well," Mr. Larsen said, making no effort to conceal the happiness in his tone. "You have cost my company quite a bit of money as it is. Let's be glad this nightmare is behind us."

"What are you going on about?" a gruff voice said. "Adele, did you see that? Passengers leaving."

Adele turned to find John scowling and approaching the two of them. His shadow stretched behind him, caught by the same sunlight illuminating the river and the seabirds.

"Executive's orders," Adele said, gritting her teeth in frustration. "Mr. Larsen, here, says he doesn't know of anyone who might've stowed onto the ship."

"Forget what he says," John muttered with a grunt, completely ignoring Mr. Larsen now, and circling Adele to position himself so he blocked sight of the small man completely. "I found something very interesting. The CEO of Sightseeing Inc. was on this boat."

Adele blinked. She felt her throat go dry. "The CEO?"

"Hang on?" said Mr. Larsen, hurriedly. His head peeked around John's large shoulder. "Eicke Rohm?"

John glanced back. "That's what the captain called him. They had dinner together two nights ago," John continued, facing Adele once more. He paused for a moment, then frowned, glancing back at Larsen. "Do you mind?"

"Not at all," said the lawyer, making no move whatsoever to distance himself. John reached roughly back, pushing the man away. "They had dinner together," he continued, "one night before our third victim was killed. And he apparently likes to move from ship to ship. He has fun sailing around, using rooms or having food without paying."

Adele stared, her dry throat now spreading, until her whole body felt like it was tingling. "You don't think he had anything to do with it, do you?"

“That asshole?” muttered Mr. Larsen, “Probably.”

Adele stared at him. “Excuse me?”

The liaison just waved a hand, dismissing the comment.

John, meanwhile, shrugged his bowling ball-sized shoulders. "I don't know. But you said to look for someone anonymous on the boat. Well, there you have it. Nothing more anonymous than a man who doesn't register, buy a ticket, or pay for anything. And, by the looks of things, no one wanted to tell me about him, because they were worried he'd be incriminated in the murder."

"You're saying Mr. Rohm is a suspect?" Larsen said from behind John, where he continued to linger.

"I said *do you mind*?" John demanded, spinning around now. The tall man looked back at Adele, raising an eyebrow.

“Is that all?” she insisted.

"One other thing; a small one. But I don't know *where* in the hell he is. He isn't in his room. I checked. It's empty, tidy. Nothing left behind. But according to the crew, he was still on the ship last night."

"So he was here the evening of the murder?"

"Exactly."

Adele watched the lawyer for a moment, studying his expression. Normally a conversation like this wouldn't happen in front of a someone so intimately connected with the company run by one of the suspects. But she needed a clue, some help, and watching him, she could see his eyes flicking one way, then the other, the gears in his mind spinning and whirring.

"What do you know about Eicke Rohm?" Adele said, slowly. She watched Mr. Larsen closely. Had it just been her imagination? No. There. His eyes flashed again. This wasn't a man particularly fond of the CEO. She knew jealousy when she saw it. It was in the tightening of his jaw, the clenching of his fist against nothing else besides the mention of the man's name.

"It's very possible that he was on this boat," said the lawyer, slowly, choosing his words delicately. "But that doesn't prove anything, as I'm sure you know. Being on a boat that he runs isn't a crime."

"No, but killing people is."

"I see." The liaison licked his lips, like a hyena eyeing a lion's meal, wondering if now was perhaps a chance at the feast. He considered his position a moment longer, and then looked up at John. His tone was carefree, dismissive, even. But his words resonated. "I understand why you might suspect him. Especially with his connections to the victims' families. But I can assure you—"

"What connections?" Adele said without batting an eye.

The liaison made a made a big show of wincing and putting a hand to his mouth as if he couldn't believe what he'd said. "*Connections*? Did I say—I meant to... oh my. Well, silly me. Look, it's probably nothing at all."

Adele shared a look with John. "Was Mr. Rohm connected to the victims?"

The liaison again made a big show of minimizing what he'd said by shaking his head and flicking his hands up, but at last, he said, with a little shrug, and a soft, nearly whispering voice, "I don't know much. I do know, though, and *this* is public record, I might add, that the Everett family, from the German motor company, had agreed to invest into the touring boats. However," the liaison tapped his fingers together, glancing down, and shaking his head, "a real pity. Truly."

"What's a pity?" Adele pressed.

The liaison winced. "I really shouldn't say."

Adele just went quiet, watching him. She knew he wanted to say. Men like this couldn't resist the opportunity to stab someone they didn't like in the back. The CEO, whoever he was, had clearly gotten on Mr. Larsen's bad side. Then again, she wasn't sure the man had anything *but* a bad side.

If Larsen was aware of her growing contempt for him, he didn't show it, and instead, after a bit more playacting, he gave a long sigh, his nostrils flaring, and he said, "It's really a pity. But, they ended up pulling out." He winced and shrugged. "And I'll remind you, this is all public record. I never had anything to do with that, legally speaking."

Adele shook her head. "You're telling me that Anika's parents were going to invest in Sightseeing Incorporated?"

"I'm not telling you that. I'm just saying they got cold feet on a business decision."

"And the CEO. He was in charge at the time?"

The liaison shrugged, in a noncommittal way, but nothing about it suggested he wanted to do anything but communicate an emphatic *yes!*

"You said he had connections with a couple of the victims. Who else?"

Here, though, the liaison just glanced off to the side, and he scratched at the side of his chin, and said, "You should probably take that up with someone else. I wouldn't want to involve myself with Mr. Rohm's past companies."

"Past companies?"

The greasy man grinned now, wagging his head. "Certainly had nothing to do with my company that I currently represent. If it did, I wouldn't say anything."

"Of course not," Adele said.

"Wouldn't dream of it," John added.

"Exactly. But," he said, emphasizing the word, "I did hear rumors, before starting here, that Mr. Rohm," he cleared his throat, and added, "a man that doesn't seem to know how to keep his hands to himself at Christmas parties when other people's wives are around," his eyes narrowed, "also had an altercation with his last place of employment. It just so happened to be with a Board of Directors overseeing a famous culinary enterprise. A chain of restaurants, in fact."

Adele shot a look at John, and then back, sharply at Mr. Larsen. "Are you saying the CEO used to be employed by Abigail Havertz's parents?"

"Christ, Adele," John said, "that gives a motive for two of the victims."

It still left Zeynep, but perhaps there was a motive there as well. Or maybe he'd simply chosen her as camouflage, to try and disguise his true victims. But what were the odds? This CEO seemed to go out of his way to piss people off. Mr. Larsen clearly wanted nothing less than the man's job. Not only that, he'd been slighted by the second victim's parents, when they pulled out of a deal. Adele would have to double check the reliability of the information, but if it was indeed public, it wouldn't be hard to search for it online. And on top of it, if Mr. Larsen was telling anything even close to the truth, then that meant Mr. Rohm had once worked for the company run by the third victim's parents.

"What happened on his last job? Adele asked, eyes glued to Mr. Larsen.

The liaison placed a hand to his mouth, and winced, in a playacting way, shaking his head. "I feel like I've said too much. I was just trying to help."

"What happened?"

The liaison was now grinning again, and he made a tutting sound. "I hear he was fired. That would make me mad. After all the work I put into a company. If they just up and fired me, as some sort of scapegoat," he clicked his tongue, "it would make me murderously angry."

"Adele," John said, peering over the railing, "they're leaving."

"I know."

"Do you think he's gonna be among them?"

Already, a large group of passengers, who'd been roused by the rest of the crew, were making their way down the dock. At least thirty of them had reached the gate at the far end. There was nothing Adele could do to keep them any longer. If the CEO had given a fake name, he was slipping away, even as they spoke.

"Do you see him?" Adele said, suddenly, pointing at Mr. Larsen.

The lawyer looked over the railing, and sniffed, shaking his head. "I can't tell."

Adele cursed, and began to move hurriedly towards the stairs, stepping down, and racing towards where the passengers were now streaming out onto the dock. Nearly seventy more passengers, who'd been in the rooms, along with employees, grateful to finally be released, were queuing up, preparing to leave. She tried to move past, but a couple of the passengers yelled, and screamed at her, "back of the line!"

"Police!" she retorted.

But the passengers were packed like sardines, bags and suitcases in hand. They seemed loath to relinquish their spot to anyone, regardless of a badge. They'd already spent a night trapped on the boat, and clearly, their sympathies towards law enforcement had dwindled.

Adele sighed in frustration and looked across the sea of heads.

Nothing stood out. She didn't even have a picture of what the CEO looked like. He could have been any of them. That man in the low baseball cap. Or that fellow with the upraised hood. Or that guy, his head ducked, moving quickly along with a woman towards the gangplank, and passing the waiting officers.

The stream of passengers grew longer, moving from the ship, out across the dock, to the street.

They didn't have cars. So many would either have to take buses or taxis or call for a ride.

Or, she considered, carefully...

Would the CEO do that? Would he risk leaving a paper trail? After all the efforts he'd gone to remain incognito, would he want to get in a taxi? Many of them had cameras now, for security purposes.

Or maybe, this close to the river, he'd do the next best thing.

Adele turned sharply, away from the gathering of passengers, and away from the milling people moving down the ramp and disappearing hurriedly.

She didn't have time to try and stop each and every one of them. She wouldn't be able. The executive had been clear. The judge's order had come in. The officers would comply, but that didn't mean she couldn't track Eicke Rohm down.

The CEO had been here the night of the murder. He had connections to two of the victims, providing clear cut motives.

And what if he was going to get on another one of his boats?

"John!" she called towards where the tall Frenchman was standing near the base of the stairwell. "I need you to check: are there any boats from the touring company nearby heading back down the river?"

John frowned for a moment, but then just as quickly, his eyes widened, and he hastily began to fish for his phone.

Adele could feel a rising sense of certainty. If another one of the touring boats was nearby, *he* could board it and be gone as quick as thought.

Rohm was their man. Now, all they had to do was catch him, before he reached his next victim.

CHAPTER TWENTY NINE

Their own taxi sped up the streets under Adele's insistent gaze and John's barking orders. Their driver knew French, a mercy for John and a curse for the driver who winced every time John bellowed in his ear, "Go faster—faster, damn it!"

Adele sat in the passenger side, her hand gripping the handle above the window, her eyes fixed through the greasy, unwashed windshield of the taxi.

Her gaze flicked to the windshield-mounted GPS unit, tracking the thin, purple line and then darting to the ETA in the bottom corner. Twenty-three minutes remaining.

She gritted her teeth, glancing back over her shoulder. "When does River Metro Eight leave Petersworth?"

John glanced at his phone, pausing mid-bellow, and then hissed. "Twenty minutes," he said. "Damn it. Go faster!"

The taxi driver winced, his knuckles squeezing the steering wheel so tight, Adele thought one might pop.

They continued picking up pace, veering through the morning traffic, down the river-side roads, and along the Danube.

Adele could feel her heart hammering wildly. Twenty minutes until the next boat left. Maybe the CEO *had* taken a taxi. He would have had to risk it—to reach his boat. But he'd had a head start. He'd left before the rest of them.

The killer wasn't done. She was nearly certain of it. Three down... but a fourth was on the horizon. He'd started writing notes, sending flowers. This taunting wasn't the action of a man who intended to hang up his murderous tendencies.

Which meant, sticking to the MO, the killer would strike on another one of the River Metros.

"Damn it!" Adele said, snapping a hand against her knee if only to feel something to jar her out of her mounting frustration.

She glanced at the GPS unit again.

Twenty minutes until arrival. She glanced at the clock. Only eighteen minutes until the boat left.

They had shaved off a minute... But would it be enough?

***

Tires screeched against the parking lot asphalt outside the dock, along with a similar sound of frustration bursting from Adele's lips.

"John! There!" she yelled.

A large, three story blue and white boat was moving, pulling out of port. The dock was nearly empty, suggesting a load of passengers had already been picked up.

John shoved a crinkled fifty euro note into the cabbie's hand, but was already lurching out of the backseat, followed closely by Adele. The two of them hurried away from their driver, moving rapidly towards the ticketing booth which led to the dock.

The ship was already fifty feet from the dock. No jumping that gap. No swimming either.

"Damn it, John! What's the next stop?" Adele said, her pulse racing. She stared at the boat. The CEO had to be on it, didn't he? Free ride, anonymity—the perfect place to lay low from police.

And now, his escape vehicle was on the move.

"Adele," John said, slowly.

"Next stop?" she yelled, louder. "Where?"

"Adele!"

"What?" She snapped, spinning around and fixing her partner with a furious glare.

But John was ignoring her, his phone still in his pocket. "Forget the next stop. Look, there!"

She frowned, staring, and then went still. Three pleasure crafts were roped off at a smaller dock, about a hundred yards away from the River Metro's port. Two of them were secured to the dock and bobbing vaguely on the water.

One, though, had three young men stepping into it, laughing and clinking glass bottles. Loud music blared from this boat's radio. One of the young men, shirtless—though he probably shouldn't have been—was busy untying the boat, looping a rope around and around.

"Adele... We might not have time to wait for it to reach the next port," John said, insistently. "If he's targeting someone else—chances are, she's on that boat. He might have timed it so he would get off in time to reach his next victim."

"Damn it, we don't know that."

"We have reason to assume," John returned.

Adele winced. The music was blaring louder now from the small, green speed boat with the three frat boys. One of them had dropped his swim trunks and was now peeing into the river.

The River Metro Eight was now well up the river, heading away from the dock and the agents, carrying its passengers and, most likely, its CEO out onto the water.

"Adele, *follow* me, hurry!" John broke into a sprint, racing towards the three young men and their speedboat.

Reluctantly, Adele heaved a sigh, but broke into a jog as well. She supposed she'd already admitted to herself why John's methods were so effective. No point in putting up a fuss now. Besides, it wasn't like commandeering a civilian vehicle was unprecedented. At least there were no paparazzi involved this time.

John had already reached the boat as Adele hurried over, glancing every so often in the direction of the riverboat, as if making sure it wouldn't vanish on the horizon.

John was busy trying to communicate to the three drunk frat boys. "Too early to be drinking," John was saying, wincing against the blasting music. The man who'd been trying to untie the boat was protesting, his words slurred. But one look at the holster on John's hip, and he went white.

The man stuttered to his friends on the boat. The one peeing into the river, glanced back, but the second one, who'd been reclining in the back of the speedboat, yelped at the sight of John and Adele and quickly darted to the dock, accidentally jostling his urinating friend.

This unfortunate fellow tumbled, splashing into the river. The other two stood on the dock, staring at John, wide-eyed and horrified.

"Keys!" John demanded, jutting out a hand. "Please. Keys! Now! We need them!"

"Interpol," Adele added, wincing.

The shirtless fellow, who was already developing a bit of a sunburn, slowly reached into his swimming trunks and pulled out a key with a small, black buoy on the ring. He handed it to John. "Don't hurt her," he said in German, his voice shaking. "She's all I have! Please!"

John patted the man on the bare shoulder, a bit harder than perhaps the fellow had been expecting, though, at least, Adele knew he'd meant it to be an encouraging gesture. Where Renee was involved, it was hard not to interpret intimidation.

But now, John was already stepping into the boat. It rocked, where it was now untethered from the dock. He reached the wheel, jamming the keys and lowering the outboard motor a second later, into the water.

Adele followed, nodding in gratitude towards the three frat boys. Two of them were now helping their friend out of the river. John pushed the throttle, slowly at first, guiding the motorboat away from the dock, and then, once they were clear, he gunned it.

The boat jolted, jarring forward, and Adele stumbled back, bracing herself against one of the cushioned seats. Cold spray and warm sunlight met on her skin, and Adele winced against the sudden flurry of wind. She glanced back at the white trail left in their wake, and the three forlorn figures standing on the dock.

John clicked the music off, leaving the only sounds to come from the churning engine and the splashing water and the rising wind as they tore up the river in pursuit of River Metro Eight.

Had the CEO found his next victim? Were they too late already?

"Come on," Adele murmured. "John! Is that how fast it goes?"

The Frenchman shoved at the throttle in explanation. It was already full speed. It felt so, so very slow, but as they cut through the water, hurrying up the river, they were drawing nearer and nearer to the large riverboat.

Adele's hair whipped around her as John guided their speedboat up alongside the large touring vessel. A few passengers stared over the rail, watching in curiosity at the rapidly approaching watercraft. Adele raised her voice over the sound of the choppy water and the rising wind, "John, pull alongside!" she shouted.

But Agent Renee had another idea; he kept the throttle maxed and pulled in front of the large boat. He started zigzagging back and forth in front of the vessel, churning up water.

The larger vessel leaned on its horn, and it sounded like someone had set off a bomb. Adele's hands clapped to her ears against the explosive noise, but John was undeterred, and he continued to zip back and forth, slowing as he did, and waving one hand over his head wildly, gesturing for the vessel behind them to stop.

Adele licked her lips nervously, looking back, and examining the nearing riverboat. If it didn't stop, it would run over them like a tank over a toy car.

John began to lean on his own horn, though it sounded like the yapping of a chihuahua in comparison to the roar of a lion. River Metro Eight's horn blared again, and Adele grit her teeth, her hands still clasped to the side of her face.

John, though, continued to slow. Soon, they were matching the riverboat's speed. More passengers and some crew members were now staring at them from all three decks.

Was the CEO one of them?

The riverboat seemed to realize the horn wasn't doing the trick and began to try and move around John. But the tall Frenchman directed his speedboat, tongue tucked inside his cheek in concentration. Adele knew how much John hated the water, but he was also masterful when given something to pilot or drive. A boat wasn't his vehicle of choice, but John was a wizard at any wheel. He continued slowing down, blockading the larger vessel; the riverboat was also stalling, trying not to crush the small speedboat.

At last, after two more attempts on a blaring horn, and another attempt to try and move around the smaller boat, the larger vessel behind them came to an idling pace, its engines grumbling quietly, like the growl of some woken grizzly. The river's current lazed in the opposite direction of the boat's momentum, counteracting, and seeming to stall the boat for a moment.

"Now!" John said, hurriedly. He turned the vessel back and moved alongside the riverboat now, their nose bumped against the much larger, metal hull. A dangling, rubber safety barrier, bounced against the side of them, preventing collision, and John grabbed the prickly, sodden rope, tethering the speedboat to the rubber guard.

Then, breathing heavily, his eyes wide with excitement, John gestured at Adele, one hand gripping the rope and the other extended towards his partner.

Adele accepted John's help, and moved across the rocking, swaying boat. Together, they pulled up, latching onto the bottom of the rail, and then clambering onto the vessel itself.

Passengers watched with wide eyes. A couple of crew members were approaching rapidly, scowling. But one look at John, and a flash of Adele's badge, they pulled up, their expressions morphing from fury and outrage to worry.

Just then, a voice peeled out, "What is the meaning of this? You're going to jail! How dare you!"

The voice bellowed and accompanied a small man, who couldn't have been much taller than five feet. He moved with a waddle, and his back was hunched, his shoulders broad, giving him a look like a small troll doll. The man's hair was spiky and gelled back, and he wore two earrings in the shape of butterflies. He was shaking his spiky head wildly, his voice booming from his small body, and he was gesturing at the crew. "Grab them. Hold them until the police get here!"

Adele blinked, but John, frowning, stepped forward. He pointed towards the small man. "Are you Eicke Rohm?"

The short fellow frowned, crossing his small arms over his thick chest. "I don't answer to you. What the hell do you think you were doing out there? You could've gotten yourself killed. You could've gotten *us* killed." He trailed off, muttering darkly, and cursing a few times, and Adele caught words like, "travesty...investors..." and "...nightmare."

"You're the CEO of Sightseeing Incorporated?" Adele said, pointing at him.

The man looked at her, frowning. The fact that one of them knew his name, and the other knew his position clearly put him off. Adele pulled her wallet out again, showing her ID once more, and the man's bluster and fury faded. He stared and started to stammer.

"Eicke Rohm," John said, growling, "you're under arrest."

The tall Frenchman stepped forward, and the diminutive CEO of the touring company just stood rooted to the spot, his eyes wide, his face pale and frightened. He kept shaking his head and muttering in disbelief.

Adele watched as John grabbed the small man, and turned him around, cuffs coming out.

Was this the killer?

She could think of a single, surefire way the man's innocence could be proven.

If she got a call about another body somewhere else.

Adele shivered, but then heard the quiet *click* of the cuffs, and followed after John as he began to lead the small man along the deck.

CHAPTER THIRTY

He adjusted his glass eye, wincing. Normally he liked to wash it first thing in the morning, but he had barely slept. He'd also been forced to abandon his borrowed car the night before. The police were tracking that too.

He walked along the river, moving slowly towards the dock entrance. The chain-link fence at his side gave him ample vision of the waterway beyond. He spotted River Metro Eight in the distance, the name of the boat written in looping purple letters on the front of the hull. The boat was stalled, however, short of the dock, in the middle of the Danube.

The painter scowled; he didn't think it was normal for one of the riverboats to pause before reaching its next destination. "What in the hell," he murmured beneath his breath.

He sighed in frustration, lowering his hand from his face, and rubbing his knuckles against the inside of his palm.

His injuries were beginning to ache. The cuts from being thrown through that window, the limp, the bludgeoning from the Sergeant were all cashing checks his body had reluctantly written.

A groan curdled his lips. He wished he could've stayed in that borrowed car. He needed to find another one.

The painter continued to limp along the sidewalk, hands in his pockets, head low. Small, frail, no bigger than a child.

People didn't look upon someone like him as a threat.

But he had always considered himself an artist. A misunderstood creative genius. And all geniuses suffered. Hadn't he been imagining Van Gogh's own pain? That's what he got for wanting to be like one of the greats. He had to pay the price with his own agony. So be it. He just wished it wouldn't take so long. He watched the riverboat stalled on the water, and for a moment, he thought he spotted a small speedboat moving along the side of the thing. A police boat?

He froze, motionless, staring through the chain-link fence. But no, just a civilian craft. He thought he spotted two, tiny figures, though it was hard to make out in this distance, especially through the trees and across the water.

The sun was reflecting off the river in just such a way that it made metallic hues blend with blue.

He took another step, and that's when he realized he'd been distracted. Sleepless, in pain, injured, watching the strange motion of the stalling riverboat, he hadn't been paying attention to the street.

There was a sudden whine, and then a flash of blue lights.

He turned sharply and spotted a police car pulling up behind him.

Shit.

He kept his head forward now, eyes fixed on the sidewalk, breathing in, out, slowly, with shuddering breaths. He felt the chill shiver along his spine.

"Hello?" called a voice behind him.

He just kept walking, head down, hands jammed in pockets. He could feel one hand wrapped around the blade of his backup knife.

"Excuse me, sir," said the voice behind him, suspiciously. Another cop, likely with pictures of the painter's face emanating from his phone and vehicle dashboard. Everyone seemed to be looking for him.

Dammit. He continued to stroll along as if he couldn't hear. He began humming slowly to himself, using the sound, if only for a moment, to calm himself.

"Excuse me, sir," said the voice behind him. Another voice could be heard, through one of the open windows of the police car, talking into a radio.

He picked up a couple of words, "...small man. Hang on, looking for confirmation."

They hadn't seen his face yet. They were just checking. By the sound of their weary voices, these guys hadn't had much rest either. Their night, likely, same as his, had been spent awake, on the move, on the lookout.

Looking for him.

Could he use this to his advantage?

He wasn't sure. He continued to move forward, his head still ducked, his hand still bunched, one fist tight around the grip of his knife.

He continued humming.

"Sir," said one of the voices, sharply, "I need you to turn around sir."

The siren wailed again, chirping once, then turning off. The blue and red lights were casting across the asphalt and sidewalk now. The chain-link fence, rusted in portions, and galvanized in others, carried only the faintest gossamer strands of the whirring lights.

He turned now, facing the fence, pausing, and staring through it, watching the boat. He continued to hum. He reached up with one free hand, pressing at his ear as if he had earbuds in. Earphones were so small these days, they were nearly impossible to notice. He could only hope, now, that they would think he was a jogger out for some exercise. They would have to get close.

Still, he could hear the sound of static, and the voice of the second officer in the car, saying, "...we're checking. He stopped. I'm not sure. It looks like a child. It might not be anything."

And so he stood, facing the opposite direction, frozen to the spot, feet shoulder-width against concrete.

And he waited. Waiting had always been one of his best strong suits. Planning, preparing, staving off chills and fear and doubt and worry.

Waiting was easy.

He heard the sound of a door opening, and then the screech of tires, suggesting that one of the police was already getting out of the car before it come to a complete stop. He heard another burst of static, and then the sound of footsteps, and the door slamming as one of the officers began to approach.

No one up the sidewalk, but a couple of people, down the other way, likely watching now.

Witnesses. Or, better yet, an *audience*. He'd never performed live before, but every true creative had to face new challenges. It was the only way to grow as an artist. To stretch himself. So, perhaps he would have to take on a live audience for a change.

From what little he knew about the police, and he knew quite a bit, the one on the radio would be in the passenger seat. The car would be turned off, momentarily. The man now approaching had been the driver.

So he waited some more.

"Excuse me, sir? Young man?" The voice spoke slowly, hesitantly.

He heard more shuffling steps. And the painter reached up again, still pretending he had an earbud in.

"Sir," the voice said, even more crisply. "Turn around, *now*."

But again, he ignored it.

The ball was in their court. They wouldn't shoot him. They still weren't even sure if he was a child or not. They wouldn't want to risk everything just because he was being a little bit obstinate. And for all they knew, he couldn't hear them. Maybe listening to music, maybe deaf.

How stupid canvases could be.

He could feel eyes on him now.

The eyes of the rapidly approaching officer. The eyes of the pedestrians down the sidewalk, keeping an eye on the scene ahead of them. The eyes of the man in the passenger seat of the police car waiting for confirmation.

And then, he felt fingers rest on his shoulder, and a voice say, "Sir, please turn around. Police."

The painter began to allow himself to be wheeled, firmly, as the hand on his shoulder turned him.

But he didn't wait for the full revolution. As he was halfway, he moved, pivoting fast and sharp, whipping his knife from his pocket, and sending it slicing back.

His aim was true. He'd known it would be. Ten thousand hours to master one's craft—that's what they said. And he had mastered it.

The knife cut through the cop's throat. It wasn't a deep enough cut. And so he slashed again and again, in rapid succession.

The follow-up cuts went deeper than the first. Arteries pulsed.

Blood exploded down the police officer's neck, down into his blue uniform, soaking his walkie-talkie.

The man stared out, stunned from beneath his hat. The fellow was mid-fifties, maybe. He had a wedding ring on. Strange the things one would notice. But a painter had to pay attention to the details.

A gurgling, desperate sound, the fingers on his shoulder were no longer gripping, but scrambling, as if begging for help.

The painter just reached out and pushed.

The man fell to the ground, choking and gasping and dying. Blood pooled beneath him against the sidewalk.

The other police officer in the car screamed suddenly. "*Shit*. It's him! It's him!"

But the painter was now moving. He didn't have time to admire his own work. He would have to hope the audience would do it for him. He sprinted. There was a gunshot. Concrete exploded to his left. He ducked behind a row of cars parked along the street. He heard a shout and a curse behind him. The sound of a door opening. The police officer hesitated, gun in hand, seemingly caught. An old military tactic—don't ever *kill* the enemy outright. Rather, wound a friend. That way, instead of taking out one enemy, you take out three. The injured fellow and the two who rush to help him.

Compassion—what a stupid vice.

The police officer snarled, taking a couple of steps towards the killer, gun-raising, but then a pitiable sound of pain emitted from his fallen partner. The cop cursed and spun on his heel, racing towards the injured man now and moving towards his fallen partner. He wouldn't give pursuit. Two for the price of one. Stupid canvas.

He heard yelling. The sound of more sirens in the distance.

A smile, now, tempted his lips. For an impromptu performance, that had gone wonderfully. He continued to run forward, teeth set, moving rapidly. He couldn't afford to move around in daylight anymore. He would have to find a place to hunker down, to hide. An alley, a parking lot, some unsuspecting apprentice's car. Maybe even someone's house.

The thoughts continued to swirl through his mind, compelling him forward, and he raced away from his latest work of art. Sloppy, quick.

But even the greats had to sketch sometimes.

He supposed he couldn't get on that boat now. No, hang tight. Stay low. Wait for nightfall. And then make a new plan.

CHAPTER THIRTY ONE

Adele stood across from the CEO of Sightseeing Incorporated. They had taken him to a stateroom. Large windows overlooked the river, and the CEO was shaking his head while muttering darkly beneath his breath.

Every time John tried to speak to the man, he would just insist, "Lawyer."

Adele stood in one of the larger rooms she'd seen on the riverboats. A stateroom, according to the crew who'd allowed them access—normally reserved for of the overseeing company managers. Two king-sized beds faced across from a private bathroom with a jacuzzi.

Adele could feel her mind spinning. The man cut a less intimidating figure than she'd anticipated, but she wouldn't discount someone because of their size. Not again. Besides, he could easily have hired someone.

She felt a flash of frustration and fury. She thought of her father, of the attack.

She needed to focus.

She swallowed, considering it from all angles. "Sir, I need you to answer my questions. I understand you're frustrated. I understand you don't like that you're in cuffs. But we're trying to do our jobs. You were connected to two of the victims on your boats. You were on the same boat where the third victim was killed," she said, emphatically but still with her voice under control, "that very night. You were seen."

The small, hunched man turned in the seat, near the bed, shaking his head. "So what?" he said, also calm, controlled. The worry and muttering seemed to slip from him all of a sudden like a duck shedding water off its feathers. He seemed to have reached some sort of decision, considering his options, planning a strategy, and now executing. And his strategy seemed simple enough. "*Lawyer.*"

Adele swallowed, leaning back against the door, the carpet thick beneath her feet. She could hear the sound of murmuring outside the door. They'd been followed by some of the crew. Everyone seemed to be waiting, poised. Passengers had been milling around as the CEO was arrested, and crew members had stared in horror.

"Sir," Adele said, quietly, "I can't impress on you how serious this is. I need you to give me an account of your movements over the last few days."

"Lawyer."

She thought about it for a moment, and said, "Truly? Because funnily enough, it was a lawyer who told us about you."

The man looked at her and snorted. "You're stupid if you think I killed anyone."

Adele glanced at John. At least he was speaking to them. She didn't mind being insulted if it meant they could make progress.

"Look," she said, quietly, "you need to give me something more than that. Maybe I am stupid. But the evidence is pointing towards you. You were on the boat where the victim was killed last night," she said, tapping one finger against another. "You didn't register your name, and you have a habit, I'm told, of moving from boat to boat. Anyone would see that as opportunity." She tapped a second finger. "And," she said, her voice hardening, her eyes narrowing. "Most of all, you had motive with two of the victim's daughters. One of them, the Everett motor company, pulled out of your touring venture last-minute, leaving you high and dry." Adele spoke confidently, having already read a couple of articles online from business tracking blogs. "And also, you used to work for the same company as the third victim's parents. You were in charge of the restaurant's finances. But they fired you."

"I was a scapegoat," he snapped. "And so what? Once you get to a certain income bracket in Germany, everyone knows each other. That's not the same thing as motive. If I killed everyone who cut me during a business venture, half of Germany would be dead."

Adele shook her head. "You're going to have to do better than that."

"Lawyer."

"Try and help me to help you. We have a killer out there if it's not you."

"Lawyer."

Adele huffed in frustration and clenched a fist against her thigh. Staring at the small man, she could feel her own temper rising. Perhaps it was the lack of sleep, the exhaustion of it all. Perhaps it was frustration at her father, frustration that she couldn't help him. Perhaps she was simply angry. Maybe, in her gut, she'd already indicted this man for the deaths of three women...

And now he was lawyering up. Hiding behind a bigger kid on the schoolyard.

She could feel her temper, could feel John's eyes on the side of her face. Her bunched fist began to tighten. "Don't test me," she snapped. "Fine. You want a lawyer? How about Mr. Larsen. He seemed to be a real big fan of yours."

Her tone, her temper, and then suddenly dropping that name seemed to jar something. The CEO blinked. He was a small man, but that didn't mean he was stupid. His eyes shifted from John to Adele, and he considered things for a moment, tracking. "That bastard," Mr. Rohm said suddenly. "Is he the one who put you up to this? I'm telling you I didn't have anything to do with the deaths. Just a coincidence. Why would I kill their kids? I've been fired before. That's no reason to murder anyone. Besides, have you heard anything about that restaurant business? Half of them are going under. Their overhead is too high. This touring company was a blessing in disguise. I should be thanking them, not killing anyone."

He made the case well, emphatically, and his hands, though they were handcuffed in front of him, where he sat, seemed on the verge of gesticulating as if Rohm wanted to spread his arms. Perhaps not a very powerful presence physically, but this man was no stranger to orating.

"I'm sorry, but that's not enough. Why didn't you register your name on the manifest?"

He snorted. "I'm the CEO. I don't have to buy a ticket. It's one of the few perks of the job. I'm not the only one who does it, either. Anyone on the board has access."

Adele shifted uncomfortably. She didn't like the idea of other potential suspects out there, moving like ghosts on the ships, without anyone to say one way or another.

"I'm sorry," she repeated, "but that's still not enough."

He heaved a frustrated sigh, "How can I convince you? It isn't me. So fine. Let me help you. You *need* something. You're desperate if you're coming after me. I'll make it easier. What can I do?"

A negotiator as well it would seem. She knew to be careful where such people were concerned. There was nothing inherently wrong with negotiation, but those who were good at it often could wield words to their target's demise.

"I don't need anything from you. Except for you to tell me what you been doing this last week."

"What I always do. Keeping an eye on the business."

"On the boats?"

"That's my business. What do you expect?"

"I expect you to tell me what connection you had with the first victim."

"Who?"

"Zeynep Akbulut."

"I'll be honest with you agent. I'd never even heard of that girl until I saw it on the news. And my first reaction was grief—I have children of my own. Two daughters and a son. But after I heard the news, I knew the threat it would pose to my business. And hang on," he said, in a wheedling, careful voice, "don't take that to mean I'm just being callous. I'm explaining to you that I have a lot of money tied up in the success of these boats. I'm part owner. Did you know that?"

Adele blinked. "I assumed as the CEO you might have some stake."

"And did you know that our revenue is in half, today, compared to the last few weeks? All because of this horrible business with the murders?" He pressed, like a boxer who'd realized he's cornered his opponent. He was staring at her, fixated, trying to measure her, to figure out a weakness.

"What's your point?"

One finger sprang out, though his hands were still cuffed. "First, I don't know anything about Ms. Akbulut. Second, though I was connected, briefly, with the parents of these other two wealthy girls, that doesn't mean anything. I'm connected with a lot of wealthy people. And besides, getting fired from that restaurant business was the best thing that ever happened to me. I'm twice as wealthy as I was then." A third and final finger sprang out. "And lastly, why would I kill these women on my own boats? It's ruining them. It's tanking the business."

Adele shook her head. "I don't know why. I just know what the evidence is saying."

"You need to take a closer look at that evidence."

He was good. Convincing, earnest, sincere. Equal parts angry and reasonable. He played the aggrieved victim well. But this was a powerful man. Powerful men often knew how to present themselves to get what they wanted. She wouldn't allow his spin on things to convince her. She needed to look at the evidence.

But then again, was the evidence in his favor? It was true that he would move from boat to boat. It was true he did so anonymously. It was also true he had been very careful to dodge her question about his whereabouts the last few days. But on top of that, even if he had been on all those boats, he only had connections to the first two victims. Adele didn't know of any connection with Zeynep. It was also true that

Rohm was financially invested in the success of the touring company. Why would he ruin that?

He didn't seem like an impulsive man. He was holding his temper in check as best as possible. He seemed to be angry, but not rageful. Was a self-controlled man the sort who'd let some violent urge ruin their own business? Would he be the sort of person to kill for vengeance or pleasure? Did he write that note, taunting the parents?

It was a note targeted primarily at Zeynep Akbulut's parents. If he was really trying to hurt the two families that had wronged him, why had he spent most of his time in that note only talking to the victims he had no connection with.

A red herring?

Adele felt a hand brush her shoulder and looked up towards John. The tall Frenchman's palm was warm as he leaned in and whispered, "Still no call back on connections with the Akbuluts. It's been twenty minutes since I called it in. That's not promising."

Adele nodded quietly, and she said, beneath her breath, "That's fine." She turned and took a couple of retreating steps towards one of the large windows. Beneath her breath, in a ghost of a voice, she murmured, so Rohm couldn't hear, "John, I'm worried it's not him."

Renee winced. "I was afraid you'd say that. You always say that."

Adele could feel the trickle of worry along her spine. "If it's not him, that means the killer is still out there."

The CEO had gone quiet, and was breathing a lot less heavily now, simply watching, trying to listen. "I can help!" he volunteered from where he was cuffed. He leaned forward on the chair, his legs not even reaching the ground. "Anything I can do. I can help. I don't want another person to die. For their sake even more than my business."

Adele turned away from him now, her shoulder blocking her mouth, and she whispered, "If it's not him, we need to know."

John switched from English to French, "How should we know? He has connections to two of the victims."

She winced, considering this. But the CEO had made sense. Why would he target people on his own boats? And if it was true that he'd made more money after being fired by the restaurant company, which apparently was tanking now, wouldn't that be vengeance enough? She didn't know how these killers worked, but this seemed like a self-controlled man. At least at first glance.

She closed her eyes, standing there, feeling the warmth of the sunlight through the large windows, feeling eyes fixed on her. She could hear the sound of the crew outside, the couple of members who'd followed them waiting, murmuring to each other.

"If what you say is true," she said, reaching a decision, and turning back towards Rohm, "then you do need to help me. I want access to the information you have on all the wealthy guests from all your boats. All the young women who come from money."

CHAPTER THIRTY TWO

Adele felt like she was in a river herself, just trying to keep up with the current. The more she talked to Rohm, the more she looked at him, the more difficult it became to try and peg him for the murders. He was too small. Could he really have subdued all three of those women? It didn't seem likely. And he would have been seen. The CEO would have stood out.

She could feel her convictions about his guilt crumbling like sandcastles on the seashore beneath a sudden tide.

"Anything you need," he said, instinctively. "I have access to that information on my own phone. I can keep track of all that. I tend to go over it daily."

"Daily?"

He wagged his head, adamantly. "This company is successful because of my efforts. Don't let anyone tell you otherwise. I keep a tight eye on the finances, especially after..." he trailed off and shook his head. "Let's just say I've been burned before. And," he added quickly, "I didn't kill anyone over it. I had business partners embezzle from me. And I haven't hurt them. How much less so would I want to hurt someone who kicked me out of a dying job. I wanted to leave the Havertz company anyway."

"Mutual breakup," John muttered. "It's never the case."

The man looked over, shaking his head. "Be that as it may, if you want that information, I can get it for you, quickly. It's on my phone. Just uncuff me."

Adele considered this for a moment. She couldn't see the threat, though, and she nodded once towards John.

The small man was unarmed, outnumbered, trapped in a room. Giving him his hands didn't seem too dangerous. Reluctantly, John moved forward, key out, and loosed the cuffs.

The CEO made a big deal of rubbing his wrists. He eyed John, then looked at Adele, a flash of relief crossing his face. "I didn't have anything to do with this."

"Help us, and that will help clear your name. You still have to account for your connection with two of the victims."

Instead of answering her though, he reached, slowly, into his pocket, one other hand raised in an abundance of caution. He fished out his phone, and then began to type.

It was one of those old-fashioned devices, with a keyboard built in. She watched, frowning, as he continued to jab at the small keyboard. John leaned against the chair behind the man, in the stateroom, his head beneath the light fixture. And then, John said, "What's that?"

"Financial compiler," Rohm returned. "It keeps all the ticket information. For the more wealthy customers, we also have names."

"We have comped tickets for the victims," Adele said, quickly.

The CEO frowned, looking at her. "We don't comp tickets."

She sighed. "That's what Mr. Larsen said."

"Well, you usually can't trust that bastard. But in this case, he was telling you the truth. We have nothing to do with comping tickets. That's someone else."

"What's that?" John said, just as quickly.

The CEO sighed through his nose, but then in a patient tone replied, "A search feature. It helps us narrow in on a target audience in markets. When we know where people are boarding, it gives us a better idea where to advertise the tours. We're going to be working on riverside attractions as well. I have contacts with a carnival who are going to agree to set up near Steinheim."

"And how does that help us?"

"It doesn't. It's just how I'm going to narrow down what you want. You said you want young women who come from wealth, right? Well, there are certain areas that are known for their wealth, and others that aren't. I'm narrowing based on that. Just hang on."

"What's that?" John said, just as quickly.

The CEO ignored him, though, this time. He said, "What ages exactly?"

"Twenties," Adele said.

"Nationality?"

"We don't know."

"How do you have access to all that information?" John said.

Here, the CEO smiled. He hid it just as quickly, but said, "You'd be amazed what the financing companies share with us. Your credit card alone has your name, first and last, your birthday, and often zip code associated with it. We know who you are, where you live, and when you were born. We can also ping the banks, querying to see what available funds are in the account. Not technically something we're supposed to do. But I know of some," he coughed, "less reputable businesses who do it to figure out which clients to focus on re-targeting with ad spend."

John visibly shivered at the thought, his hand moving instinctively towards his pocket, as if wondering if he should take out his wallet and fling it across the room.

Adele couldn't blame him. This stuff gave her the creeps. But, hopefully, at least in this case, too much information could help them save a life.

"Alright, here we go. A wealthy, young woman who comes from means of her own. I found one. The suite she has booked is one of the more expensive ones."

"And you said you don't comp."

"That's right."

"There's only one name?"

The CEO wagged his head, turning his phone towards Adele. "Only the one."

"Who?"

"Martha Velz; who, actually, I happen to know." He raised his eyebrows significantly. "Like I said, in Germany, everyone of a certain bracket knows everyone. She's the daughter of a wealthy production agency who funds German movies. A bit of an actress too."

Adele set her teeth, "And which boat is she going to be getting on?"

The CEO shook his head, frowning. "She's already on a boat. Has been for a day. This is her second night. River Metro Ten," he said. "It's departing Ingolstadt in fifteen minutes."

This time, he didn't look at his phone to say this, as if the departure schedule were simply memorized off the top of his head. Impressive. Eloquent, smart, persuasive. Adele wasn't sure she could trust this man. And yet her instincts were telling her this wasn't the killer. She couldn't let him go. They had to keep an eye on him, but it wasn't like they could do anything until backup arrived to take Mr. Rohm to the police station for further questioning. And in the meantime, Martha Velz was in danger. If what the CEO was saying was true, she was already in her second night on a ticket bought for her by the killer.

"Alright, dammit," Adele said. "How do we contact this River Metro Ten? There a phone number?"

The CEO hesitated, but then said, softly, "I'm helping, aren't I?"

"As noted."

"I didn't have anything to do with this."

“Just keep helping."

"I have the captain's number right here. Do you want me to tell him to dock the boat?"

Adele hesitated. Rohm wasn't behaving like a guilty man. "Ingolstadt that's not far from here, is it?"

The CEO shook his head. "No, but River Metro Ten is going to be passing us, heading in the opposite direction."

Adele hesitated. "And you say it's leaving the dock in fifteen minutes?"

The CEO frowned but nodded once.

"What are you thinking?" John murmured in her ear.

She kept her own voice low but could feel her excitement rising. If the CEO really was innocent, and she was beginning to think so, then the killer would be hunting his next victim. Only one name matched; a wealthy, young woman with three nights booked. Only one potential target remaining. Which meant, whether Adele liked it or not, Ms. Velz was bait.

"I need you to call that boat," Adele said, quickly, "and tell them to keep an eye on Martha Velz. Put crew with her or something and take her to her rooms. Make sure she's safe. At least two people watching her at all times. And watching each other."

"Noted." The CEO began to raise his phone. "Anything else to help the fine law enforcement officers from France?"

"Yes. Tell them to continue on their route, but to come past us. I don't want this bastard to get a chance to go overboard. And I don't want him to get off on some dock if he thinks something is up. Have them come past us, directly. How long will that take?"

"Maybe an hour to reach us. They're supposed to have another stop before they get here."

"Tell them to skip it. If the killer is stuck on that boat, we're going to be able to find him.”

"Think we should warn Ms. Velz directly?" John said.

Adele nodded adamantly. "Yes, tell the captain to tell her. For now, though, make sure they don't dock a second time. They have to come towards us, past our own boat."

The CEO sighed, leaning back, staring up at the ceiling of the stateroom, but then he completed the call, and someone answered nearly instantly. Adele heard a voice in the background. Mr. Rohm said, "Look, Dodd, you're not going to believe this, but I have some special instructions for you. Listen closely."

CHAPTER THIRTY THREE

Adele braced one hand against the rail, her hip pressed hard into the metal bar. She stared up the river, watching, wide-eyed at the approach of River Metro Ten.

Was the killer on board? She frowned—more importantly, was Martha Velz still alive? She gritted her teeth, and called over her shoulder, "John, any word about them yet?" She glanced back towards where Agent Renee was standing with his phone pressed to his cheek, his eyes narrowed. He winced, shaking his head. "Nothing," he called back. "They can't find her, Adele. Martha is missing."

Adele wet her lips with her tongue, feeling the spray from the water below. Their own vessel moved slowly, lazily against the current.

River Metro Ten, however, was baring full steam ahead. The CEO had already advised the captain of the other ship to come alongside the stalled boat.

Adele inhaled, held the breath and then loosed it, her hand still tight around the railing, her knuckles as white as snow. She could feel her heartbeat hammering, could feel the eyes of the passengers, the crew above and behind watching the spectacle. No backup this time.

Just her and John, and two moving boats. They couldn't alert the killer they were coming. Couldn't let him know they were on to him.

If she was right, then the killer was stuck on board, right where she wanted him.

It had seemed a good plan at the time, but now... Martha Velz was missing. The crew had called back—they hadn't found her in her room, or in the dining compartment. They'd checked the lower decks as well.

Nothing.

"Damn it," Adele muttered. What if she was too late? What if the killer had already struck...

She couldn't afford to think like that; she needed to focus. Especially for what she was planning to do next.

"John," she said, her throat dry all of a sudden, "You ready?"

"Hell, Adele, you sure about this?"

"Just be quick," she said. "And..." She glanced down at the churning water between the two boats and winced. "Don't fall in the crack."

John muttered darkly behind her. "Heaven forbid any of us fall in the crack."

"Shut up. It's getting closer—get ready!"

River Metro Ten continued its approach, heading along with the current. She could glimpse faces on the other boat now, glimpse lights flashing from windows, could hear music softly pulsing from the nearing vessel.

"Almost!" she called.

The opposite boat's rail swished by like the metal on a train track. It was moving far faster than she would have liked. Her hand only tightened further on the railing, and she grit her teeth, counting down in her head. *Just do it,* she thought to herself. *No idling. Just jump.*

She hadn't wanted the killer to have a chance to get ashore. Hadn't wanted to alert him.

But this...

Maybe this was a mistake.

The railings were now passing each other. Two tracks of metal and glass and thick hull. Eyes on the deck above, eyes on the deck behind her.

River Metro Ten was larger than any of the other boats she'd seen so far. Even now, as she braced, she glimpsed an entire swimming pool on the first deck, towards the prow, beneath a concave gap. Bright red and white umbrellas extended above the pool. Was it her imagination, or could she smell chlorine?

She waited a second longer, feeling her anxiety pulse through her one last time.

One... Two...

On three, she'd go, no matter what.

John suddenly lurched past her, yelling as he did. The tall Frenchman struck the opposite rail, hard, and let out a loud gasp of pain, but at the same time, he hung on, and tilted his body, depositing himself over the rail.

Adele said, out loud, if only to summon her last nerve, "Three."

And she jumped.

For a moment, as she launched over the railing, propelling herself across the gap in the water, she felt a jolt of terror. What if she missed? What if she landed *between* the two giant boats? What if she was caught under the enormous—

Thump.

She struck the rail, hard, gasping, the wind knocked from her lungs. For a moment, wincing, she worried she'd broken a rib. But just as quickly, the throbbing sensation faded, and Adele managed to cling to the opposite rail. River Metro Ten's guardrail was colder, in her assessment, and thicker. The lager boat loomed up and around her. A couple of older women in bathing suits—far too revealing to match well with the accumulation of wrinkles and cellulite scars—had gone still, both of them holding small glasses of red drinks with miniature umbrellas.

One of them, who'd been sucking on a cherry, opened her mouth so wide, the small fruit fell out, and hit the deck.

John, gasping, reached his feet first and hurried over to Adele. She wheezed, ignoring the attention of the nearby passengers, while allowing John to help her over the rail and onto the deck.

It took her a moment, breathing in, slow, out—exhaling longer. She waited, trying to calm her nerves, and then, she straightened, forcing down her swirling emotions, forcing down the slew of *what-if* scenarios sparking through her mind.

They'd made it. That's all that mattered.

And there was a killer on board—his potential victim now missing.

"John," she said, still breathing raggedly.

His hand gripped her elbow, and she wasn't sure if he was steadying her, or himself.

"Let's not do that again," John muttered.

Adele shook her head. "We need to find her, John," she said, shrugging off his hand. "Before it's too late. Did the CEO say where her rooms were?"

John nodded, wincing. "Yeah. Room thirty-four. Third level. Want me to check?"

"Yeah, you go there. I'll start looking in other places."

"Crew said they couldn't find her."

"Damn it, *we* will!" Adele pushed away from John now, moving up the deck, eyes narrowed. "Just go check her rooms!" she called over her shoulder.

She didn't look back to see the expression on his face. Now wasn't the time for sentimentality or discussion. Now was the time to find a potential victim, and then the predator himself.

Were they too late? Was Martha Velz, even now, stowed away somewhere, dead? Had she been thrown overboard?

Adele moved faster, practically jogging now, accidentally stepping on the fallen cherry, crushing it into juice as she made her way in the direction of the swimming pool. Where would the crew not have checked?

She could only think of a few places. Bathrooms, for one, perhaps. They'd already checked Ms. Velz's room, the dining hall, and other public places. But they'd also been told to check the bathrooms, and as of yet, no call—which meant no body, living or otherwise.

So where else might Martha Velz be?

Was she hiding or dead, or oblivious to the whole thing?

Adele moved faster now, still jogging, breathing heavily, her side aching from where she'd careened into the rail.

***

Perhaps he was a killer. Disputing it seemed incongruous with his nature. Was it really so bad? Killing had always been a part of human endeavor.

He twirled the rose between his fingers, staring at it for a moment, eyes narrowed. Not quite frowning, but his lips didn't smile either.

Expressionless, emotionless.

The anger was gone too, now. It had been rising, swirling, but now—all at once—it had vanished. Almost as if he'd been lied to. He wasn't left with peace, but rather a grim emptiness. Something... something in himself had also been killed along with those young women.

He stared at the rose, plucking one petal, eyeing it, and then lifting it to inhale. It barely smelled at all, though; perhaps that was due to the overpowering odor of chlorine. The splashing and giggling of swimmers around him gave him a bit of a headache. How much would he have enjoyed, once upon a time, coming on a boat like this, enjoying a pool.

He wondered how many of the children splashing around, screaming and scooping water, and diving after toys, knew how lucky they were.

He twirled the rose once more, and then examined the small note he'd written. Only three words this time... The emptiness had sapped him in more than one way. Even the taunting had lost some of its flavor.

Our deepest condolences, he'd written.

Perhaps he should have said "my." But no—he preferred it this way.

Three simple words. The same words on the card they'd sent him.

And besides, he wasn't alone. She was watching over him, from beyond. She was part of all of this—it was on her behalf after all. She'd been treated like scum and died in her own vomit.

And now, because of it, he was setting things right once more.

He stared at the drink tray on the small table next to him. Three glasses empty—but even they didn't help the emptiness.

Each of those drinks had cost more than a week of groceries not too long ago.

Times had changed...

He waited, watching for a moment across the pool.

There she sat. Martha Velz, chatting with an older man next to her, clearly uncomfortable. She wore a modest bathing suit with a sundress over it. Her cheeks were lathered in sunscreen, despite her darker complexion, and her eyes kept moving off to the side as if looking for some way out.

He waited impatiently, feeling his temper rising.

The old man kept gabbing, but finally, extricating herself from the conversation one inch at a time, until there was a ten-foot gap between them—and the old man still kept yammering—Martha winced, gave a little excuse and a sidelong glance, and then moved, heading towards the steam rooms.

He watched her leave through hooded eyes.

Maybe he didn't need to kill her too...

The anger was gone, stolen from him somehow. Emptiness was all that remained. Live or die, what did it matter?

He watched her move towards the steam room, pushing in past a couple heading the other direction.

Maybe she didn't deserve to die...

Three was enough, wasn't it?

Martha paused for a moment in the door, shooting a nervous glance towards where the old man was still watching her, waving cheerfully. She waved back, and then turned, disappearing into the steam room.

At the same time, two uniformed crew members moved through the small black gate circling the pool. They began to circle the tables and sun chairs and swimmers, frowning and glancing at their phones, then at faces.

He froze for a moment, feeling his nerves rising again.

Fear.

Fear was as good as hatred for now.

He got to his feet, as casually as possible. Were they looking for him? How was that possible? Clearly the crew were searching for someone.

No time to wait, they were drawing nearer. By the looks of things, they hadn't found their target—not yet. They kept looking, glancing at swimmers, making them uncomfortable.

He moved, lazily, stretching his legs, as casually as possible, heading directly for the steam rooms.

CHAPTER THIRTY FOUR

Adele paused by the small, black gate which opened to the swimming area. The same older women from before jostled past her, doing their best not to spill their drinks as they moved towards a couple of sun chairs.

Adele frowned. Two employees were moving through the swimmers, checking phones and faces. By the looks of things, they hadn't found Martha Velz either.

Adele gave a little huff of frustration.

Not the pool, then. In the water?

Adele scanned, but most the swimmers were young children. She shook her head, eyes settling on the passengers around the pool, watching for any odd reaction at the employees. A couple of young women in bikinis looked uncomfortable at the scrutiny and covered themselves with towels beneath their umbrellas. But neither of them matched the description of Ms. Velz.

An older man, who was smiling, with far too much sunscreen on his nose, began to question one of the employees, chattering away with a wide grin. The employee tried to move off, but the old man kept following him, still talking.

Nothing there, either.

Just then, Adele spotted someone in a swimsuit rise from a sun chair. Next to the chair, there was an empty tray of drinks. The man in question had a scar on his back, near his left kidney. A donor? A recipient?

His back was to her, his hair dark, but not particularly distinguishable. He wore an expensive watch, and his shoes, which he hadn't taken off, seemed similarly valuable.

But why was he leaving his shirt and small backpack next to the sun chair, untended? Did he have family nearby?

Didn't seem like anyone was watching the items. He wasn't heading for another drink, either, as the waiter was on the opposite side of the pool.

Adele watched with mounting curiosity as the man strolled the edge of the pool towards another black, exit gate on the opposite side.

An employee with a phone began to move towards the man all of a sudden.

The fellow with the expensive watch paused, bending to one knee and tying his shoe, his back still to Adele. He ignored the employee, face down.

Of course, the employee was looking for a young woman, so he didn't even notice the odd behavior.

But the man's shoes were both tied.

Why was he ducking, then? Unless...

He didn't know who they were looking for—and Adele desperately wished the crew had been told to be more subtle about it...

But what was the man hiding his face for?

Once the employee passed, the dark-haired fellow with the fancy shoes moved out the small, black gate, and towards a wooden door marked *Steam Rooms.*

He slipped inside, his shirt and small bag still left untended behind him. And there... beneath the chair...

Adele felt a slow shiver prickle up her spine. A single, red rose petal discarded on the damp ground.

"Excuse me," said one of the employees, waving at her. "Excuse me—are you with the police? I have a question about this search."

Adele cursed. Perhaps standing in a full suit by a swimming pool wasn't the best of covers. She ignored the employee though, racing towards the steam rooms, feeling the prickle along her spine turn to a buzz.

It felt like walking in a cloud. Adele winced, feeling the sudden damp against her cheeks, her shirt, her trousers. She narrowed her eyes, waving a hand in front of her face to clear the steam, but even then it only seemed to swirl the puffs of vapor.

"Martha?" she called out, hesitantly, quietly.

She spotted movement towards the back of the room, but then the motion ceased, and another gust of steam obscured her vision.

Adele frowned to herself. Slowly, she reached towards her holster—hesitated for a moment, but then withdrew her weapon. She kept it aimed low, at the ground, but could feel her spine still tingling. Could feel her anxiety mounting.

She resisted the urge to call out again. She spotted wooden benches on either side of her, and porcelain bowls with flowing water splattering into the basins. One of the faucets had been left turned on.

She spotted a wooden stand with coals—a metal mesh covering

over the top, protecting it. Someone was standing by the coals. She frowned, drawing nearer, but then went still. A young man in an employee's uniform poured water on the coals and another gust of steam spewed into the room.

Behind the benches, and the porcelain bowls, she spotted a length of hall, moving off to four separate rooms.

Adele kept her gun low, eyes fixed on the first door down the hall. She stepped through this new burst of steam, wincing against the heat on her face, against the humidity and the way her clothing now seemed heavy and thick about her.

Adele puffed a breath, and the vapor swirled in front of her lips.

Come on... she thought to herself. She didn't call out, though she wanted too. Was Ms. Velz in here, with her? Where was that man with the expensive shoes? She couldn't seem him anymore. She winced at another hissing sound from behind her. More steam.

Great. Less vision.

She wished John had been there too, but no time to wait.

She spotted movement—someone in a towel crossing from one room to another. She heard a soft swishing sound, like swirling water.

Adele frowned, pausing for a moment. But the figure, like a ghost through mist, was gone again—into the furthest room in the corner. Adele walked up the wooden hall, beneath dull lights in waterproof glass casings above. She winced against the orange glow.

Adele paused at the doorway and reached out, slowly, feeling her fingers tremor. For a moment, she felt another swirl of anxiety, even more acute than when she'd jumped from one boat to another. But then, her hand touched the cool, plastic doorknob, and twisted.

Locked.

She frowned. She tried again, harder, pushing her shoulder against the wood. Nothing.

Now, she could feel her pulse quickening. Adele rapped her fingers against the wood, quickly. She spoke in nearly a whisper, "Ms. Velz, are you in there? This is the police! Let me in, please."

She knocked again.

Nothing.

Was Martha dead? Was the killer in there with her? Adele began to reach for her phone to call John, wondering now if she ought to shoot the lock.

But just then, the door suddenly opened wide, and mist swirled and twirled around her.

A young woman, wearing a towel, stood in the doorway frowning. Dark complexion, beautiful features, a nose gifted by a scalpel.

"Martha Velz," Adele said, suddenly, feeling a burst of relief. "Thank God."

The woman blinked, pulling her towel a bit tighter around her. "I—sorry, who are you?"

"My name is Agent Sharp," Adele said, quickly, not bothering to reach for her wallet. Guns usually did enough talking.

Ms. Velz's eyes found the weapon a second later, widening above the swirling mist. "I—did you say *agent*?" she said, nervously. "I'm sorry—is this about my father?"

"What? No... I don't think so, at least. Look, Ms. Velz, you need to come with me. Now! Do you have clothing nearby?"

"I'm wearing my swimsuit under this," she said, quickly, pulling the towel aside to reveal a modest one piece. "What's the matter, agent; you're scaring me."

Adele heard a creaking sound behind them all of a sudden. She felt her pulse race and cursed. She reached out, taking Ms. Velz gently by the hand and tugging insistently at the woman's wrist. Adele made sure to keep her gun angled off to the side.

Martha's eyes were still round and wide, but slowly, she allowed herself to be coaxed back into the hall.

Another creaking sound behind them. Adele felt a shiver up her back. "Come," she said, firmly. "Please—hurry. We need to get you out of here."

CHAPTER THIRTY FIVE

Adele turned and, thankfully, Martha finally followed. One hand held her towel about her, the other bunched at her side in a defensive gesture. Fear emanated from her form, but she allowed Adele to guide her hurriedly back towards the room with the coals and benches.

Fog and steam swirled. Another hiss from the room beyond. Another creaking sound. What was that?

Adele neared the end of the hall, feeling her pulse racing. Almost there. *Almost...*

A form suddenly emerged in front of them, blocking the exit.

"Hello, Martha," said the voice in a strained tone. "It's good to see you." The form was cut in shadow and steam. Nearly impossible to determine features.

Was he holding something? A weapon?

"Get down!" Adele yelled, suddenly, yanking firmly at Martha, and pulling her back. At the same time, she aimed her gun towards the man. "Don't move!" she yelled.

She heard a sound of rapid footfalls, and the figure disappeared around the mouth of the doorway, now, vanishing in the steam.

Adele winced, staring. Had he moved *back* out into the main area? Or had he stepped into one of the doorways in the hall in front of them? She couldn't tell through all this fog.

"Come," Adele whispered, fiercely, pulling Martha along with her, back towards the far end of the hall, away from the exit—at least for now.

They hurried quickly, disappearing into the steam. Adele guided Ms. Velz towards the same room she'd found her in.

She pushed Ms. Velz into the room and stood in the door, waiting. Adele held up a finger to her lips, though she wasn't sure if the gesture was visible in the mist. Then, standing in the doorway, gun in hand, she waited, eyes wide in the humid air, watching, seeking any motion at all.

She winced against the glare of the orange lights above, her back braced against the wooden frame. Her own breathing sounded like an echo in her ears and the steam danced in rhythm with her exhalations.

No sign of movement, or motion.

She could only hope the man with the watch was having a similarly difficult time navigating in the steam.

Adele could hear Ms. Velz hyperventilating in the room behind her. She risked a glance back, and wanted to offer something in the way of encouragement, or comfort, but any sound could attract the attention of the man in the mist.

As she stood, waiting, hoping he'd left, she felt a buzz in her pocket.

Adele frowned, briefly, and then her eyes widened in horror.

Her phone. It would ring on the third buzz.

Damn it. Shit. Adele frantically reached for the device, her fingers scrambling. She yanked the phone from her pocket by the second buzz, her fingers fumbling for the volume buttons. But the phone emitted a loud, chirping noise for a brief moment, a split second before she muted it.

Adele cursed beneath her breath, holding her silenced phone against her damp suit.

The sound had peeled out in the steam rooms, echoing along the hall, like a flare of sound.

And then, a figure suddenly burst from one of the rooms up the hallway.

Adele yelled—gun rising. The figure barreled into her, moving fast and Martha Velz screamed.

Adele went down with a shout, her gun—miraculously--still gripped tight. The figure on top of her, though, seemed to realize the threat. He was snarling now, his body weight pressed against her, smothering her. She tried to kick, but his legs pinned hers. He smelled of alcohol and sweat and he cursed beneath his breath, desperately grabbing at her wrist. Fingernails gouged into her wrist, and a hand clamped over her face, fingers pushing against her eyes as if trying to pluck them out.

She yelled, shaking her head and dislodging his hand; she couldn't push the man off—he was too strong, but every man had a weakness.

Instead of trying to rise, instead she twisted and launched her knee *up.* She caught him in the fork of his legs, and the man let out a wheeze like a whoopie cushion.

His grip on her wrist slackened somewhat, and Adele kneed him again, in the same spot. The man gagged, rolling to the side, desperately scrambling to avoid her weapon. Adele cursed, trying to aim from the ground, but he kicked at her hand, stumbling back at the same time, regaining his feet.

She sat up now, aiming once more, but the man ignored her now, looking around the steam room like a wolf searching for prey. Martha Velz screamed again.

"Get back!" Adele yelled, trying to fire, but the man with the watch shoved her to the side, sending her tumbling. She struck the opposite door, *hard,* her shoulder aching.

The man emitted a snarling sound, like a wounded animal. "I'll tell them they'll miss you!" he screamed, his voice peeling out. And then he football-tackled Ms. Velz, bringing her to the ground beneath his weight. There was a sickening crunch of flesh and bone against hard floor.

Martha let out a gasping whimper. The killer's finger scrambled towards her throat, her mouth, something in his hand. Was that a rose? He seemed to be trying to shove the thorny stem past Martha Velz's lips.

The man was crazed, completely ignoring Adele now, as if she wasn't even there.

"Get off her!" Adele yelled, aiming.

But he ignored the call. No choice. She couldn't risk hurting Martha, so she aimed towards one of his upraised hands, which he'd braced against the wall, while using the other to attack.

The blast of gunfire jolted through the steam rooms. The man on top of Martha yelped, his arm slamming against the wall like a slab of beef. A spurt of red splattered the wood grain.

Martha's lips were sealed, but she was breathing wildly through her nose, nostrils flaring.

The killer had dropped his rose and was now clutching at his arm, moaning in pain.

"Get down!" Adele screamed.

But the man wasn't done. He rolled off of Martha, but then grabbed her, dragging her to her feet with him. She hung limply in his grasp, trying to make herself as small as possible, sobbing now and pleading with incoherent words.

"Let her go!" Adele shouted.

"You don't understand," he gasped. "Go away! Go!"

"No—not until you let her go. Then we can talk. I can get you some help for that arm."

For a moment, the man almost seemed to smile in the mist, a bout of sanity falling over him. "Wound me, then offer help? You're like a mechanic." He chuckled. But then his features morphed in pain again, and the steam around him fell about, swirling and making his features hazy.

"I mean it!" Adele yelled, "let her go."

He set his teeth and gripped Martha *hard* by the shoulder. "Don't you get it—this is just desserts. That's all! It's my right!"

"Your right?" Adele said, quietly, trying to engage, looking for a clear shot. As long as he was talking, he wasn't attacking. She needed an angle, some opportunity. But nothing yet, so she pressed, buying time, "What gives you that right?"

"Her own parents!" he snapped, shaking Martha, roughly. The young heiress squeaked and played possum, limp in the man's arms.

"They killed my sister as sure as if they'd put the cancer in her kidneys themselves! They did it!" He was shaking now, white, trembling like a leaf. "It spread... I donated a kidney. I tried. But it spread. There were complications..." he spoke now as if narrating a movie in his mind, his eyes wide, vacant, gasping to himself as he stuttered.

"Your sister died?" Adele said, softly. "Is that what this is about." She tried to take a step forward, but he snapped at her, and squeezed Martha's neck.

Adele went still. Hastily, she said, "I'm sorry for your loss. But how is that Ms. Velz's fault?"

The killer spat off to the side. "Her parents—I worked for them. Once upon a time. You get all sorts of interesting work as an electrician. Worked for their production company—oh, don't try to speak, I know all about little Martha Velz."

He spat, now, still bleeding, haggard, pale. "Why *should she* live, when my sister died? Why? Hmm? Why's that fair? You tell me! Why!"

Adele gritted her teeth. "I'm sorry. I'm sorry your sister—"

"Choking on her own vomit. Dying in the most horrible way—it took months. She didn't deserve that! She didn't!" He screamed now, shaking Ms. Velz by the throat. But the anger was like a flash of lightning, appearing once, then vanishing a second later. He didn't seem to be able to keep his fury kindling, as if it took all his energy just to remain standing upright.

"And the others," Adele said, still stalling. Still no angle—wait, *there!* His shoulder... No. He moved, shifting again. Damn it. "What about the others?" she said, trying not to let her frustration show. "You killed Zeynep Akbulut, Anika Everett, and Abigail Havertz. Why?

What did they do to you?"

"I didn't kill *them.* I killed an idea," he spat. "The haves and the have-nots, a tale as old as time. I worked for the Akbuluts, and the Everetts. Worked on motors and worked on runway lighting. The Havertz' too—while I was freelancing, needed help with wiring their restaurants. It's amazing how much you can do for *them.* And how little they do in return!"

Adele could feel her pulse racing; she forced herself to listen to the man if for nothing more than forestalling the inevitable, like watching a hangman's hand gripped on the hatch lever. She swallowed and, in a ghost of a voice, managed to eke out, "I don't understand."

"They knew my sister was dying! I told them! Begged them for help. It wouldn't have cost them *anything.* It bankrupted me—bankrupted my sister. But for them—they spend more on their seventeenth car than it would have taken to save my sister's damn life! Don't you understand?"

She tried to force down her fear, her worry. Tried to swallow the terror swirling through her. She tried to listen—to *really* listen to the man's ravings. In a way, for a glimpse of a moment, she felt a flicker of sympathy. But the emotion was drowned out by an even greater bout of sympathy for Ms. Velz. "I understand that's frustrating. Let Martha go. We can talk later."

"It's not about the money," he said, which wasn't a direct answer to anything she'd said, and Adele wondered, vaguely, if he was even listening to her. "I had a settlement from the company she worked for. The cleaning fluids caused the cancer. Ha!" he shook his wrist with the watch, then winced at his arm. "Money, money, money. Gave me some nice clothes, gave me a watch. Didn't give me my bloody sister!"

Martha Velz was crying now, shaking in the killer's tight grip.

Adele felt another pang of fear at the look on Martha's face. Her own body was prickling and buzzing from adrenaline and nerves. If she wasn't gripping her hand so tightly around her weapon, she was nearly certain her fingers would start trembling. Still, she kept her face placid, her tone even, "This isn't going to help your sister either. It won't. Let her go, please." The final word cost her even more, but she needed to de-escalate emotions.

"You don't get it! They sent me flowers! Roses. They sent me a note, giving their condolences. That's all they did! They could have saved her life, but instead they taunted me. They mocked her death."

Adele felt another jolt of sympathy, a stronger one this time. She looked at the man and felt a flash of compassion. An odd thing to feel for a serial killer. But he'd started as human once upon a time. Before grief had consumed him. To her surprise, she meant her next words, "That's sounds horrible, and I'm sorry. But I don't—"

"A month after she died! That's when I got the flowers. A month after! That's when I knew. Four roses. That's what they thought my sister's life was worth. Meanwhile, they're buying cars and boats and their tenth house. Going on vacations that could have saved my sister's life! And they sent me four measly damn flowers! And so yes, damn it, yes I killed them! So what! Hmm? I killed them! I'd do it again! Happily. Four flowers for four flowers. Isn't that right? I sent a note too. My own condolences. I'm sure that'll make them feel better."

Adele gritted her teeth, wincing against the barrage of words. She didn't blame the man for his grief, or even his anger. But none of it justified his actions. Not even his anger.

"Look—you're not getting out of here. Give me Ms. Velz. I'll tell the judge you were cooperative."

He breathed heavily, his eyes darting side to side, his face pale from blood loss and fear. At last, though, he seemed to make a decision. His tongue darted out, briefly, licking his lips. "You want her so bad? Take her!" He shoved Martha towards Adele, hard, sending the young woman stumbling.

Adele grunted against the sudden impact, her gun jarring off to the side. At the same time, as Adele tried to catch Ms. Velz before she fell, the killer bolted back through the door and up the hall. Adele didn't risk another shot—remembering the employee from earlier at the end of that hall, and the deck full of passengers outside.

Still, she yelled, "Are you okay?"

Martha was shaking horribly, one hand pressed to her lips. There were bloody marks across the lower portion of her face, where the thorns of the rose had been dragged like cat claws. But other than that, she seemed well enough. Shock, no doubt. But she'd make it.

The killer, on the other hand, couldn't be allowed to escape.

"Hang tight," Adele said, patting the woman firmly on the shoulder. "You're going to be okay. I'll send help. Don't move!"

And then, she broke into a sprint, moving back after the killer's retreating form. He'd already made it to the door in the main hub of the steam room and slipped back out into the swimming area.

Adele spotted the employee glued to one of the walls, frozen, as if trying to hide. His eyes were as wide as saucers, staring over the metal container of coals.

"Go help her," Adele snapped, pointing at the man. "Back there—a passenger. Help her! Now!"

The young man snapped out of his panic, and nodded dumbly, hurrying towards where Ms. Velz was still sitting. Adele raced towards the door and burst back out onto the deck as well.

Her eyes flicked about. Then she spotted him. The killer, with his expensive watch and shoes was hastening towards the edge of the deck, gasping, blood spilling down his arm.

"Stop!" Adele yelled. "Hey—stop him!"

The man glanced around, panicked now. His eyes fell on her and flared with fear.

Good. Fear was what he deserved.

For a brief moment, Adele was given a long look at the killer. He had plain features, with a blunt nose. His eyes were gaunt, and strangely vacuous, as if some sort of spark were missing. He was clean-shaven and had the thick arms and the calloused hands of a laborer, which didn't match his watch and shoes, or the three expensive drinks she'd spotted on his table by the swimming pool.

Adele kept her gun low. She couldn't risk firing on the deck. Passengers were now staring after the man with the bloody arm. Some of them watched with gaping mouths, others gathered their belongings and loved ones, scattering like hens with chicks tucked beneath their wings.

"Stop right there!" Adele shouted.

But the man seemed intent. He reached the rail, stared into the river and then tried to climb it. His bad arm buckled, though, and blood continued pouring down his hand, to his fingers.

"You don't understand!" he screamed over his shoulder. "Get away from me! She's the criminal! Arrest *her!*"

Adele picked up the pace, cursing. He was going to jump. She didn't want to have to go fishing for a killer in the river.

The man managed to clamber, with one working arm, onto the rail now. His body and swim trunks were slicked with blood.

The gaunt-eyed fellow paused, winced, and then he jumped.

Adele felt her stomach drop, but just then, she froze in surprise.

A large figure lurched forward from the surrounding passengers as the killer dove. A thick, muscular arm darted out. A hand grabbed the man around the throat, catching him in a headlock and slamming him against the rail.

Adele stared at where Agent John Renee's large form angled over the railing, holding the killer in place.

The man was kicking, his hands scrambling, gagging and choking where John's arm wrapped around his windpipe, holding him taut.

"John, pull him in!" Adele said, feeling a spurt of awe and relief. "Good job! Bring him in! You're choking him."

John looked back at her. Waited a bit longer as the man kicked and squirmed, then flashed a thumbs up with his free hand, and, with rough motions, dragged the bleeding murderer over the rail and onto the boat.

He tossed the man unceremoniously onto the ground at his feet as Adele arrived next to him.

"You're under arrest," they both said, between panting breaths.

The man didn't look up, preferring to close his eyes, groaning, and clutching fingers against his bloodied arm, while desperately gasping for air.

CHAPTER THIRTY SIX

Adele stepped off the riverboat, with a sigh of relief matched only by John's great, bellowing exhalation.

"Damn boats," he muttered, refusing to look back, as if scared the water might beckon.

Adele's gaze was fixed on the small fleet of police cars lining the dock, and the street. No fewer than eight officers were escorting Ian Moffat towards the waiting vehicles.

A strange case, Mr. Moffat. Adele stood on the dock for a moment, frowning at where the police were guiding their suspect into the back of a cruiser. The killer's arm was bandaged now, and his hands were behind him, cuffed.

Adele let out a weary little sigh. For a moment, Moffat looked across the parking lot, his eyes landing on her for a moment. He watched her, and she stared back, eyes narrowed.

"Let's go," John murmured. "Nothing here for us."

Adele continued to stare as Ian Moffat was pushed into the back of the waiting cruiser. Other police returned to their own vehicles, and began to pull away from the curb, escorting the killer. Lining the sidewalk, cameramen and news reporters looked for a shot of the notorious River Killer, who'd taken three of Europe's wealthiest heiresses.

Even from here, as the door shut, and he stared out through the tinted window, his eyes seemed strangely *empty.* As if the spark of life had been snuffed.

"What a horror story," Adele murmured, wincing as she did. She crossed her arms, glancing back at John.

He reached out a steadying hand, guiding her towards where their waiting taxi was idling by the curb. "Nothing to do about it now. Ms. Velz is alive because of you."

"You should have heard him, John. Back in that steam, in that heat. He was so angry. So... broken."

"He was jealous of their money."

"I don't think that was it. I think he wanted help, and they didn't give it."

John snorted. "Everyone in the world needs help. I wonder how many times Mr. Moffat chose to watch some TV, go for a vacation, go for a drive to clear his head. I wonder how many people he felt responsible for when he was simply living his life. It's easy to blame others for how they use their resources—not just money, but time, too. Easy to think you're better. Moffat was a bastard. A killer. Nothing else."

Adele sighed, giving a soft little, sad shake of her head. She wasn't sure she entirely agreed. Mr. Moffat was right. He'd worked for four of the wealthiest companies in Europe. Any one of them could have helped his sister. Saved her with a treatment.

But John was right too... If Adele wanted, she could easily have gotten a second, or even a third job. How much more money could she make then, and give it to charity, or help others. She could skip dates, or jogs, or home cooked meals, just for an extra ten minutes here or there—each investment another meal to someone starving. What if she cut back on sleep?

Everyone could give more. But was it really up to her to decide how much?

She hated the thought. She didn't know—couldn't be sure. And now, Mr. Moffat's sister was dead. Three young women had died too. Families ruined, lives broken. Greed, jealousy, murder...

She massaged the bridge of her nose, approaching the taxi with John and reaching into her pocket as she did to slide out her phone.

She frowned, glancing down at the number that had called when she'd been in the steam rooms. The same phone call that had nearly cost Ms. Velz her life.

An unknown number.

Strange.

Adele paused, but then lifted the device, stopping on the curb in front of the taxi. She waited, hearing it ring.

Then, a second later, a voice: "Agent Beatrice Marshall. Is this Agent Sharp?"

Adele frowned in surprise. "Hello, Agent Marshall—this is Adele. I'm returning your call."

A pause, then a hurriedly cleared throat. "Look—you mentioned I ought to call you with anything pertaining to the man who attacked your father."

Adele felt a shiver up her spine, and her breathing came in a quick gasp. "What about him?"

"We found him. He killed one of our officers in Gremheim." The voice became rather constricted at this part. "We're looking for him now. I heard you were in the area—we could use all the help we can get. Especially if you know this son of a bitch."

"I'll be there right away," Adele said, quickly, her tongue feeling strangely numb.

She lowered her phone, exhaling softly and standing in silence for a moment by the taxi. The Spade killer was nearby... Gremheim—where was that, again? She paused, frowning, and then her eyes widened. They were only a ten-minute drive away...

"Adele?" John said, his voice quiet. "Are you okay? What is it? You look like you've seen a ghost."

"John," she said, suddenly, looking at her partner. "We need to go to Gremheim right now."

"What's the—"

"I'll tell you on the way! Get in the damn car. Now!"

Adele was already moving, slamming the taxi door shut behind her and barking instructions as she did. She didn't even hear her own words, her body on autopilot.

He was nearby. Close.

They were going to catch him. *She* was going to catch him.

Not in a week, not in a year. No.

Right now. He was in her sights. And she was going to pull the trigger.

"Faster!" she yelled as the tires screeched and the taxi pulled them out of the parking lot, racing towards Gremheim and onto the warm trail of her mother's killer.

CHAPTER THIRTY SEVEN

It looked like every police car in Germany had been emptied onto the streets of Gremheim. Adele could still smell the river air lingering over the industrial outskirts of the small town. She watched officers move about, in groups, some of them led by dogs on tight leashes. They moved through the factories, in a sweeping pattern, searching every floor, behind every window.

Adele could feel her stomach tighten. A hazy, oppressive series of memories hovered over her. Memories of her mother, *bleeding, bleeding, always bleeding*. Thoughts of Robert, dead, in front of his fireplace, beneath his favorite red leather chair, cut to pieces in his own home.

She glimpsed the small, dull-eyed little man. The way he'd grinned at her, and then fled when she'd confronted him in his apartment. The memories came fast and made it difficult for her to focus.

"Agent Sharp?" someone was saying, "Excuse me, Agent Sharp, so, what do you think?"

She felt John nudge her from behind, and she snapped out of her momentary reverie, and glanced towards the police captain who was standing in front of her. Three other officers, all of them high ranking were circling the captain, staring at the map he had spread on the hood of the SUV in front of them. Adele pressed a hand to the metal of the police vehicle's hood. It was warm beneath her fingertips. She lowered her hand, staring at the map.

"What was the question?" she said, her heartbeat still pounding.

"Where should we search?" The police captain repeated, rubbing a hand against his bristling mustache, not quite dissimilar to Sergeant Sharp's own facial hair.

She thought of her father, wondering if he'd had the good sense to return to the hospital. But no, of course not. Her father was probably at home, eating soup, or watching TV. She hated that he wouldn't look after himself.

But the killer wasn't out there anymore.

Not now. Not for this moment. He was on foot, according to the police. He'd attacked a cop and then ran away. He was here, somewhere, skulking about. Trains, planes, and now, at her insistence, even boats were being monitored. Everyone was looking, double checking identifications. Everyone had a description of the Spade killer. He was an easy man to pick out of a lineup.

"He won't be in the factories," she said, quietly.

A couple of the ranking cops behind the police captain shared a look. "You're sure?" the captain said. "It provides cover, is hard to search. Some of them have chemicals which would make it difficult for the hounds to detect his scent."

"I'm not saying it wouldn't make sense for a normal person, but he's not normal. He thinks of himself as some sort of twisted artist. He wouldn't want to be in a factory."

"Where then?"

Before Adele could answer, though, one of the sergeants cleared his throat and interrupted, "Sir, we're already gearing up to go through these buildings. We've searched three already. It would be a mistake to call it off now."

The captain nodded, showing he'd heard, but then gestured towards Adele, as if to say, *please continue.*

She bobbed her head once. "Look," she said, "he's not going to be in some grey, dusty, bleak building, with boring windows, and cement floors. He'll hate it. Plus, on top of that, there are too many entrances, too many windows. He won't go into a basement, either, because there are no escapes."

"Well, where then?"

Adele looked around, glancing at the map, but then deciding it wouldn't help her. The aesthetics of the building, the aesthetics of it all would matter. She remembered the way, back at that apartment of his, he had painted on the walls, drawing figurines and smiley faces. He seemed to enjoy decorating his home. He liked to taunt Adele, by decorating his victims too.

She shivered.

"I need you to take me back to where you last saw him."

The captain frowned. "We've been over that place three times already. There's no sign. We have a couple of police still patrolling, but he isn't there anymore. He's on the move."

Adele shook her head. "That's fine. Me and my partner can go. Can you let us borrow a car?"

She wondered if she should press further and insist that they send backup. She needed to track the Spade killer, retracing his footsteps, and she could use all the help she could get.

But on the other hand, she didn't *want* the help. In fact, part of her resented the notion. She didn't need help. She wanted to catch him on her own.

"I'm afraid we need those vehicles," one of the sergeants began to say, but the captain cut him off with a shake of his head. "That's fine. You can take mine. Contact us if you find anything. There's a radio in the car."

The captain's mustache twitched, but the rest of his expression remained stony, impassive, as he fished keys out of his pocket, and handed them to Adele. The keys were surprisingly cold compared to how warm the hood of the car had been. She nodded in gratitude, and then moved over towards the indicated vehicle the captain waved towards.

John fell into step, lost in the midst of a sea of German. He followed after Adele, narrowly avoiding a hound on a leash, who was sniffing and growling.

"What's the plan?" John muttered beneath his breath.

Adele had to speak loudly to be heard, now that the captain was barking orders again.

"We're going back to where they saw him last. I'll drive."

"Did you ask them where it was?"

Adele nodded. "Near one of the River Metro docks, of all things. What are the odds?"

John sighed, but nodded, sliding into the passenger seat as Adele took the driver's side.

He said something else, but Adele didn't quite hear him, her eyes fixed on the road. She couldn't even make out his words, as if his voice was muffled or coming down a deep tunnel.

She was closing in.

He was nearby.

She would find him.

***

She stood by the chain-link fence, her eyes moving towards the police car parked on the other side of the road. Orange traffic cones and caution tape cordoned off the area. She could see the stain of blood on the sidewalk, which they had attempted to scrub away. She shivered, staring at the crimson mark.

There was a chain-link fence behind her, and through it, she glimpsed the river.

"Well, what now?" John said, quietly.

Adele looked one way, then the other. She paused, her eyes on the distant water tower, and then her gaze flicked to a bridge spanning the river.

She crossed her arms for a moment, scanning the street.

Low buildings, some shops. Witnesses, potentially. Nothing stood out about any of it.

The water tower, though, had a big pink fox painted on it.

She frowned at the thing.

The bridge itself, seemed old, and well-constructed, beautiful in a way, with stone pillars lining it, and holding the thing aloft, more than a hundred feet in the air above the water.

"He's there, or there," she said, quietly. "A high vantage point. Alluring structures—the sorts of things he might find fascinating. Plus, an easy landmark to track, while moving through the streets, away from police cars. The water tower won't have people around it, nor the bridge, beneath it. Seclusion, high vantage point, safety. He's in one of those places."

"Are you sure?"

Adele paused, and began to shake her head. Of course she wasn't sure. It was like picking a needle out of a haystack. They had narrowed in on the Spade killer's location. But that didn't help unless she was able to find the needle.

"We need to split up. You want the water tower or the bridge?"

John frowned at the words, shaking his head. "We can't split—"

"No choice. He's going to get away if we wait for nightfall." She glanced up at the sky, as evening continued its descent. "Which one do you want? You can take the radio from the car, too."

"You take the radio."

"I'll use my phone. It's fine. He probably won't be there anyway. We can reconvene at the car if neither of us find him. Keep an eye out for any other landmarks or something that might attract the eye of the psychopath."

"You sure?"

"I already answered that."

And with that, Adele began to walk hurriedly, stalking towards the bridge, moving along the sidewalk next to the chain-link fence, the river rushing in the opposite direction of her own motions.

Would he be beneath the bridge?
What would she do if he was?
She picked up the pace.
Evening loomed above, and night threatened. Once night fell, the cover of darkness would help the Spade killer get away.
She couldn't let that happen.

***

Adele shivered softly. She remembered her first time returning to France in ten years. That case had started with a bridge as well. Beneath the bridge, a young woman, killed. And now Adele was back to a bridge. It seemed fitting somehow.
She could hear the sound of traffic above her as she took the steps on the side of the bridge and began to move down towards the river walk.
On one side, she spotted people strolling the walkway, and others riding bikes.
But on another, behind a low, concrete wall, there were only support columns for the bridge itself. And shadows.
She paused, one hand braced against the low, concrete barrier. She felt a shiver up her spine. For a moment, she looked off into the distance, staring at the water tower. The bright, pink fox was still visible.
Had she sent John into a trap all alone?
She shook her head, fighting the thought. Agent Renee knew how to take care of himself, and she couldn't afford to allow her own distractions to cost her. Too much was riding on this.
She began to move, quietly, stepping over the concrete wall, and beneath the metal supports for the giant bridge above. Shadows swallowed her and fell across the ground. She could smell the faint odor of urine and mold. The scent of something decaying wafted nearby. She paused, frowning, towards a small tent hidden in an alcove.
Her hand went to her holster, and slowly, she approached.
She didn't speak, didn't warn. Instead, she moved quickly, shoving the tent open, and pointing her gun.
Empty. The smell of sweat met her nose, and she pulled back sharply.
Adele frowned, but then moved away from the tent, heading deeper into the shadows beneath the bridge.

Something glinted.

She stiffened, her pulse racing.

There, she spotted a small service ladder; it moved up to the higher portions of the bridge above.

She stared. The lock was broken on the security gate.

Her fingers tingled as she approached, and she gripped the gun even more tightly in one hand.

Adele looked up, her eyes tracing the ladder towards a metal service platform above. She licked her lips, remembering the last time she'd ascended a ladder, behind a building in search of the Spade killer. He had trapped the exit.

Was he up there?

Adele approached, slowly, one hand still gripping her gun; the other pulled open the safety gate, and she moved into the small cage. She stared up, exhaled, and then holstered her weapon. She would need both hands to climb.

The rungs were cold and still had dust on them. Had he been this way? It didn't seem like it.

There weren't many places left for him to hide.

And so she climbed, one hand in front of the other, the cold metal dusty and rigid beneath her fingers.

***

He'd been clever. No one would find him here. The canvases were all too stupid. They played in two dimensions, while he was on the way to discover a fourth.

The painter smiled to himself, staring at his fingers.

They were stained with dry blood. How had that happened? He frowned.

Oh, yes, the police officer whose neck he'd slit.

Pity that. A rushed work.

Still, his pulse hammered from the adrenaline, from the excitement of it all. He shivered beneath the shadow of the structure above, crouched on the metal platform like a gargoyle. He peered over the railing, down, down, down, watching, in the distance, small canvases move about.

He'd lay low until nightfall, maybe even a couple of days. Then, he'd slip out right beneath their noses.

He'd been so very, very clev—

A sudden noise behind him. He frowned, glancing back—but no motion. Just the strain of metal in heat, no doubt. Still, he'd have to keep his wits about him. At least for another couple of days.

***

Adele moved slowly at first, but then picking up her pace. The soft clanging and slaps of her hands against the rungs seemed far too loud now.

She shivered in anticipation as she reached the top.

No shouts, no movement, no sudden sound of clattering footsteps.

She reached up, her fingers braced against the metal platform.

She gave another sigh, and then pulled herself, moving into the darker shadows beneath the bridge above.

She froze.

And so did *he*.

For a moment, she stared, unable to believe her eyes.

His eyes widened, one of them dull, the other vibrant and excited all of a sudden.

He was there. The small, childish form of the Spade killer hunched over the edge of the platform, staring towards the river, like some leering vulture.

The moment her fingers had hit the platform, he turned, and now, for a brief instant, Adele Sharp locked eyes with her mother's killer. Robert's killer.

And now, like an animal let out of its cage, the Spade killer went stiff, staring right back at her, a hood raised, casting his face in shadow, except for his eyes.

The pause didn't last long, though. With a sudden yell, Adele burst into action, adrenaline fueling her.

The killer cursed, and reached down, grabbing a discarded brown bottle and he threw it at her, hard.

It ricocheted off the platform next to her knuckles, shattering against the wall behind her.

Adele ignored it completely, yelling at the top of her lungs. It didn't even cross her mind to try to retreat and call for backup. There was no retreating.

"Hang on," the killer began to shout, "One moment!"

She ignored him. The time for talk was long over. All that was left was action.

She surged up the ladder, clambering like a spider from a drainpipe.

The killer didn't react in fear, though, calm as ever, calculating. As she neared him, her hand reaching towards her holster, he turned and began to sprint along the walkway beneath the bridge above.

Rust was beginning to eat at some of the bars, and a portion of the platform was completely worried through, an orange-ringed crater staring down at the river below.

"Stop!" she yelled.

But he didn't call back. He kept sprinting, his footsteps clanging against the metal, and he leapt over the gap in the platform, bridging it with one giant surge.

She spotted a small ladder at the other end of the bridge and knew that's where he was headed.

She cursed, raised her gun. And for a moment, she sited. A clean shot. No way she could miss. He couldn't dodge left or right; the platform forced him to run in a straight line.

Her finger squeezed on the trigger, but just as she fired, she jerked to the right.

She didn't want to kill him. Not now, not this way. He needed to pay for what he'd done. This would be too quick. Too clinical. Too painless.

He needed to suffer. The way she'd suffered. He needed to face what he'd done. The way she had to every night.

She fired, winging him, aiming for the same arm she'd shot on Mr. Moffat.

She hit the Spade killer.

He yelped, twirling like a top, and slamming to the rail. She fired again, a warning. "Stop!" she screamed, all self-control gone from her voice.

The Spade killer breathed heavily, leaning against the rail, bleeding. He seemed to realize if he broke into a run again, she'd shoot once more. He stared at her, shaking his head, his one dull eye not quite looking in the right direction. He gasped, his voice croaking, "This isn't how it was supposed to be, friend," he said, his voice low, and singsong, sending chills up her back.

"Shut up and get on the ground. Now!"

She stood, gun in hand, pointed towards the little monster.

He was still bleeding, but instead of trying to stop the blood, he stared at it; he reached out with a finger, tracing it through the liquid, and lifted it up. Then, he pressed his finger to his forehead, winced against the pain in his arm, but using the blood from his own body to make a swirling pattern. Then he tapped the symbol. "I have plans," he said, in that same singsong voice. "This isn't how it ends, my friend. Not yet."

"Shut up. Get on the ground," she screamed. "I will kill you. I will."

He looked her deep in the eyes. She refused to look away, but neither did he. Neither of them blinked for a moment, one of them holding a gun, pointing towards the other's head. But the other gave a simple, soft shake of his head.

"No you won't."

And then, he bowed, like a stage performer after a production. With his uninjured arm, he raised his hand, and gave a flickering little wave.

"I'm warning you," she began, taking a step closer.

But then, he pushed himself over the edge of the rail.

She yelled in frustration, firing. She missed. She watched the Spade killer fall like a ragdoll, plummeting nearly a hundred feet.

And then, he hit the water below, with a splash.

Adele cursed, surging to the rail, gun in her hands, pointing towards the ring of white spreading in the churning blue.

She waited, but there was no motion.

She watched for him to surface. But he didn't.

"Dammit!" she yelled. "Shit!" she said even louder.

For a moment, she just stood there, gun in hand, pointing towards the water, waiting, watching, breathing heavily.

No movement. No motion. No one resurfaced from the water.

The river was traveling fast, the current quickening.

Nothing.

She'd shot him, hadn't she?

A hundred-foot fall. He couldn't have survived that, could he?

She felt a vibrant flutter of, *something*, but she couldn't quite place the emotion in her chest.

Had she killed the Spade killer?

Was it finally over?

She gritted her teeth. She needed to know. They needed to search the bottom of that river. She needed divers, searchlights, watchdogs. She needed *everything*.

With trembling fingers, she reached for her phone.

To her surprise, she felt moisture curling down the inside of her cheek.

She reached up, quizzically, wiping away a tear.

What was that for?

This wasn't over yet. She needed to see his corpse. Only then, *then*, would she take a moment to grieve everything he'd cost her.

***

Three hours of searching well into the night turned up nothing. Not even with the floodlights blaring down, or the helicopters above, searching back and forth and back and forth.

Adele stood by the river, arms crossed, watching as three new divers emerged from the water and looked up at the police captain next to her. The divers winced, shaking their heads.

"Just once more," Adele said, through gritted teeth, "he's down there. They have to find him."

She felt a hand on her shoulder and looked over to see John standing next to her, staring across the river.

The police captain sighed. "It's night, Agent Sharp. We won't be able—"

"One more time," she insisted. She didn't yell, but the force of her words struck like hammer blows.

The captain met her gaze but seemed to find something there. He nodded once, and said, "All right, one more search. I'll have the helicopters go back down river and check the banks. We have police cars searching within three miles of here, Agent Sharp. We're not going to find him tonight. It may take days to drag the river."

"Once more."

The police captain nodded. The divers readjusted their masks, and turned, dipping back beneath the water.

Three hours.

No sign of the body.

No sign of the Spade killer.

Maybe she really had killed him.

She wasn't sure if she wanted that to be true or not.

EPILOGUE

Adele stepped from the taxi out onto the curb in front of her old childhood house. She paused for a moment, staring up at the two-story affair, with the white porch. Along the side of the house, she spotted a window, with cardboard covering it, and caution tape used to secure it in place.

She sighed, allowing the car door to swing shut behind her with a quiet *thump.* And then she marched forward. She waved towards the two, burly men sitting in an unmarked vehicle in front of the house. They waved back. She wondered if they recognized her.

She wasn't sure her father talked much about her with his friends. Still, they didn't move to intercept. She wondered, also, if they'd heard the news about the Spade killer. Alive or dead—no one knew. They'd have to drag the river in the morning.

But she wasn't optimistic about what they'd find.

Still, she was alive. John was alive, and on a plane, heading back to France.

And her father...

Also alive.

She took the creaking stairs and reached the front door. She raised a hand, but before she could knock, the door suddenly opened, the screen creaked, and a man wearing a plain white t-shirt and boasting an impressive walrus mustache, stepped out onto the porch, carrying two bowls.

One of the bowls sloshed, and a green, gunky substance dripped down his fingers. Her father winced and placed the bowls on the glass table on the porch.

"Er, hi Dad," she said.

"Soup," he replied.

He sat in one of the spindle-backed chairs, and then looked at her, waving towards another chair. "I made extra."

"What type?"

"Pea."

"Hmm. Thanks. I'm not hungry."

"Eat."

A sigh. “Alright. It's good to see you moving about.”

“The rat got my arm, not my legs.”

She spotted the thick bandage wrapped around her father's forearm. “They said he stabbed you.”

“Shallow cuts.”

“Are you on pain meds?”

“Don't trust 'em.”

Adele slowly lowered into the seat, inhaling the salty scent of pea soup. “You really should be at the hospital.”

“Adele, you promised. I said no talking about hospitals. You're welcome on that one condition.”

“Welcome on your porch, more like. You're worried I'm going to see the mess he made, aren't you?”

She glanced towards the door, which her father had shut behind him. “Is it really that bad?”

Joseph Sharp grunted. “His thick skull busted my window. Couple of chairs. Not horrible.” He grinned. “I have a new fishing knife.”

Adele frowned, but then felt a shiver up her spine as she realized what he meant. She massaged her nose and shook her head in disbelief. “You're not keeping that, are you?”

“Psh. Not going to waste a good knife. How are you, Adele? I heard you winged the scum bag.”

“I shot him. Yeah. In the arm.”

“So that's that, then.”

“I... I'm not sure. But he jumped off something high... I, I think he might be dead, Dad... I think I might've got him. We'll know soon enough. They'll drag the river tomorrow. But it all might be over.”

Even as she said it, she wasn't sure she believed it. Adele let out a little sigh, leaning even further back in her chair. She tapped a finger against the side of the pea soup, watching the surface tension shiver.

Her father took a sip of his own, wiping a hand across his mustache and saying nothing.

“Good,” he managed to eke out at last. “Good on you, Adele. I knew you had it in you.”

She blinked. This was suspiciously close to praise. “I... Thanks. Mom deserved better.”

“Damn right.”

“Thought you didn't cuss, Dad.”

“Sometimes you have to. Elise deserved better.” He shook his head and sniffed softly. For a moment, it almost seemed like his eyes had gone misty, but just as quickly, he cleared his throat and glanced across the porch, sighing once more. At last, Joseph Sharp looked his daughter in the eyes.

"I always knew you were smart, Adele. I'm proud of you. I hope you know that."

She blinked. "Umm... You are?" She didn't mean to fish, but the words were surprising.

"Of course. You're the best they have. I've tracked your closure rate. I know how good you are."

"Right. Well, thanks, Dad. That means a lot coming from you." She wasn't sure how much she meant it. On one hand, she felt a flicker of pride at her father's words. She *was* good at her job. On the other, though, she wished it didn't take a career to make him proud. She'd never much liked performing for someone's affection, least of all her father's.

Still... Maybe she was being too hard on him.

He'd started that trend, though. In this very house. He'd been a hard man—a cold man. But wasn't that what she'd needed? To become the person she'd become? Would her mother's killer have been caught if not for her?

She doubted it.

Her father, in a way, had helped train her, guide her.

She stared past her father now, her eyes tracing the cheap siding, flicking to the windows, to the closed door.

Maybe, just maybe, the place wasn't so intimidating as it had once been.

But it wasn't home.

She knew that now. Sitting there, in front of two bowls of pea soup, facing her father.

This wasn't home.

She thought back to her small apartment, the one she used to share with her mother back in France. A whisper of a smile tempted her lips. She thought about Agent Renee. He'd promised to clear up the report he'd made with Foucault, though she doubted he would. Still, it was the thought that counted. Whenever things got hard, he was always there, by her side.

Plus, it didn't hurt that he was tall and handsome and tough.

She couldn't hold back the smile now, but she tilted her head, staring at her hands in her lap. No, this wasn't home.

Paris was. France was. She'd come to think of it as home, because the people who cared most about her in the world were from France. John, her mother, Robert... Two of them were dead, now. But that didn't rob the memories.

Memories made in Paris. And with John, memories still to be made.

She wasn't sure why, but this realization almost seemed to lift a burden from her shoulders. She swallowed once, looked at her father, and said, "You did a good job, raising me. As best you knew how. I'm proud of you too."

He stared at her, as if he'd been smacked. This time, she was certain a tear had crept into his eye. And also, this time, he didn't look away.

"I mean it," she murmured. "Things weren't perfect. But you did the best you could. I... I like my life. And in part, I have you to thank for what I've been able to build. So thank you."

Her father let out a little sigh, and then turned his attention to his pea soup.

Silence stretched, and the emotions seemed to dwindle like sparks caught in the wind. Daughter and father sat on the porch, one of them sipping soup, the other staring at the bowl in suspicion.

NOW AVAILABLE FOR PRE-ORDER!

<u>LEFT TO PREY</u>
(An Adele Sharp Mystery—Book 11)

"When you think that life cannot get better, Blake Pierce comes up with another masterpiece of thriller and mystery! This book is full of twists and the end brings a surprising revelation. I strongly recommend this book to the permanent library of any reader that enjoys a very well written thriller."
--Books and Movie Reviews, Roberto Mattos (re Almost Gone)

LEFT TO PREY is book #11 in a new FBI thriller series featuring Adele Sharp (the series begins with LEFT TO DIE, book #1) by USA Today bestselling author Blake Pierce, whose #1 bestseller Once Gone (a free download) has received over 1,000 five star reviews.

On a sunny day along a religious pilgrimage in Spain, two hikers find a mangled corpse. When more bodies up across the 500-mile trail, it is clear a deranged serial killer is at work. FBI Special Agent Adele Sharp is summoned to enter the dark mind of this cross-boundary killer and stop him before it's too late.

Meanwhile, Adele mother's killer, bent on vengeance, resurfaces in the US, and he knows just what to do to hit Adele the hardest. Can Adele return in time to save the ones who matter most?

An action-packed mystery series of international intrigue and riveting suspense, LEFT TO PREY will leave you turning pages late into the night.

Books #12 and #13 in the series—LEFT TO LURE and LEFT TO CRAVE—are now also available!

Blake Pierce

Blake Pierce is the USA Today bestselling author of the RILEY PAGE mystery series, which includes seventeen books. Blake Pierce is also the author of the MACKENZIE WHITE mystery series, comprising fourteen books; of the AVERY BLACK mystery series, comprising six books; of the KERI LOCKE mystery series, comprising five books; of the MAKING OF RILEY PAIGE mystery series, comprising six books; of the KATE WISE mystery series, comprising seven books; of the CHLOE FINE psychological suspense mystery, comprising six books; of the JESSE HUNT psychological suspense thriller series, comprising nineteen books; of the AU PAIR psychological suspense thriller series, comprising three books; of the ZOE PRIME mystery series, comprising six books; of the ADELE SHARP mystery series, comprising thirteen books; of the EUROPEAN VOYAGE cozy mystery series, comprising six books (and counting); of the new LAURA FROST FBI suspense thriller, comprising four books (and counting); of the new ELLA DARK FBI suspense thriller, comprising six books (and counting); of the A YEAR IN EUROPE cozy mystery series, comprising nine books; of the AVA GOLD mystery series, comprising three books (and counting); and of the RACHEL GIFT mystery series, comprising three books (and counting).

An avid reader and lifelong fan of the mystery and thriller genres, Blake loves to hear from you, so please feel free to visit www.blakepierceauthor.com to learn more and stay in touch.

BOOKS BY BLAKE PIERCE

RACHEL GIFT MYSTERY SERIES
HER LAST WISH (Book #1)
HER LAST CHANCE (Book #2)
HER LAST HOPE (Book #3)

AVA GOLD MYSTERY SERIES
CITY OF PREY (Book #1)
CITY OF FEAR (Book #2)
CITY OF BONES (Book #3)

A YEAR IN EUROPE
A MURDER IN PARIS (Book #1)
DEATH IN FLORENCE (Book #2)
VENGEANCE IN VIENNA (Book #3)
A FATALITY IN SPAIN (Book #4)
SCANDAL IN LONDON (Book #5)
AN IMPOSTOR IN DUBLIN (Book #6)
SEDUCTION IN BORDEAUX (Book #7)
JEALOUSY IN SWITZERLAND (Book #8)
A DEBACLE IN PRAGUE (Book #9)

ELLA DARK FBI SUSPENSE THRILLER
GIRL, ALONE (Book #1)
GIRL, TAKEN (Book #2)
GIRL, HUNTED (Book #3)
GIRL, SILENCED (Book #4)
GIRL, VANISHED (Book 5)
GIRL ERASED (Book #6)

LAURA FROST FBI SUSPENSE THRILLER
ALREADY GONE (Book #1)
ALREADY SEEN (Book #2)
ALREADY TRAPPED (Book #3)
ALREADY MISSING (Book #4)

EUROPEAN VOYAGE COZY MYSTERY SERIES
MURDER (AND BAKLAVA) (Book #1)
DEATH (AND APPLE STRUDEL) (Book #2)

CRIME (AND LAGER) (Book #3)
MISFORTUNE (AND GOUDA) (Book #4)
CALAMITY (AND A DANISH) (Book #5)
MAYHEM (AND HERRING) (Book #6)

ADELE SHARP MYSTERY SERIES
LEFT TO DIE (Book #1)
LEFT TO RUN (Book #2)
LEFT TO HIDE (Book #3)
LEFT TO KILL (Book #4)
LEFT TO MURDER (Book #5)
LEFT TO ENVY (Book #6)
LEFT TO LAPSE (Book #7)
LEFT TO VANISH (Book #8)
LEFT TO HUNT (Book #9)
LEFT TO FEAR (Book #10)
LEFT TO PREY (Book #11)
LEFT TO LURE (Book #12)
LEFT TO CRAVE (Book #13)

THE AU PAIR SERIES
ALMOST GONE (Book#1)
ALMOST LOST (Book #2)
ALMOST DEAD (Book #3)

ZOE PRIME MYSTERY SERIES
FACE OF DEATH (Book#1)
FACE OF MURDER (Book #2)
FACE OF FEAR (Book #3)
FACE OF MADNESS (Book #4)
FACE OF FURY (Book #5)
FACE OF DARKNESS (Book #6)

A JESSIE HUNT PSYCHOLOGICAL SUSPENSE SERIES
THE PERFECT WIFE (Book #1)
THE PERFECT BLOCK (Book #2)
THE PERFECT HOUSE (Book #3)
THE PERFECT SMILE (Book #4)
THE PERFECT LIE (Book #5)
THE PERFECT LOOK (Book #6)

THE PERFECT AFFAIR (Book #7)
THE PERFECT ALIBI (Book #8)
THE PERFECT NEIGHBOR (Book #9)
THE PERFECT DISGUISE (Book #10)
THE PERFECT SECRET (Book #11)
THE PERFECT FAÇADE (Book #12)
THE PERFECT IMPRESSION (Book #13)
THE PERFECT DECEIT (Book #14)
THE PERFECT MISTRESS (Book #15)
THE PERFECT IMAGE (Book #16)
THE PERFECT VEIL (Book #17)
THE PERFECT INDISCRETION (Book #18)
THE PERFECT RUMOR (Book #19)

CHLOE FINE PSYCHOLOGICAL SUSPENSE SERIES
NEXT DOOR (Book #1)
A NEIGHBOR'S LIE (Book #2)
CUL DE SAC (Book #3)
SILENT NEIGHBOR (Book #4)
HOMECOMING (Book #5)
TINTED WINDOWS (Book #6)

KATE WISE MYSTERY SERIES
IF SHE KNEW (Book #1)
IF SHE SAW (Book #2)
IF SHE RAN (Book #3)
IF SHE HID (Book #4)
IF SHE FLED (Book #5)
IF SHE FEARED (Book #6)
IF SHE HEARD (Book #7)

THE MAKING OF RILEY PAIGE SERIES
WATCHING (Book #1)
WAITING (Book #2)
LURING (Book #3)
TAKING (Book #4)
STALKING (Book #5)
KILLING (Book #6)

RILEY PAIGE MYSTERY SERIES

ONCE GONE (Book #1)
ONCE TAKEN (Book #2)
ONCE CRAVED (Book #3)
ONCE LURED (Book #4)
ONCE HUNTED (Book #5)
ONCE PINED (Book #6)
ONCE FORSAKEN (Book #7)
ONCE COLD (Book #8)
ONCE STALKED (Book #9)
ONCE LOST (Book #10)
ONCE BURIED (Book #11)
ONCE BOUND (Book #12)
ONCE TRAPPED (Book #13)
ONCE DORMANT (Book #14)
ONCE SHUNNED (Book #15)
ONCE MISSED (Book #16)
ONCE CHOSEN (Book #17)

MACKENZIE WHITE MYSTERY SERIES
BEFORE HE KILLS (Book #1)
BEFORE HE SEES (Book #2)
BEFORE HE COVETS (Book #3)
BEFORE HE TAKES (Book #4)
BEFORE HE NEEDS (Book #5)
BEFORE HE FEELS (Book #6)
BEFORE HE SINS (Book #7)
BEFORE HE HUNTS (Book #8)
BEFORE HE PREYS (Book #9)
BEFORE HE LONGS (Book #10)
BEFORE HE LAPSES (Book #11)
BEFORE HE ENVIES (Book #12)
BEFORE HE STALKS (Book #13)
BEFORE HE HARMS (Book #14)

AVERY BLACK MYSTERY SERIES
CAUSE TO KILL (Book #1)
CAUSE TO RUN (Book #2)
CAUSE TO HIDE (Book #3)
CAUSE TO FEAR (Book #4)
CAUSE TO SAVE (Book #5)

CAUSE TO DREAD (Book #6)

KERI LOCKE MYSTERY SERIES
A TRACE OF DEATH (Book #1)
A TRACE OF MURDER (Book #2)
A TRACE OF VICE (Book #3)
A TRACE OF CRIME (Book #4)
A TRACE OF HOPE (Book #5)

www.ingramcontent.com/pod-product-compliance
Lightning Source LLC
Chambersburg PA
CBHW030618310726
48979CB00003B/779